SURGE

by

ROD TANNER

First published by AuthorHouse 04/29/04

ISBN: 1-4184-5510-5 (e-book)
ISBN: 1-4184-3150-8 (Paperback)
ISBN: 1-4184-3151-6 (Dust Jacket)

Library of Congress Control Number: 2004091882

This book is printed on acid free paper.

Printed in the United States of America
Bloomington, IN

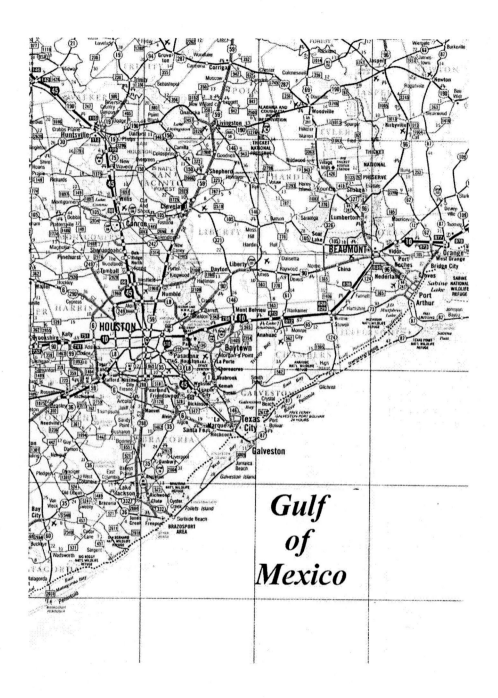

Gulf of Mexico

ACKNOWLEDGMENTS

I would like to thank all the people who helped bring this book to completion: To my wife, Diana Meade, and Karen Estep for having the courage to tell me I could make it better. To my friend Gene Rutt, who gave me the idea for *Surge,* and helped me with the cast of players. To Elliot Jennings, Emergency Manager of Galveston, for his valuable input and for always taking my calls for more silly questions. To John Hughes for his expertise on guns and boats. To my monthly writer's group cohorts, Karen Estep, Lora Lawrence and Diana Meade for reading my mistake filled, early drafts and giving me tons of encouragement. To my agent, John Downey, for believing in me. And to all the fine folks at AuthorHouse.

Map provided courtesy of Five Star Maps, Inc.

Author photograph by Cathy Bottoms

DEDICATION

To Diana, the love of my life.

PROLOGUE

The man had been listening to the pounding on the roof of his pickup for a long time. It sounded like it was raining gravel. The light show outside was non-stop and the wind howled like a wounded animal. He squinted through the water as it battered the windshield and could barely make out the large eighteen-wheeler beside him. *It's now or never*, he thought. He struggled to get the door open, bracing himself as he stepped into the assaulting rain. In seconds he was drenched from head to toe. Fighting his way through the wind, he mounted the running board of the semi and climbed into the cab.

As Mother Nature raged and revealed her bad side to the world, he sat unmoved and unconcerned. Putting the flask to his lips, he felt the whiskey slowly burn its way down to his stomach. Finally, he turned the key until the powerful diesel engine rumbled to life. *I'd better deliver my little surprise before J.D. and the boys miss me.* He put the truck in first gear and eased out into the darkness just as a fractured bolt of lightning lit up the sky. *Hell of a night for dying.* He knew people would die tonight. He was going to kill them.

CHAPTER ONE

She is an accident, but then so many creations are. The conditions can be exactly the same and nothing happens but today is different. The right cell merging with another right cell and suddenly energy is everywhere. Molecules acting and reacting at a frantic pace. Ions and protons smashing into one another at a random chaotic rate. The combination of water and the perfect temperature inside the natural womb she is growing in, is giving her energy and life. Soon she will be in search for more, like a hungry werewolf on a full moon night. She has no shape or form, but she is already moving and growing stronger by the minute. She even has a name.

"Goddamn it." J.D. slammed the door on his ten-year-old battered blue pickup. He walked to the front of the truck and opened the hood. "This is all I need."

"What you need is this." His wife Beverly came out of the back door waving his lunch in her hand. "I swear you'd forget your head if it wasn't tied on."

J.D reached for the lunch box and set it on the fender. He took the crescent wrench in his other hand and banged it twice on the starter.

"Would you get in and give it a try?"

"It's what I live for." She climbed into the truck and turned the key. The starter turned over a couple of times and then the engine caught. "You probably weren't holdin' your mouth right," Beverly deadpanned as she slid out of the truck.

"Probably." J.D. tossed the lunch box into the front seat and gave Beverly a kiss on the cheek. He climbed in behind the wheel and shut the door.

"Besides, Thelma likes me best." Beverly had named his old truck Thelma, and her worn out station wagon Louise, because she said they really should be driven off a cliff.

"If we win the lottery Saturday, you can buy a brand new starter." She tossed him a smile over her shoulder and headed for the back porch. J.D. sighed and backed out of the driveway. He turned onto the frontage road that ran beside the Twin Oaks Mobile Home Park and immediately entered the on ramp that would take him out over the causeway of Galveston Island and up I-45 where he would exit onto 146 toward Texas City and International Petroleum Refineries. J.D. smiled to himself as he thought of Beverly's lottery comment. How many times had he heard some guy who had just won eighty zillion dollars say that he didn't think he would quit his job, but he might get the transmission fixed on his Buick?

The first rays of morning light were peeking over the horizon as J.D. reached down and turned on the radio. Robert Earl Keen's off key voice drifted up though the speakers of his old truck. J.D. realized his radio was still on KPFT; he liked to listen to them in the afternoon driving home from work because they didn't play any commercials. He punched the button and Robert Earl was replaced mid-word by the sexy, whiskey-throated dj on Rock 105.

"This is MoJo in the morning. I'm gonna tell ya one more time to get your ass out of bed." Her sexy laugh oozed out of the dashboard of J.D's truck and made him smile. "Now here's some rock and roll for your ear holes." As Pearl Jam blasted into the cab, J.D. looked out over the water as he crossed the causeway onto the mainland of Texas and spied a large sailboat making its way down the Intracoastal Waterway. *I would spend some lottery money on one of those.* As he imagined himself and Beverly moored in a secluded Caribbean cove, skinny-dipping in the clear blue water, he didn't have the slightest inkling, that in a week, none of his world would exist.

He pulled into the parking lot of International Petroleum about forty-five minutes later and looked for a space close to the front gate. He cruised the lot for five minutes before giving up and going to the back of the lot where he parked every day. *Hell, maybe that's what I'll buy if I win the lottery, a parking space by the front gate,* he thought as he got out of the truck and laughed to himself. Doors slamming and cursory grunts of hello mingled with the sound of work boots on the gravel parking lot as the seven to three shift shuffled toward another day. He merged into a group and headed for the entrance gate. As he passed the row of reserved parking, he spotted his supervisor Lloyd Boone getting out of his truck.

"Hey Boone." Boone looked at J.D. and shut the door of the truck without a word.

"Shore looks good." J.D. slid a hand down the rear fender over the sparkling white paint job.

"It'll do." Boone trudged to the front gate. J.D watched Boone check in with the guard. He glanced back at the pristine Silverado. Not a scratch or a speck of dust to be found anywhere. *He must wash this thing twice a day.* He shook his head, then turned and walked toward the guardhouse. Tom Callie, the guard at the front gate, looked up with clipboard in hand.

"Morning, J.D." Tom made a check on the clipboard with his Bic.

"Tom," J.D. drawled as he pulled his plastic ID card out of his pocket and clipped it on the front of his shirt.

"You gonna get ya a Sliverado like Boone's?"

"Nope, don't want nothin' like Boone's."

He heard a couple of laughs behind him.

"Ain't that the truth?" Tom said with a grin. "Have a good un."

"You too." J.D. waved as he passed through the gate. He headed for the shop and his locker to get his hardhat and put away his lunch box. He thought about Boone as he followed the yellow arrows on the pavement. J.D. had never met anyone as pissed off at the world as Boone. He seemed to hate everything and everybody. He told Bev one time, "I don't think you can call him a racist or bigot because he hates everybody equally."

"No, but you could damn sure call him an asshole and nobody would argue with you," she had replied in that manner of hers that cut right to the heart of the matter. J.D. smiled when he thought about that. Twelve years and four kids later she was still the center of his existence. He remembered the first time he saw her. He was sitting in world history class listening to Mrs. Weaver drone on about dead people, when the principal, Mr. Larry, brought Beverly in and introduced her as a new student at Alvin High. She had an air of self-confidence that radiated out of her in the way she returned the stares of all the students sizing her up. She never looked down or away; she took them all in and gave it back with attitude. She was tall and her demeanor broadcast loud and clear that she knew she had a good body, liked it, and wasn't sharing it with any of the horny adolescents leering back at her. He loved her immediately. This took J.D. aback. He was dating Shelly Morgan, one of the most popular girls in school, was on the student council and played on the football team. He thought everything in his life was just as it was supposed to be. And it was, until that moment.

4

Mrs. Weaver was one of those teachers who didn't take bullshit from anyone, including Mr. Larry, and had over the years, perfected a line of caustic sarcasm that could cut the biggest halfback down to his knees.

"Miss Knight, I'm in the middle of discussing the Christian crusades which you and Mr. Larry have interrupted. Now quit standing there like you're on the cover of some fashion magazine and sit right over there." She motioned to an open seat in the front row. Mr. Larry's smile immediately slid off his face, as Mrs. Weaver's jab sliced through the air and poked him in the chest, but Beverly's expression remained exactly the same.

"You should know a good fashion model never passes up a runway. I think I'll sit back there." Beverly strolled down the aisle in a flawless imitation of a fashion model and sat down at the back of the classroom. J.D. knew this wasn't some high school crush he was suddenly having for a teenage girl who was trying to act cool in an awkward situation. She was the real deal. He was hooked.

The shop was a large concrete block building located in the heart of the plant. During shift change, it was full of men and women opening lockers and standing around talking in small groups.

"Hey J.D." J.D. turned to see Roy Huggins standing beside him.

"Roy boy, made it through another shift with all your arms and legs intact, I see."

"What can I say?" Roy placed his hands together as in prayer. "Another miracle." A number of people standing close by laughed, some nervously. J.D. dialed the number on his combination lock, opened it and put his lunch box inside. He retrieved his hardhat and work gloves.

"Can I buy you a cup of coffee?" Roy dug in his pocket for some quarters.

"You can." There was a small break room in the middle of the building with food and drink dispensing machines along the back wall. Roy found the correct amount of change and bought two coffees. He handed one to J.D.

"Thanks."

They flopped down at a table in the corner of the room.

"Nuthin' earth shattering last night, I take it?" J.D. blew on the liquid in the cup.

"Thank God. They got this son-of-a-bitch running wide open, that's for sure."

"I know. The last two weeks have been the worst I've seen. I walk on egg shells the whole goddamn shift." J.D. took a sip of coffee.

"They're asking for another one, and it ain't gonna to be pretty."

"You'd think after the last fireworks, they would get the message."

"Bullshit. The only message these assholes understand is money." Roy opened a fresh piece of gum and stuck it in his mouth. J.D. knew he was trying to quit smoking. Roy told him that drinking coffee always made him want to light up.

"I would have thought a two million dollar fine would have grabbed their attention." J.D. shrugged.

"Not likely. It probably took all of ten minutes of running wide open like we are right now to pay for that slap on the wrist. They make too much money doing it this way. Besides, fires, explosions, lawsuits; it's all built into the cost of doing business. Safety is what throws the profit margin out the window."

They drank their coffee in silence for a moment. Roy played with the gum wrapper, wadded it into a tiny ball and thumped it in the direction of the trashcan. The room was beginning to thin out. The new shift was starting.

"All I know is I can't take much more of this." J.D. stood and threw his empty cup away.

"What'cha gonna do?" Roy stood up stretching his arms outward, stifling a yawn.

"I got a line on a plant up in Arlington that's supposed to be hiring next month. They make cans."

"Cans? That sounds exciting."

"Hey, they don't have shit blowing up. Now, you might slice a finger off but hell, that ain't no big deal."

"It would be for you, how you gonna pick your nose?" Roy laughed as he slapped J.D. on the back.

J.D. grinned and headed for the door.

"Hey let me know before you ride up north, I might want to ride shotgun with you."

"Will do," J.D. said over his shoulder. "Now I'm gonna go put on some of that well known cologne, unleaded octane."

J.D. pulled into the Chevron Mini Mart on the corner of Texas Avenue and 146. He pumped five dollars worth of unleaded into Thelma and went inside. He stopped at the barrel full of ice inside the front door, dug down to the bottom and pulled out a cold Bud. He paid the cashier and went back out to his truck. As he was opening the door, an Atlas Moving van cruised by. J.D. put his hand up to shade the late afternoon August sun from his eyes and watched until it was out of sight.

J.D. was Vernon and Maxine Younger's only child. He was named after his respective grandfathers, Papa John and Papa David, but everyone called him J.D. from day one unless he was in trouble, and then it was JOHN DAVID. He had loved his dad very much; he just hadn't seen him very much. Vernon had driven a truck for Atlas Moving and Storage. Most long haul, cross-country drivers work

7

out of a main terminal and run to one coast or the other and back again. Not so with moving companies, you go out and work your way back home. Sometimes Vernon would be gone for six to eight weeks at a time. Even though he missed his family, he loved the road and driving. Vernon had tried other jobs; stationary jobs, he called them. He told J.D. one time, "those are the kind of jobs where you don't go anywhere."

J.D. became the permanent man of the house shortly after his fourteenth birthday. Vernon was killed coming off Tehachapi, a dangerous mountain pass outside of Bakersfield, California. He was loaded to the hilt with three families' precious possessions when the pin that connects the trailer to the tractor snapped. When the pin broke it also cut the hoses for the air brakes on the trailer. Vernon sideswiped a half-mile of mountainside and fence post trying to get the runaway trailer off his back, to no avail. He lost control and ended up in a ravine, which stopped the cab almost immediately, but not the fifty thousand pounds of furniture following him. It took the highway patrol and EMS almost four hours to cut what was left of Vernon out of his truck. It was not an open casket funeral.

J.D. slid his lanky six-foot frame into the seat, cranked Thelma and headed for Galveston and his children. He had never been away from his kids for more than one night at a time, and he liked it that way. He smiled to himself when he wondered if Beverly's hair would be the same color as when he left her. This morning while shaving, he had spotted the telltale sign of an unopened box of L'Oreal on the bathroom vanity. Beverly was prone to changing it quite often. Sometimes two or three times a week until she got the color that scratched her itch. It was one of the many quirks that Beverly had that J.D. loved. He told her he liked coming home to a different woman every so often.

One person who didn't approve was J.D.'s mom. Maxine was a no-nonsense, get-down-to-business woman who happened to be a beautician. She had gone to beauty college in Houston right after she and Vernon were married. She had worked at a number of beauty shops in Alvin building up a clientele, and when J.D. was five, Vernon had converted their unattached two-car garage into Maxine's Hair Palace. Maxine had graciously done Beverly's hair for years, but she refused to recolor it at the frequency of one of Beverly's whims. She told Beverly one time that if she didn't quit coloring her hair so often they'd be calling her Kojak because every hair on her head would soon fall out. Beverly had just winked at Maxine, pinched her cheek and said, "Who loves ya baby?" and walked off.

Both Beverly and Maxine were strong willed women who were accustomed to getting their own way, and since J.D. tried to stay on the good side of both of them, he had learned a long time ago to stay out of any disagreement they might have. They always worked it out and they were a formidable force when they teamed up against him. He was lucky they had his best interest at heart.

J.D. stopped behind their old station wagon and got out. The door to the double wide flew open and a stampede of children rushed out. He stood beside his truck waiting for the onslaught.

"Daddy-O," Dallas, his four-year-old, cried as he ran up to him.

J.D. reached down and swept him up into his arms.

"Me too, me too." Dallas's older brother Austin was grinning from ear to ear.

"Okay." J.D. kneeled down to hug both of them. Sometimes he was overcome with the pure joy that he felt in coming home to these little guys. The unvarnished affection that they showered upon him every day more than made up for whatever problems may have plagued him that day.

They were surrounded by three of the neighbor children. The Younger home was a kid magnet in the neighborhood. Beverly thrived on it and the truth was, so did J.D. He turned around and grabbed hold of the five-year old that lived two trailers down.

"Hey Jimmy, give me five." Jimmy slapped J.D's hand and giggled.

Paris, his eleven-year-old daughter, came out on the porch, opened book in hand. She read night and day, despite all the uproar and distraction caused by her three younger brothers. She blew him a kiss and went back inside. J.D was honored that she tore herself away from whatever book she had her nose stuck in, to welcome him home.

"How 'bout me?" a sexy voice said.

J.D. smiled at Beverly standing on the back porch holding Tyler, their youngest, on her hip. She had strawberry blonde hair as opposed to the light brown she was sporting that morning.

"Oooh Madonna," J.D. said, getting up.

"How was your day? I didn't see any mushroom clouds over your way," Beverly said as she stepped down off the porch.

J.D. laughed, gave her a kiss and took Tyler. He felt at ease, now that he was home. "The only thing that blew up was Boone when he found out that we're gonna have to work overtime this weekend."

"Again? Well it's probably a good thing." Beverly frowned.

"Why, what happened?"

"The water heater croaked. I found out this morning when I was turning into Madonna."

They stood looking at one another for a moment.

"Come on guys, supper's almost ready. Time for y'all to head to the house," she said to the other kids. There was a chorus of byes and see ya later as they took off in different directions. Austin and Dallas raced up the steps.

J.D. set Tyler down and watched the eighteen-month-old stutter-step toward the house. He leaned up against Thelma's fender as he watched his family disappear into the house. He knew he had to find another job. One that was safer. He was driven by two concurring thoughts. He couldn't let his kids grow up without a dad, and he couldn't stand the thought of not seeing them grow up. He didn't know which was stronger.

CHAPTER TWO

Lex leaned against the rail, looked out over the blue water and watched the whitecaps as they rolled onto the beach. This was his favorite time of the day. Late afternoon. The hottest part of the day was over but the heat seldom bothered Lex anyway. He was cool under pressure and for some unknown reason he seemed to remain cool in the face of whatever heat and humidity Galveston could throw at him.

The winds had died down and the sun was sinking slowly in the west. He took a sip of his martini and then stirred the olive around in his glass. After a moment he sucked it off the toothpick it was impaled on and sat down. He leaned back in the large blue and white striped chair and set his glass on the round wrought iron table. He put his feet up on the matching ottoman and gazed up at the few white puffs of clouds floating overhead.

The balcony was off the master bedroom and ran the length of the house. The sliding glass doors led into a huge master bedroom with a fireplace and sitting area. There were two more bedrooms, three and a half baths, a den, a game room, living room and kitchen that would rival most restaurants. In all, it covered a little more than seven thousand square feet on an acre of prime beachfront property, and Lex's wife, Sarah, had designed it. The most amazing thing about the house, though, was that it was probably the only project Lex had ever built where he hadn't cut corners or used shoddy material. That was due to the fact that Sarah had supervised every aspect of the building from the ground up. The house had been her vision, and she was so focused on the outcome that she'd nearly driven the contractors, the suppliers and Lex nuts with her rabid fanaticism to make the house a reality as she saw it. But, that was the way Sarah was when she only had the one project to fixate on. Lex could get a little fixated occasionally as well.

He stared out over the water and slipped into a little daydream fantasy involving himself and the new salesgirl in his office. He had hired her only a few days ago and had been thinking of her almost continually since then. She was about the same age as Sarah was when they first met, but much more stunning. The best part was that she seemed awestruck to be working for Lex Levin Developments. The jingle of his cell phone jerked him back into the real world.

"Yes," he snapped into the small palm size phone.

"Mr. Levin, Mr. Ramsey's office called and wanted to know if you would be available next Tuesday for a meeting on the West Beach project?"

"Perfect," Lex said. "Clear my schedule."

"Yes sir."

Lex hit the end button on his phone and laid it on the table. Collin Ramsey was the Mayor of Galveston. Lex had been trying to meet with him for weeks. He picked up his glass and drained the rest of the martini as if it were water.

"All right!" he said out loud.

Lex was in the kitchen mixing his third martini when he heard Sarah's Lexus wheel into the driveway under the house. A few minutes later she came through the front door peeling off her silk jacket and kicking her shoes off onto the Terrazzo tile floor. She tossed her briefcase onto an overstuffed chair in the living room. Lex came out of the kitchen holding two martini glasses.

"Could you use a drink my dear?"

"Bring the fuckin' bottle." Sarah plopped down on the sectional that took up half the room and stretched out her long tan legs.

"Bad day?" Lex handed her the glass.

"Bad doesn't come close."

Lex moved her briefcase and sat in the overstuffed chair.

"Which one today?"

"The Miller project." Sarah leaned her head back and wearily closed her eyes.

He waited. This was their pattern; he drank, she bitched. Lex sipped his drink. After a moment Sarah opened her eyes and stared into her glass.

"Now they want to completely re-think the kitchen and den."

"It's tough dealing with people who can't make up their mind." Lex was patronizing but Sarah didn't seem to notice.

"I know. They want to change everything, every time some distant relative has a new opinion or some friend says 'Oooh, I don't like that'." Sarah made a face for the last part. "Bitsy Miller's real name should be Bitchy Miller." Sarah took a drink. " Trust me, she hasn't done more in the kitchen than open a can of diet Coke since she married Marvin. Now she's become an expert on kitchen design and Marvin is pissed at her about something so he contradicts her at every turn."

Lex started to say something, but before he could get his mouth open, Sarah plowed on.

"And I've got to keep him happy so he stays on the same page I am about the safety features. I had to be a goddamn marriage counselor and referee just to keep them from killing each other in my office." Sarah drained her glass.

"That's what happens when you take on every project that . . ."

"Let's don't go there, okay," Sarah interrupted. "I don't need a fucking lecture from you tonight."

Lex knew better than push it. He got up to mix another drink. When his back was safely turned, he smiled to himself at the irony of Sarah acting like a marriage counselor.

It was a little after nine the next day as Lex strolled into his office.

"Good morning, Mr. Levin," Karen said, as she handed Lex his messages. "These two are from yesterday, and this one came this morning."

Lex took the messages into his office and sat down at the sleek mahogany conference table that served as his desk. There were two original Eames chairs and a small coffee table at the other end of the room in a sitting area. Karen, who had followed him, placed a cup of coffee in front of Lex and left. He didn't look up or acknowledge her presence. He tossed the two messages from yesterday aside and looked at the one from this morning. It was from Dennis Johnson. This wasn't good. *Yesterday was great and now this shit.* He knew something was in the wind a couple of weeks ago when he'd heard from Marcy out of the blue. He crumpled the message up and threw in it in a wastebasket by his feet. He hadn't called her back either. *It has to be the Haven Estates project.* He had known better than to get involved in that little scam, but he had needed the money at the time. He considered his options. He was sure there was no paper trail leading back to him so he decided that he was not going to worry about something that might never happen. He would cross that bridge when he came to it.

He got up and walked over to the expanse of glass. His office was on the top floor of the Frost Bank building in downtown Galveston. The area, known as The Strand, was a big tourist attraction for the city. In the 1850's The Strand was filled with wholesalers, hardware and dry goods, cotton agents and insurance companies.

Charter banks had not been approved by Congress so financial transactions were handled by the mercantile firms. The Strand became "The Wall Street of the Southwest." The combination of the hurricane of 1900, which wiped out the island and killed over six thousand people, and the growth of upstart Houston as a port, almost turned Galveston into a ghost town. Then in the 1920's through the 40's, it became one of the top resorts in the country boasting gambling casinos and the nation's top entertainers. When the state cracked down on gambling and closed the casinos, Galveston was devastated once again. The third resurrection of Galveston took place in the 1980's with the revitalization of The Strand, that included restaurants and shops located in renovated old buildings such as his. The Mardi Gras had become a huge event for Galveston every year and was held on The Strand, swelling the normal population from sixty thousand to over a half million people for the weekend.

Lex first learned about Galveston when he was in high school. As a bored junior, in boring American history class at Council Bluffs High, in the boring state of Iowa, he had discovered Jean Lafitte and other pirates who made their home in Galveston. He was fascinated and read everything he could find about Galveston and the area. Then in 1991 when he read an article in the Wall Street Journal about the revitalization of The Strand and Galveston, he decided this was the perfect place for a budding real estate developer.

Lex could see the cruise ship from the Carnival line as she sat moored to her dock at Pier Two. He watched the passengers as they clamored up the boarding plank for a cruise in the Caribbean. If things went well at next Tuesday's meeting with the Mayor, a cruise might be in order. Maybe Ashley, his newest addition to the sales force, would want to see the Virgin Islands.

Lex stopped next to the construction site office that sat on blocks in front of the fourteen-story office project known as Levin Towers. He slid out from behind the wheel of the deep green Jaguar and looked up at the glistening glass and fake stone. Workers that far off the ground looked like ants bred on speed. Bill must have put the fear of God into them. He had an uncanny knack for getting more work out of people than anyone Lex ever met in construction. He walked over to the office and went inside.

"I thought you said you were going to have the ninth floor finished by this week," he said to the man bent over a small desk. He was studying a blueprint with a phone to his ear.

"The week's not up yet," the man growled without looking up. The desk was covered with sets of blueprints and a stack of dog-eared spec books bent double. He motioned in the general direction of a small chair in front of his desk.

"Damn it, I'm looking at the specs. It calls for two-gauge wire and you sent three-gauge so when the invoice comes in you're gonna be crying because we ain't paying."

Lex sat down in the chair and looked around the office of his project manager. Bill Medlin was in his mid-fifties, but looked much older and would probably age another ten years before this project was finished. Lex had met Bill years ago in Des Moines and they had been working together ever since. It was hard to find a good project manager who didn't mind cutting a few corners or knew how to squeeze blood out of a sub-contractor or supplier.

Whoever was on the other end of the phone said something and Bill grunted, "Fine," and banged down the receiver.

"It'll be finished by Saturday," Bill grumbled at Lex.

"I guess that is the end of the week." Lex grinned.

Bill got up and walked over to the kitchenette in the corner of the room and picked up a pot of coffee and poured a cup. He held the pot up and gestured to Lex. Lex shook his head no.

"I've got preliminary code inspections coming up Monday on the first five floors. Are the wheels greased?" Bill walked back to his chair, reached into his pocket for a pack of unfiltered Camels, and lit a second cigarette. There was one already burning in the ashtray.

"Ten grand greased. We will be completely up to par."

Bill shook his head and took a sip of coffee. He took a long drag and exhaled the smoke slowly. "If we get through with this project without getting caught, I'm through. I'm retiring,"

"Do I need to remind you that you have said that on every project for the last ten years."

"Fuck you."

"And fuck you too," Lex said with a smile.

Sarah Levin's office was in an old house she had remodeled when she and Lex had first moved to Galveston from Minneapolis. It was in a middle-class neighborhood off of 13th Street and Broadway. It wasn't a large house, but it was a charming old Victorian style that had survived many years of Gulf Coast weather and social changes. It sat on a corner lot surrounded by palm trees.

The first in a series of trust funds had kicked in shortly after they had moved to Galveston, and Sarah had used her own money, or rather, daddy's money, to turn the old home into a beautiful showcase. Lex had resented her using her own money because it meant less money for him to get his hands on, and he thought she was pouring it down a Victorian remodeling hole. Lex hated quaint, picturesque, gingerbread houses. Emotional dalliances he called them. Lex liked his architecture sleek, shiny and new, the way he liked his women.

In public he was always so proud of his wife and would never say a disparaging word about her financial independence, which of course was the same financial independence that he had married her for. Sarah knew that if she had come to him for money to remodel the house, he would have found every excuse under the Galveston sun to say no.

Sarah sat at her desk and looked at the plans she had drawn for Marvin and Bitsy Miller's beach house. *Why did I take this project?*

Sarah had sat on enough therapists' couches to know that she was looking for her father's approval. She had tried to convince herself otherwise; that all this work was to prove to herself that she knew what she was doing, that she was a fine architect, but in the dark of night, she still fantasized that her father would finally see what he had missed all those years. Her father was a world-class architect, famous for designing coveted projects and winning awards and industry accolades. She was barely a blip on his radar screen. She was his daughter from his third marriage, behind sons cut from the old man's cloth who already had a significant head start on vying for his affection. Her mother had evidently been a stepping-stone in a long line of unsuccessful unions.

Sarah had been surrounded by nannies paid to give her some attention when she wasn't parceled out to a succession of high-dollar boarding schools. She had made it her business to read everything she could get her hands on about her father and his work so that when she did have an opportunity to see him, she would have intelligent questions to ask. She had even interned in his office during summers while she was in college, which she thought would have led to a job offer, but her father had been in Buenos Aries overseeing a new cultural center project when she had been recruited by another firm, and he had been too busy to return her phone calls until it was too late.

After they had completed their house, there had been a ton of publicity about it. She was sure that her father's clout had influenced the *Architectural Digest* spread, but she didn't care. It was a small crumb he could throw her way, and she would take it. Lex had tried to tell her she would have lots of business. He had cautioned her against taking on every project that came her way. Sarah had told him she would be very selective, but so far she hadn't been able to turn down a single client out of the steady stream that had knocked on her door. She was looking for the perfect client who was ready to back her ideas with a fat pocketbook.

She looked at all the notes Bitsy Miller had scribbled on the plans yesterday during their meeting. *These people are so full of shit.* She sighed heavily. People would always start out telling her they wanted to build a house that could handle any kind of weather and then start backing out when they saw the cost. *When am I going to learn to tell these hicks to go fuck themselves*? She rolled up the plans and eased them into the large tube labeled Millers. *God, I need a vacation.* She looked at her daily planner and punched the button on her intercom.

"Uh, Miss . . . uh . . ." *Shit! What is that idiot's name*? Sarah had gone through two secretaries already this year and had been using a temp agency for the last two weeks.

"Taylor," the voice said slowly.

"Oh yes, would you get Mrs. Welks on the phone for me?"

"Yes ma'am."

Sarah glanced at the picture of her and Lex's house on the desk. It had taken her almost two years of talk and lots of sex to convince Lex. In the end she had to threaten to leave him. That finally did the trick because he was not about to let all that inheritance money walk away.

She had come up with the design when she was in college. Sarah graduated from the School of Architecture of the University of Virginia with the highest of honors and had taken a job with an architectural firm in Minneapolis. She had met Lex at a conference of builders and architects where he was being touted as the hot new developer in town. He had just moved there from Iowa. She was attracted immediately. They began dating and were married six months later. Lex's charm soon faded completely and was replaced by a large self-centered ego. Even though she had foolishly disregarded her father's advice and had not made Lex sign a pre-nuptial agreement, she was seriously considering leaving when Lex told her he wanted to move to Galveston. She jumped at the chance. For her, it was the opportunity of a lifetime. Sarah was positive she had designed a hurricane-proof house.

CHAPTER THREE

She was only twenty-four hours old and had no recognizable shape or discernable movement. She was simply feeding and growing.

Boone pulled into the driveway and stopped in front of the closed garage door. He got out and picked up the water hose lying beside the sandstone walkway leading up to his front door. He walked over to the small faucet peeking out from a dying bush in the flowerbed and turned it on. The water came regurgitating through the hose and began spitting out the end. Boone put a thumb over part of the opening and the water shot out in a narrow stream. He walked around the Silverado spraying the top, back and sides. He continued this until the truck glistened in the hot August sun. He turned the water off and walked past the brown dying grass without so much as a glance. He took out his keys, opened the front door and stepped inside. The house was dark and deathly quiet. Death hung in the air. It was in the closed drapes over the front windows and the twenty-year-old couch and chair that sat in front of them. It was in the carpet, the walls and the ceilings. The smell of death permeated every square inch of Boone's house. Every person Boone had ever loved was dead and so was he, his body just didn't know it yet.

Bonne's whole family had worked for IP as long as anyone could remember and they were staunch company employees. They had bought the company bullshit, hook line and sinker, but in a blinding flash on November 6, 1997, everything that Boone had turned a blind eye to become perfectly clear. The safety short cuts, shoddy equipment, overtime and mental exhaustion were all for one simple reason, to boost the bottom line.

His mother had died a year after the big bang in '97 that had snuffed his brother and his dad. She had simply withered away. She had become withdrawn, then transparent and finally invisible.

The last person to die in Boone's life was his wife, Libby. The big C got her and it was ugly. He was positive International Petroleum had contaminated and killed her the same as the rest of his family; it had just taken longer. After an agonizingly painful six-month crawl to the finish line, the end had come eighteen months ago, but to Boone it felt like yesterday. He reached into his pocket and pulled out the small gold band that he carried with him always. He gripped it in his palm and then slipped it on his pinky finger where it would barely go over the first knuckle.

Somebody was going to pay and pay big. And not some paltry ass settlement like the one that had bought his new Silverado and paid for Libby's funeral. Boone reached into his boot top and pulled out the silver flask, but could tell immediately that it contained no more forget medicine. He walked into the kitchen, got a cold beer out of the fridge, shuffled into the dark living room and flopped down on the couch. He sat there sipping his beer, wrapped in the boiling rage that kept him breathing.

23

CHAPTER FOUR

"You got it on Rock 105. Let's see who's on the line. This is Mojo in the morning, talk to me."

"Uh, hi, this is Richard."

"Girls! We got a dick on the line." Mojo hit the button on the console in front of her that controlled over four hundred voice tracks and sound effects.

"Oooh really?" gushed a group of female voices.

"Uh Mojo, I think I need the Mojo hand," Richard said.

"Okay. Got problems huh? Well you've come to . . . wait, where are you calling from? Your car? Don't you listen to the Mojo?"

"Yeah, everyday."

"Well then you ought to know how I feel about car phones. Pull over and stop."

"Mojo, it's seven fifteen in the morning and I'm on the Gulf freeway; I am stopped."

"You want to talk to me; you pull over to the side of the road," Mojo said and hit the disconnect button on the phone. "Folks, you know how I feel about car phones. If God wanted us to talk on the phone while driving our car, he would have had Alexander Graham Bell invent the Model T," and Mojo was off on one of her well-known rants.

John Scott laughed and winced at the same time as he listened to Mojo's cell phone bit. As General Manager of Rock 105, he knew he would be hearing from Harris Cellular Phones, one of their biggest local sponsors, by ten o'clock. John loved the high ratings Mojo brought to the station, but they were always tempered with the problems that came with having a controversial jock on the air.

Mojo's real name was Bonnie Sloan. She had come to the station two years ago from a radio station in Austin and started on the lowly all night show. It took her six months to move to the morning show where she had the highest ratings in Houston radio. She was twenty-eight years old, single and probably had more men in her life than any woman in town, but they were all nameless and faceless and at the other end of her microphone. The primary target of Rock 105 was eighteen to thirty-four year old males, and she played to them like a dancer at Rick's Cabaret. She made every one of them think she was hot for just him. Bonnie found it easy. She didn't have a very good history with men, but she sure knew how to punch the right buttons when she was on the air. Bonnie was smart and sassy and not only did you hear her voice, you could almost see it as it curled up out of your radio like little wispy twists of smoke. Her sultry, earthy delivery was thick with a sensual presence and like fragrance out of a bottle of expensive perfume; it seemed to attach itself to your body.

Bonnie hit the button and the guitar riffs of Three Doors Down began filling thousands of radios in Houston.

"Damn that was fun," she said to Doc Holiday who was coming on next. She pushed her chair back from the console and hung her headset on the hook next to the stack of CD players.

"Mojo, I'm a grown man, and I haven't got half the balls you do. That crack you made about the Mayor caused me to almost wreck my car."

"Well, I'm sure General John will have something to say about it. He's got to rake my ass over the coals for something. Got to justify his gig, you know." Bonnie gathered up the note pad she doodled on and stuffed it in a Louis Vuitton leather bag. She slung it over her shoulder and headed out, "I'm going to the beach."

She was almost to the lobby when John Scott caught up with her.

"Mojo, got a minute?" John asked.

"Always for the boss man," Bonnie wheeled around with a smile.

"Harris Cellular didn't think the car phone bit was very funny," he said, fooling with his tie. It was a habit he had when he was nervous.

"What'd you think?" Bonnie stared him in the eye.

"Uh, I, uh I thought it was hilarious."

They looked at one another for a moment.

"Well, let me ask you another question. Who runs this station? You or Harris Cellular?" Before John could answer, Bonnie was out the door.

She had stopped and changed from her normal working clothes, a pair of faded jeans and a Rock 105 T-shirt, into a sun dress with her bikini swimsuit underneath. She had the top down on her red Mazda and a basket in the front seat beside her filled with an Antone's sandwich, chips, a bottle of wine, beach towel and Huston Curtiss' *Sins of the Seventh Sister*. It was Friday afternoon, and she didn't have to be back at work until Monday morning. She had made herself a promise not to think about radio all weekend.

Bonnie had poured her heart and soul into her radio career for the last five years, and the attention she was getting now that she was a big star was a rush she'd never known before, but something was missing. Her run-ins with management were occurring on a regular basis, and she had heard rumors that corporate over in San Antonio might be replacing John Scott. That was a little unnerving, not because she liked John so much, but because he was a real radio guy from the old school who loved radio and had worked his way up from dj, to programming, to management. Most of the new breed of radio management came out of sales and were stuffed-suited assholes that knew nothing about radio and didn't care to. Their passion was the corporate world.

But it was more than that, radio didn't give her the instant reaction she now realized she needed. Being a dj was sitting alone in a small room talking to a wall. It was great when someone came up to her and complimented her on something she'd said, or told her how funny she was, but that was much later, sometimes days. She had been seriously thinking about trying stand-up comedy.

Her mind drifted as she headed south. Bonnie loved the beach. Galveston was a far cry from the white beaches of Pensacola, Florida where she had grown up, but it was beach, and it would do. As she passed one of the freeway exits she saw the huge billboard for Rock 105. It still stunned her to see such a large picture of herself, but mostly she was pissed she had let management talk her into the pose. It was a picture of her behind the console. You could see her face but she was turned slightly and it appeared she was wearing only a headset. In giant letters under the picture it read, IF YOU CAN GET IT UP BY 6AM, SHE'LL ROCK YOUR BRAINS OUT. MOJO 6 TIL 10. ROCK 105. *If Mama could see that she'd shit.* She hit the accelerator and kept her head lowered as if someone might recognize her at seventy miles an hour.

Her mother and father were Pentecostal missionaries. When Bonnie was growing up she thought that's what they called all people from Pensacola. Pentecostals. She smiled to herself as she thought about that. *Man, could I do a*

27

stand-up routine on them. She laughed out loud. Her parents were rigid, religious, weird people whom she hadn't had contact with for almost ten years . . . and that suited her just fine.

CHAPTER FIVE

The eye that she had developed overnight offered her no vision but instead was an eerie calm that pierced her from top to bottom.

Collin Ramsey was into his second two-year term as Mayor of Galveston, and he was beginning to think politics might not be quite as bad as he had first envisioned after all. He hadn't really wanted to get into the political world, but a group of fellow businessmen had urged him to run. They said they were tired of the old family money running the city and needed someone pro-business who would look after their interests. Collin reluctantly agreed, and was surprised to find that not only did he enjoy the spotlight, he was genuinely supported by the community. He came in thinking he would do one term and then go back to overseeing the family business which consisted of a motel, a curio shop which rented bicycles, pedal carts and converted golf carts, and two small bars along Seawall Boulevard.

"Mr. Abernathy is on line one," his secretary said as she stuck her head inside his office.

"Thanks, Sue." Collin frowned as he picked up the phone. "Jason, what can I do for you?"

Jason Abernathy was the Emergency Management Director for Galveston. "Got something out in the Caribbean I wanted to let you know about."

Collin sat up in his chair. "Storm?"

"Yeah and it's developing pretty fast. We just noticed her yesterday, and she's already getting pretty organized."

"Shit," Collin cursed, leaning back in his chair.

"Hey it might not even come into the Gulf. I just wanted to give you a heads up."

"'Tis the season," Collin said, trying to keep the edge out of his voice.

"I'll keep you updated," Jason replied and hung up.

Collin hung up the phone, turned his chair around and looked out the window toward the Gulf of Mexico. Collin had been blessed with almost perfect weather as long as he had been in office. The only storm to come close to Galveston in the last three years was Tropical Storm Allison. She turned out to be one of the most costly storms to ever hit Houston, but Galveston had escaped unscathed. She had formed quickly not far off shore and moved over land before she had a chance to grow into hurricane strength. She had only caused some minor flooding as she crossed over the island on her way up to Houston. Allison passed through Houston quickly and traveled over a hundred miles north before she turned completely around and came back for a second look at the Bayou City. This time she sat over Houston for two days and dumped over thirty inches of rain. By the time she left, sections of the city, which hadn't flooded in a hundred years, were under water, twenty-two people were dead and she had racked up over five billion dollars in damages.

Collin did not want to be put in the situation that every mayor dreaded: evacuation. Not only is the decision to call for an evacuation expensive in financial terms, it has another cost that has to be weighed. The public relations hit. If the storm doesn't come in, apathy makes it much harder to get the citizens' attention the next time, and even though the decision to call for an evacuation is made by a committee of the emergency managers of the various cities in the area and the mayors, it's the mayor who takes the heat because he is the only elected official. The emergency managers are appointed.

Another reason the call is so dicey is that it takes over thirty hours to evacuate Galveston Island and at thirty hours out nobody knows where the storm is going to land because it can turn in any direction at the last minute. Most hurricanes coming into the Gulf of Mexico are traveling from east to west and usually make a right turn at some point.

There are three ways to get off Galveston Island under normal conditions. The most traveled route is Interstate 45 over the causeway bridge. The other two exits are the Bolivar ferry off the east end of the island and FM 3005 off the west side. During storm conditions, FM 3005 goes underwater with very little tide and the ferries stop running due to high seas. That means over the causeway and up Interstate 45 is the only way out, a route that is fairly congested all the time.

The reason it takes at least thirty hours to evacuate Galveston Island, a city of about sixty thousand people, is that you also have to evacuate the residents that live in Galveston County and the other bedroom communities on the mainland that are in low lying areas. There are another three to four hundred thousand people who use Interstate 45 as their primary route into Houston.

But that wasn't what was on Collin's mind at the moment. He couldn't afford to call for an evacuation, period. He picked up the phone and punched the button for his secretary.

"When is my meeting with Lex Levin?"

"Next Tuesday at nine a.m."

"Okay, thanks." Collin hung up the phone. He walked over to the window and looked out. He could barely see part of a large cruise ship. He thought about another ship that had departed from that dock a few years ago.

Collin had just gotten settled into his new office and new job as Mayor of Galveston when the special interest groups began lobbying for special favors.

"We really appreciate you seeing us Collin, I know you have a lot on your plate right now." John Hamilton's voice oozed with the practiced polish of a lifelong politician.

"Yeah I just found the men's room yesterday." Collin laughed. "But no problem, glad to meet with you fellows. I think your project will be great for Galveston."

"Good, so do we. We just wanted to meet with you personally so we could extend an invitation for our maiden voyage. We think that your attendance would give us the endorsement we need. Bring your wife. We'll give her the royal treatment. She'll love it."

"I'm up for that. I don't know if Joan will make it or not, she's not much on boats, especially out in the Gulf."

"Well, we only go out seven miles to international waters, but I understand. Some people don't want to go out more than waist deep." John flashed a smile that he had spent many an hour in front of a mirror perfecting.

Collin was in the main casino of the gambling ship *Lucky Star*. It was like looking at a Christmas tree loaded with presents and they all had your name on them. There were rows of slot machines on one side of the room and blackjack and roulette tables on the other. The energy of the room washed over him in waves. He had never been in a casino. Up until now, Collin's gambling had consisted of Tuesday night poker games in college and the occasional football pool.

"Enjoying yourself?"

Collin turned around to see John Hamilton standing beside him with a perfect ten hanging on his left arm.

"This is great," Collin almost shouted.

"Collin, I want you to meet Shanna Black," John said as she held out her hand.

"Miss Black, nice to meet you," he said, shaking her hand. She held on to his hand and looked him straight in the eye.

"I'm not letting go until we are on a first name basis," she said with a smile that sent a small charge through Collin. Being Mayor had perks he hadn't anticipated.

"Shanna it is." Collin grinned.

"Shanna has volunteered to show you around." John patted them both on the shoulder.

"Now, this is the red carpet treatment," Collin laughed.

"Let's go have some fun." She took Collin's arm and began leading him toward the blackjack tables.

And some fun they did have. Collin came home with over three thousand dollars cash in his pocket.

"How was it?" Collin's wife asked him without opening her eyes as he slipped quietly into bed beside her.

"Oh, it was okay," Collin said in a dull monotone as he lay on his back with a smile from ear to ear.

"That's nice," Joan mumbled into her pillow.

Collin hit some good licks in that first year. The *Lucky Star* wasn't so lucky though and went bankrupt in its thirteenth month. By the time the *Lucky Star* had rolled snake eyes, Collin's occasional itch had developed into a full-blown plague. John Hamilton turned out to be Collin's personal Typhoid Mary. First, he started making trips over to the casinos in nearby Lake Charles, Louisiana, but as his habit grew, Vegas became his monthly destination. The first year-and-a-half of his love affair with gambling was a constant high. He loved the energy, excitement and risks that had consumed his life. Collin had always been faithful to Joan and as far as women, he still was, but his mistress now was much more demanding and dangerous than any woman on the planet. Just when he thought life was about as good as it gets, lady luck turned her back on him. The past year had been a downward spiral of massive proportions. It had been a nauseating roller coaster ride that he couldn't seem to get off of, no matter how hard he tried.

First he maxed out his credit cards, then he began milking as much cash out of his businesses as he could. At the first of the year, he had taken a second mortgage on the house, without Joan's knowledge of course, and then three months ago, when some very serious gentlemen were threatening everything from bodily harm to public humiliation, he paid them off with money from the city's emergency fund. Money to be used only in case of an evacuation. He had been sure he could cover his secret withdrawal before hurricane season but Lady Luck was still pissed at him.

CHAPTER SIX

Beverly decided to take the kids to the beach since J.D. had to work overtime. He was supposed to have a five-day workweek, but he seldom turned down the opportunity to make some extra cash. *Where does it go?* Beverly thought to herself almost daily, and the answer would immediately come running in the door with a bloody nose or "Mama, Austin tore my new shirt."

They had two destinations they liked to visit, the beach and the local library. They were both fun and cost nothing, which carried a lot of priority in the Younger household. Beverly had started reading early to Paris, getting her interested in books and had continued the tradition with each of her children as they came into the world. Now they loved to read almost as much as she did. Books had been her companions growing up as an only child. Even though her children had each other and half the neighborhood for playmates, she was adamant that they learn to entertain themselves; books fit the bill, and they helped Beverly retain her sanity.

Beverly had thumbed through a book on time management written by somebody high in the corporate world. *If you really want to know about time management, you ought to come live with four kids in a double wide*, she had thought as she tossed it back onto a table of books that were on sale for a quarter.

"Are we gonna go to the beach?" Dallas had syrup running down his arm from the fork he was holding up with a large bite of waffle attached to it.

"Yes, but first we have to go shopping." Beverly took a wet rag to Dallas' arm. "We have to get some school stuff for Austin and Paris."

"When am I gonna get some school stuff?" Dallas pouted.

"Next year, Dallas. Now finish your waffle so we can get to the beach before the sun goes down."

"Yes ma'am."

Beverly had everyone strapped into Louise, her old Chevrolet station wagon. Paris was in the passenger seat beside Beverly and Dallas and Austin were strapped in on either side of Tyler who was sleeping in his car seat.

"We gonna get a pooter?" Dallas asked lots of questions.

"No, we're not going to get a computer. We're getting clothes and school supplies," Beverly sighed as she backed out of the drive.

"We don't need a pooter, we got you," Austin said and made a farting sound with his mouth. Paris giggled in the front seat and Beverly smiled as she glanced in the mirror at Austin.

"You're the one who poots all the time," Dallas said, trying to slap at Austin.

"Settle down. Let's not wake Tyler up any sooner than we have to."

The two boys made faces at one another around the sleeping Tyler. Beverly turned east and headed toward downtown.

"Where're we going?" Paris raised her head out of the book she was reading long enough to ask.

"There's a new thrift center that opened up over off 51st." Budget management was another of Beverly's duties as full time stay at home mom, a job she cherished.

"Aw Mom, I thought we were gonna buy new clothes," Paris groaned.

"Well sugar, they're new to us."

Paris stared at her mom, willing herself not pout. Her mother didn't tolerate much whining.

Beverly pulled into the parking lot of the new thrift center and eased in between an old Toyota and a new Buick.

"Now what are the rules?" Beverly turned the key off and listened to Louise knock, gasp and finally die.

"No running," Dallas said, rolling his eyes.

"And we stay together," Austin mumbled, looking out the window.

"And?" Beverly said after a moment.

"We use good manners," Paris sighed.

"Okay, as Charlton Heston would never say. Let's unlock and unload." Beverly got out and opened the back door. "There will be treats for everybody if no rules are broken."

A chorus of "yippies" rang through Louise as the kids bailed out. Once outside they got into single file with Paris leading and headed for the front door. Beverly reached in and took Tyler out of his car seat. He looked around sleepily then laid his head on Beverly's shoulder. Watching her troop all but march across the parking lot, her thoughts drifted to her dad. He would be proud of her well-disciplined group.

Beverly was at the opposite end of the spectrum from her dad who had been a strict military man most of his life. It was amazing that the two of them had spoken to one another, much less loved each other, but they had, fiercely. Captain James Knight had been an Air Police in the Air Force his entire career before retiring. During her early childhood, Beverly had a good daughter/father relationship. She couldn't wait for her dad to get home at the end of the day. He never failed to spend time with her and always read to her at night. When she hit puberty, her independence grew and so did the gap between them. By the time Beverly was fourteen, she had lived in thirteen different countries and had attended sixteen different schools. She and her dad hardly spoke and never agreed on anything, especially clothes, music and boys. The saving grace was that her mom, whom Beverly loved dearly, understood them both. She ran interference between the two of them and managed to keep a turbulent peace between the generations.

What finally brought Beverly and her dad together was an unknown heart defect in her mom that came to light on May 13, 1986. Beth Knight died of a heart attack in her sleep at the age of 36. What shocked Beverly even more than the sudden death of her mother was seeing how this tragedy completely devastated her father. Until then, Beverly was convinced that her dad had no feelings of any kind. His near breakdown reversed this perception; their common loss brought them together and bonded them for life.

Her dad had retired from the Air Force shortly after her mother's death and had taken a job in security at NASA, which brought them to Alvin. Even though NASA was located in Clear Lake, a small bedroom community that had built up around the space center, he had chosen to live in Alvin, an older, more traditional small town. He worked for NASA until early last year when a stroke reunited him with her mom.

CHAPTER SEVEN

As Beverly and her troop roamed the thrift store in search of school clothes, a few miles away down Seawall Boulevard, Bonnie rummaged through her bag to see what clothes she had brought to wear to lunch. She found a teal colored blouse and a pair of white shorts that she had bought on her last trip to Galveston. She glanced at the clock beside the bed and saw that she had an hour before she was to pick up Cora. She peeled off her bikini and headed for the shower to rid herself of the salt and sand from this morning's vegetation session on the beach.

As the water rained down on her she thought of when she had first met Cora. It was just about a year ago to the week. She had come to Galveston for her semi-monthly dose of beach therapy and had gone shopping on The Strand where she discovered a little shop tucked away on a side street called Annie's Treasures. She'd gone inside and found Annie had a thing for Oriental fans. Bonnie had been collecting fans since her Aunt Alice brought her one on her eleventh birthday. Alice was a missionary like her parents and spent most of her time in obscure tiny villages in China and Tibet. Her annual trip home was the event of the year for Bonnie and her sister Gail. They loved Aunt Alice and thought she was the only one in the family that was anywhere near normal. She was sweet and loving instead of cold and demanding which seemed to be the preferred Sloan personality trait.

Bonnie had over thirty fans in her collection and was always on the lookout for one she didn't have. She spotted a nineteen-century Canton gilt-metal filigree fan displayed in a small glass counter just inside the door. It was enameled in purple, blue and green with a motif of scrolling flowers. She bent down to get a closer look.

"Would you like for me to take it out of the counter for you?" a voice called from somewhere in the back of the shop. Bonnie rose up and saw an older woman squeeze past a rack of vintage clothes and a counter filled with teapots.

"It's beautiful, but I think I have one similar," Bonnie replied as the woman approached her.

"Oh you must be a collector then." The woman had a wide smile on her face.

"Well, I have a few." Bonnie smiled back. The woman went behind the little glass counter and brought the fan out and handed it to Bonnie.

"Yes, this is like mine." She gently held up the fan.

"I believe Annie told me that one dated back to around 1820 something."

"That would be about right." Bonnie turned the fan to examine it closer. "It's in very good condition," she said after a moment and handed it back to the woman. "But I think one in my collection is enough."

"Are you looking for anything in particular?"

"No, just always on the looking for something I don't have."

"Do you have any ivory fans?"

"Only one. They're hard to find."

The woman's smile somehow grew even larger as she held up her hand and wiggled her finger for Bonnie to follow her to the back of the shop. When the woman reached a counter containing a gigantic old cash register, a coffee cup with three pens and a pencil and the newspaper open to the crossword puzzle, she said, "I'll be right back," and exited through a curtain behind the counter. Bonnie nodded and looked around at the tiny shop. There were a few antiques here and there but mostly collectables from dishes to hand made dolls. In a moment the woman reappeared holding a long narrow box. She sat it on the counter and removed the top and took out a beautiful ivory fan. She handed it to Bonnie.

"Oh my god, this is exquisite." Bonnie took the fan and spread it out.

"Annie found it on her last buying trip. She said she didn't know if she could sell it or not, but I could tell you would appreciate it." It was an 18th century brise' fan, made entirely of inlaid mother of pearl ivory.

"Well, even if she decides to sell it, I'm not sure it's in my budget. Of course I guess I could sell my car." They both laughed.

Bonnie spent another hour wandering around the store and talking with the woman. Her smile and laugh reminded Bonnie of her Aunt Alice. Around four o'clock Bonnie left and told the woman she would come back to see her again. She spent another hour window shopping and aimlessly looking in stores until she noticed the clouds starting to gather. It looked like a summer storm was coming in off the Gulf, so she hurried to her car, and put the top up. She headed back to her motel and as she turned the corner and drove past the little shop with the fans she saw the woman walking down the sidewalk. She pulled over to the curb and rolled down the passenger side window.

"Do you need a ride?" The woman turned and looked at her, then as recognition spread across her face she said, "Oh the fan girl." A low rumble filled the air. The woman opened the passenger door and slid into the seat.

"Thanks. My husband was supposed to pick me up but I have the feeling the son-of-a-bitch is sailing with Captain Morgan right now . . . probably three sheets to the wind." The woman slammed the door closed.

"Sailing?" Bonnie looked at the darkening skies.

"Figure of speech, honey. Captain Morgan is a rum. The asshole is drunk."

"Oh." The language did not offend Bonnie. She was just surprised to hear it coming from this woman who looked like somebody's grandmother. She eased the car away from the curb. "By the way, I'm Bonnie Sloan," she said after a moment.

"I'm Cora Rucker. I hope I'm not putting you to any trouble," she said, not looking at Bonnie.

"Nice to meet ya, and no trouble at all."

Cora was rigid in her seat and stared intently at the dashboard of the car. After a moment she said, "I have a problem with motion sickness and I have to concentrate on one object or I'll barf and you'll have to carry me out on a stretcher."

"Okay, but you'll have to tell me where to go." Bonnie stared over at Cora.

"When you get to Broadway, take a left, then go down to 19th Street, and take a right." Cora continued to stare at the dashboard.

They rode in silence. At 19th Street, Bonnie turned right.

"Take a left up here on Avenue K and it's the third house on the left."

Bonnie stopped in front of the house.

"Thanks for the ride," Cora said as the car came to a halt. "I'm sorry about the little outburst back there. I was just a little pissed at the time."

"Oh, don't worry about it. Glad I came along." They sat in silence for a moment. Cora didn't move to get out of the car.

"Are you going to be all right?" Bonnie looked up toward Cora's house.

"Oh yeah, he's not mean. Well, not physically, just runs his mouth a lot."

"I'm sorry, I know what it's like to be with someone like that." Bonnie stared off in the distance.

"It can wear you out some time."

"Yeah, I got tired of it in a hurry. I sent his ass packing," Bonnie said as she turned and looked at Cora.

"Good for you."

They spent the next thirty minutes cussing and discussing men in general and decided to meet the next day for lunch.

Bonnie stepped from the shower and toweled herself off thinking how it was a wonder that they had become such close friends despite the age difference between them. She quickly dressed and made her way down to the beautiful lobby of the Hotel Galvez.

"Ready for some wheels?" the valet asked as she approached.

"Thanks, Rick."

In a few moments Rick returned with Bonnie's car. It was a beautiful day on Galveston Island so she put the top down, and headed toward Cora's house. She turned on the radio and heard the dj saying something about a hurricane in the Caribbean that could make its way into the Gulf. It was the fourth of the season and her name was Dolly. *Dolly, that doesn't sound very threatening.*

CHAPTER EIGHT

She was growing tall. As she supped from the warm waters of the Caribbean, she was a giant floating paradox. Her aimless, slow- moving outer shell concealed the pirouette dance inside her that increased in speed and intensity with each passing hour.

It was dusk when Boone stopped behind the line of cars on NASA Road 1. The highway was a virtual parking lot this time of day. It was the main thoroughfare through Clear Lake, the sprawling bedroom community that had grown up around the Space Center. Even though Clear Lake and the surrounding area had tripled in population in the last twenty years, NASA Road 1 had only doubled. It had gone from a two-lane highway to a four.

He was tired from the long Saturday shift. Boone hated working overtime and it had become a regular occurrence the last couple of months. He was staring at nothing when a car horn beeped. He focused his eyes and saw a shiny black CRX Honda that was in the inside lane coming toward him that wanted to turn in front of him and pull into the large strip shopping center on his right. Boone could have backed up a few feet and let the car turn in front of him, but he didn't. He didn't because he had seen too many near accidents and wrecks caused by do-gooders thinking it was the courteous thing to do. The problem was that your car blinded the person turning. Since the traffic in the outside lane could still be moving, it was easy to be broadsided by an oncoming car.

Boone sat staring at the young driver facing him who was becoming angrier by the minute. After a while, the car behind Boone backed up to let the highly irritated driver turn. As the car pulled up even with Boone, a twenty-something year old with a scraggly goatee flipped him the bird and called him an asshole. The other two boys in the car were also shooting him the finger and shouting. Boone smiled and watched the car in his rear view mirror as it turned behind him into the parking lot. At the same time the traffic in Boone's lane began moving, and he glanced in his rear view mirror and saw the lane next to him was clear. He eased over and turned into the next driveway of the shopping center. As he drove into the lot he saw the impatient driver about three rows over. Boone gassed the Sliverado and raced to the end of the parking lot. He turned right and stopped at the row the Honda was coming up.

He turned the ignition off, slipped Libby's ring off his pinky finger, and put it in his pocket. Then he reached into the top of his boot and pulled out the small silver flask that resided there and took a drink. The whiskey burned as it slid down the back of his throat. He wiped a hand across his walrus mustache and slipped the flask back in his boot top. He reached into the glove compartment and pulled out a deep blue Beretta 96 Centurion pistol, and slipped it in the top of his other boot. He watched the Honda pull into a parking place about four cars over.

He got out of the Sliverado and quickly walked over to the car. There were two boys in the front and one kid in the back. As he approached the car, the driver started to open his door, but Boone slammed it shut. The driver jumped back with a shocked look on his face. Boone motioned for him to roll the window down.

"What the fuck is wrong with you?" the kid snarled as he lowered his window.

Boone leaned down with his left hand on the windowsill.

"I was just wondering sompin'." Boone reached down with his right arm as if to scratch his leg. He pulled the gun out of the top of his boot, and in the same instant grabbed the boy by the front of his shirt with his other hand and jerked him to the window. In a flash he jammed the pistol in the boy's left ear. The boy let out a yell.

"Holy shit." The kid in the back seat who had a multitude of tattoos on both arms recoiled to the other side of the car.

"I was wondering if I pulled the trigger right now, if it would blow off that asshole's face sittin' next to you."

The passenger in the front seat who looked to be the youngest of the trio immediately slunk as far down in the seat as he could.

"Whatcha think?" Boone pressed the gun into the kid's ear a little harder. The kid could smell the sour whisky on Boone's breath, and it kicked his panic into high gear. He began moaning and sobbing.

"Aw now, look at that." Boone watched the wet spot grow in the boy's crotch. "Seems you're not as tough as you thought you were."

For a moment, time had come to a complete standstill. There was not a sound. Everyone was holding their breath because if they moved a fraction of an inch or made a sound, they knew the world would explode. Slowly, Boone moved the gun away from the boy's ear.

"Do you think you babies can be a little more courteous to your elders from now on?"

All three mumbled, "yes sir," as if their lives depended on it, and it did.

46

"Why don't we just keep this between us? I would hate to have to tell your daddy you pissed your pants."

The boy slowly nodded his head as if too much movement might be the spark that would ignite the combustible situation. Boone stared at the boy for a full minute, possibly the longest minute any of the three had endured in their short lives, then slipped the gun back into the top of his boot and strolled away.

There was a time when Boone would have never dreamed of doing something like that, and it wasn't that long ago.

Boone sat nervously leafing through the Time magazine that was filled with stories of last week's Challenger explosion while Libby calmly stared at the TV that hung in the corner of the room. *Nineteen eighty-six isn't getting off to a great start.*

"The doctor will see you now." The nurse opened the door off to the side of the registration window. Boone and Libby got up and followed her down a white hallway to a small room. There was an examination table in the center of the room and two chairs up against one wall. Boone and Libby sat down in the chairs. Neither said anything. After a moment the doctor came in holding a file folder in his hand.

"Libby, Lloyd. Good to see you," he said, shaking each one's hand. He leaned up against the exam table and opened the file folder.

"I've double-checked these tests twice and..." his eyebrows scrunched together.

"Yes." Libby leaned forward in her chair.

"I can't find anything wrong with either one of you."

Libby sighed out loud and slumped down in her chair. Boone put his arm around her.

"There is nothing physically wrong," the doctor said, scratching his head. "You should be able to conceive children."

The room was silent. After a moment Boone stood up.

"We appreciate you doing the test for us." He turned to Libby who was still slumped in her chair. "Come on hon, we need to go." She looked up at Boone, tears swelling in her eyes and stood up.

"Thank you," she said as she held her hand out to the doctor.

As they pulled out of the parking lot of the doctor's office Boone looked over at Libby leaned up against her door staring out her window.

"You want to stop at Luby's and get some lunch?"

"I'm not hungry," Libby said without looking around. Boone drove in silence for a while.

"Darlin', you know adoption is fine with me."

"I know," Libby said as she reached over and patted his leg. "That means a lot to me, but I think if the good Lord meant for us to have children, we would on our own."

Boone nodded and reached down and squeezed her hand. Boone wasn't much for religion, but Libby was and that was fine with him. It made her happy and that was all that mattered to him.

"I love you."

"I love you too," Libby said with a tiny smile.

Boone and Libby didn't give up trying for a family, but it wasn't in the cards. So they spent the next twelve years giving all the love they would have poured into their children to each other. Their passion became the Houston Livestock Show and Rodeo. They worked tirelessly year round on various committees to promote the show. They even scheduled vacation time so they could participate in one of the trail rides that took place prior to rodeo week. Boone had inherited a little over thirty acres of his great-grandfather's original farm in a secluded area down by Angleton. He had a small barn and corral on the property where he kept two horses. Boone and Libby spent many a weekend riding their horses, loving the outdoors and each other.

CHAPTER NINE

J.D. constantly checked the patties on the grill, as if that would speed up the natural cooking process. Dallas and Austin were engaged in a heated conversation of "is too, is not," over a Dallas Cowboy t-shirt. Paris had Britney Spears cranked to a level just slightly below melting earwax and Beverly was feeding Tyler in hopes of getting him down for the evening. It was Saturday night in the Twin Oaks trailer park, a rather unusual name considering there weren't any oak trees or any other form of plant life within a mile of the place, only two acres of twenty-by-eighty concrete slabs covered with rectangular boxes commonly known as tornado food. J.D. lifted the lid one more time on the old metal cooker sitting on the small wooden deck attached to the side of the trailer. There was a slight breeze blowing in off the Gulf and the stars sparkled overhead as bright as if J.D. and his family lived inside their own planetarium.

"Burgers are ready," J.D. announced to no one in particular. He began removing the patties and placing them on a paper plate as Dallas and Austin skidded to a halt beside him.

"How bout' my weener?" Dallas asked. Dallas was a hot dog man.

"It's ready too. Now get your drinks and sit down." The two boys raced to retrieve their drinks from the old red and white Igloo cooler sitting by the back door. Beverly came out of the door, and with a sleight of hand that would have impressed Mandrake the magician, caressed the crotch of J.D.'s jeans.

"How 'bout my weener?" she asked as she passed J.D. on the way to a weathered wooden picnic table standing on the opposite end of the deck. J.D. smiled and said, "Dessert's later."

"Paris, dinner bell's ringing," Beverly yelled to be heard over the CD player.

The Younger family's Saturday night ritual was underway. Beverly and J.D. made small talk and ate their burgers. The boys were constantly fighting over who mixed the mayo and mustard together while Paris ate in silence, contemplating how she was going to approach the subject of tattoos.

She only wanted a small one on her ankle, but she knew they would both react as if she told them she wanted a skull and dagger in the middle of her chest with the inscription "Up Yours" in bold letters. It wasn't fair. She knew that both her mom and dad had tattoos. Her mother wouldn't talk about it with her except to say that when she was eighteen, they could discuss it. Paris knew better than to ask her dad.

After supper Beverly and Paris cleaned off the picnic table and tossed the paper plates while J.D. took the boys over to a small park located in the middle of Twin Oaks for a workout on the monkey bars.

Later, as J.D. lay in bed looking at the ceiling waiting for Beverly to finish her bathroom routine, he thought of his day at IP. They had another close call with one of the process units. Someone had forgot to check the discharge pressure as they were cleaning a tank. Only a stroke of luck had prevented a major explosion. One of the guys had left his gloves lying on the outlet valve and when he went to get them he noticed the pressure was redlining. He had quickly shut down the operation and prevented a disaster. Another prime example of what can happen when you're working shorthanded and trying to double productivity at the same time.

Beverly came out of the bathroom and slipped into bed beside J.D.

"What were you thinking 'bout?"

"Nuthin'." J.D. lied, not wanting to tell Beverly of how close he had come to being a memory.

"Sure?" She sat up on one elbow.

"Yeah, just things in general." J.D. looked up at Beverly.

Their eyes locked for a moment, and then J.D. shifted his gaze over her shoulder. Beverly rolled over on her back beside him and stared up at the slowly turning ceiling fan.

It hadn't been love at first sight for her that day in Mrs. Weaver's history class like it had been for J.D., but she had sure as hell noticed him. He was the only boy in the class that wasn't mentally undressing her. He had more of a deer in the headlights look. It took almost three weeks for her to fall head over heels in love with J.D. He was funny, thoughtful, self-confident, and most of all, completely adored her. She had told him, when he asked her to marry him, that she wanted a big family. She had hated growing up as an only child.

"The bigger the better. I always wanted a little brother myself and I also think the sooner we get started, the better," he had said with a twinkle in his eye.

They had gotten married as soon as they graduated. Even though J.D. had played all sports, standing a tad over six feet at one hundred and eighty-five pounds, he hadn't caught the eye of any college scouts, and without a scholarship, more education was out of the question. He had gone to work for an oil field service company until it went belly up in the late nineties, then had taken the job with International Petroleum two years ago.

Beverly knew things were worse at IP than J.D. let on. A lot worse.

"Honey, I think it's time for you to get out of there. It's getting too hard to watch you drive off to an accident waiting to happen."

"You remember that gig I told you about up in Arlington?"

"Uh huh."

"They're supposed to be hiring next month."

Beverly rolled over and sat up on her elbow again.

"I think you need to check it out."

"Me too." J.D. looked up at Beverly. "I just worry about making the move, you know, uprooting the kids from their friends . . . new school and everything."

"J.D., the kids will be fine. Trust me, they can handle a move. Hell, a move ain't shit compared to losing their dad for good." Her eyes moistened as she stared at J.D.

"You're right . . . I love you." He pulled her to him. Their lips met and he slid his hand down to her butt and pressed her against him. He pulled away after moment and said, "I think your weener's ready now."

CHAPTER TEN

The sweat poured off of Jack's nose as he fidgeted at the plate trying to get his stance just right. It was a typical August night in Houston, hot and humid. He squared his shoulders and tapped the bat a couple of times on the plate. Everyone in the stands was on their feet. He turned his head slightly to the left to catch a glimpse of the blonde standing right behind the dugout. She was jumping up and down and hollering for Jack to knock one out of the park. He could see her round breasts jiggling under her blouse every time she jumped. He planned on seeing those up close after the game.

Jack turned back and stared at the pitcher on the mound and gave him a see-if-you-can-get-one-past-me look. The pitcher stared back and threw one right by him. *Damn.*

"Strike one," the ump said. Jack stepped back and tapped the bat against his left foot a couple of times. *All right Jack, quit thinking about the boobs and think about the ball.* He moved back into the batter's box and went through his routine again. He squared away and stared at the pitcher, a tall redheaded kid in his early twenties. The kid stared at Jack as he rubbed the softball in his hands and then gave Jack a tiny little smile. The next thing Jack knew, the ump had shouted strike two. *Have I stepped into the twilight zone or what?* Jack stood there with a shocked look on his face. He stepped out of the box and glanced back at the blonde. She was no longer jumping up and down, but was standing with her arms crossed. *Okay Jack, get it together*. Back into the box, he did his routine and got set. The kid wound up and let one go. Jack had it all the way. He saw it leave the kid's hand. Everything was in slow motion. He could see the stitches on the ball as it turned over. He was in a vacuum. It was dead silent. He planted with his left foot and swung with everything he had. The sound cracked through the air breaking the silence.

"Strike three," the ump bellowed.

Jack sat on the balcony of his Washington Avenue condo and looked at the lights of the Houston skyline as he nursed a cold beer. He was by himself since the blonde had left with her girlfriend before the end of the game. *Damn, Jack, there was a time when you could have had both of them up here now*. He took a swig of beer and muttered, " I know," out loud. He had turned thirty-eight a week ago and had been in a funk ever since. It wasn't because of his birthday. Birthdays had never bothered Jack; he usually made a big deal out of them. It was that damn crazy woman, the fortune-teller, reader or whatever the hell she said she was.

He had gone to lunch by himself. It was his birthday and he wanted a hamburger so he went to his favorite burger joint, Otto's on Memorial. He was about halfway through his burger when he noticed this black lady sitting two tables over staring at him. He smiled at her and she got up and came over to his table.

"Excuse me, I know this sounds strange but could I see your hand for a moment," she said with a strange accent.

"My hand?" Jack looked up at her.

"Yes, I'm a reader."

"Reader?" Jack drew the word out slowly as if he wasn't sure what that meant. Jack slowly lifted up his hand. She took it and he felt something. It wasn't like a shock of static electricity that you get sometimes from another person but there was definitely some kind of current there.

"Are you going to tell my fortune?" He asked with a nervous little laugh. "Or how about the meaning of life?"

She smiled again and he could see the flash of a gold tooth. "The right question is: What is meaningful in your life?" She dropped his hand. "Your aura is very dark, you have much sadness in you." With that she turned and walked away.

At first he blew it off and didn't think too much about the incident, but later things started nagging at the back of his mind. Little bits and pieces floated just far enough away to stay out of focus. He felt like everything in his life was a half step off.

Jack was born and raised in Houston. He was the oldest of Bob and Edna Nolte's two sons. He had worked for the Houston Fire Department for eighteen years; the last twelve in Emergency Medical Services. He was a Lieutenant with a cushy desk job that he could do in his sleep. He made good money, he was single, he was in good health and had a great condo with a killer view of downtown. Jack should have been a happy camper, but he wasn't. Instead he was full of anxiety, a feeling foreign to him.

He drained the bottle and as he got up to retrieve another from the fridge, he felt his right knee lock up. He immediately sat back down and massaged it for a minute. *Damn, first time that's happened in a while.* Jack was a high school football star at Bellaire, a suburb of Houston, and had earned a full scholarship to the University of Houston, but whatever thoughts he had of a career in pro football had gone out the window in his sophomore year with a crushing helmet-to-knee tackle.

56

Slowly, he got up and limped through the large living room, past the giant TV and into the kitchen. He opened the fridge and surveyed the contents. It contained a box with a half-eaten pizza, two large water bottles, a bottle of ketchup and sixteen Miller Lites. Grabbing a beer and leaning against the cooking island in the middle of the room, his mind wandered back to earlier that evening.

He had been looking forward to tonight's game. Jack had played in the Houston Men's Softball League for years. Most recently, he had been playing third base for a team sponsored by a beer and burger joint known as Bubba's At The Park. They were one win away from a perfect season and Jack had had the opportunity to be the big hero; something he had done many times through the years, only to go down swinging without touching the ball. What was bothering him now, was that he wasn't upset. It just didn't seem like a big deal in the overall scheme of things. Normally, he would have ranted, raved and stewed over it for weeks. Tonight, he didn't even care about the perky little blonde with the Pamela Lee Anderson tits. Jack turned the bottle up and took a long drink. He gingerly walked back into the living room and flopped down in the large easy chair in front of the giant TV. There was this tiny little knot somewhere deep down in his stomach that was connected directly to the vague uneasiness roaming around in his brain. Something was way more wrong than just missing out on a new piece of ass. *What is meaningful in my life?*

CHAPTER ELEVEN

Boone parked in front of the barn and watched a covey of quail dart behind a large mesquite bush at the edge of the horse corral. The corral was horseless and had been for several months now. Boone had sold the horses at the first of the year. They reminded him too much of Libby. They had spent many weekends riding and working on the corral and barn. He crawled out of the Silverado and stretched in the early Sunday morning sun. It was going to be another hot one, not a cloud in the sky. *I guess that could change pretty soon.* He had heard the reports of a hurricane in the Yucatan Channel. It was still too early to tell where it was heading, but Boone thought this could work out just right for the little surprise he was planning for International Petroleum. He smiled to himself as he opened the doors to the barn and stood there looking at the large silver tanker truck parked inside. He had bought the truck at an auction in Dallas eight months earlier, right after he had made the decision that it was payback time for IP. He walked back to the Silverado and began unloading the ten, fifty-pound bags of ammonium nitrite fertilizer that were snuggled up against the cab. Boone stacked the bags at the rear of the tanker.

Next came the fun part; he lifted a bag over his shoulder with a grunt and started up the ladder attached to the back of the tanker. Holding the bag with one hand, he climbed the ladder with the other. He grabbed the rung and then caught hold of the next one before he fell back. There weren't that many rungs on the ladder, but by the time Boone got to the top and crawled to the center of the tanker to open the middle hatch, he was drenched with sweat. He opened the bag with his knife and began pouring the fertilizer into the tanker.

Boone's payback plan started forming almost a year earlier on September 11, as he sat in front of the television watching the World Trade Center buildings collapse before his eyes. If that had happened five years earlier, before his family had been blown up or died a slow painful death from cancer, his heart would have ached with pain for the families of the innocent people killed. He would have automatically felt closer to everyone around him, even people he didn't particularly like, but wanted to hug because they were fellow Americans. He would have been outraged at the terrorists.

But that would have been the old Boone. The old Boone, who loved his family dearly, enjoyed his job, laughed at silly jokes and adored his wife. That Boone was dead, slowly dying little by little as each member of his family slipped out of his life. The new Boone looked and talked like the old Boone, but was devoid of love, compassion, or empathy. Rage was the only thing alive inside of Boone and it saturated every cell and fiber of his body. The new Boone stared at the TV and only related to the people who had flown the planes. He knew how much rage and hate it took to do something that horrible. All he could think of, as he watched the endless replays, was how he wished those planes had crashed into International Petroleum. He wanted the greedy little men who ran the bottom-line-obsessed corporation known as IP to burn in hell.

A few weeks later he began putting his plan in action. He read as much as he could find on the bomb Timothy McVeigh had used in Oklahoma City. Then he started buying a few sacks of ammonium nitrate fertilizer every weekend. He worked a seventy-five mile radius around Houston, hitting small feed stores, very seldom going to the same place twice. The diesel fuel wasn't a problem because he kept a 55-gallon drum at the farm for his tractor. The detonators were a little harder to come by, but not much. He called a friend of his who worked for one of the biggest demolition companies in Houston. He had met Bradley on one of the rodeo committees they had served on together. Boone told him he was clearing some land and was having trouble with some large tree stumps. Bradley met him for lunch the next day and handed him a sack with five blasting caps in it.

After Boone had bought the tanker, he had crawled down inside the tank and wired the blasting caps in place. He had spent seven months slowly filling it up with diesel-soaked fertilizer.

Boone closed the hatch and crawled off the tanker. He was exhausted and his arms ached from the ten trips up the ladder. He leaned up against the front of his Silverado and stared at his forty-foot bomb. Boone knew he had built quite a little surprise. What he didn't realize was that he had created the nightmare that petrochemical plants all along the Gulf Coast had been worrying about for years.

Timothy McVeigh's bomb that brought down the Murrah Building was four thousand pounds of fertilizer in a mid-size Ryder truck. Boone's little creation was over twenty thousand pounds in a forty-foot semi, five times as powerful as the Oklahoma City blast. Boone was about to set in motion a chain reaction that would consume the nearly three hundred chemical plants and refineries that were clumped together in the Houston-Galveston area, creating an unprecedented environmental disaster. When factoring in the people who would die from the released toxic gasses with the casualties that would result from the explosions, Boone was about to top the 9-11 body count by at least seventy thousand people.

CHAPTER TWELVE

Bonnie and Cora were giggling like two teenagers discussing boyfriends. They laughed a lot when they were together and today was no exception. They were oblivious to the looks and glances of the other guests enjoying the Sunday brunch at the historic Galvez Hotel. On a casual glimpse, they looked like a typical mother and daughter, except they were having too much fun; Bonnie with her four earrings and multi-colored hair of pink, purple and a deep maroon, and Cora dressed to the nines. The Galvez was Bonnie's favorite place to stay when she came to Galveston. It was steeped in island history and had been restored to its original beauty a number of years ago.

"So, how's Harold this morning?"

"Quiet as a fuckin' mute, if you can believe that."

"Yeah, that is hard to believe." Bonnie raised an eyebrow.

"Well, he usually is after he hangs a good one on and last night was a goddamn ten."

Bonnie stared at Cora and shook her head.

"The city changed our trash pick-up days from Mondays to Fridays. That upset his schedule."

"Cora . . . "

"I know." Cora took a sip of coffee. They had been over this territory so much in the last year that there was nothing left to be said. Cora was married to an obnoxious, opinionated drunk. That was Bonnie's take on him. Cora would disagree only slightly. Bonnie couldn't understand why she didn't leave him and Cora couldn't explain it. Of course Bonnie had only known him for a year and Cora had forty-five times that experience.

Bonnie remembered the first time she had met Harold. After many long visits at the shop and Sunday afternoon meetings on the beach, Cora had invited Bonnie home to meet Harold.

"It is purple and pink," Harold boomed as Cora introduced her. Harold was a tall man, at least six three and had the biggest ears she had ever seen.

"Yes, I've outgrown the green and blue stage," Bonnie grinned.

"Well it's nice to meet you. Come in and sit down." Harold turned and headed toward the large easy chair by the window.

"Thanks." Bonnie followed and plopped on the sofa across from him.

Harold could be quite charming when he was sober. Cora said he could also be charming when he was drunk. He could also be mean as a snake when he wanted something. Harold reminded Bonnie of the many preachers she had met in her lifetime, full of themselves, always right and righteous, and as narrow minded as a Republican banker.

"Cora tells me you talk on the radio."

'Yes sir, I've been known to do that."

"Do you know Rush?"

"Well I've never met 'em, but I've sure played a lot of their music."

Harold had a quizzical look on his face.

"Limbaugh, Rush Limbaugh."

"Who's that?" Bonnie knew full well who Rush Limbaugh was.

"He talks on the radio, tells it like it is."

"I thought that was Howard Cosell. He's dead isn't he?" Bonnie asked sincerely. Harold stared at Bonnie, not sure if she was putting him on or not.

"Never mind." Harold turned on the TV to signal that their conversation was over.

What mystified Bonnie was that Cora was no Edith to Harold's Archie Bunker mentality. Cora was smart, funny and fiercely independent. She didn't take any shit from anyone and when they were alone, Cora cussed like a sailor.

"Jesus fuckin' Christ," was Cora's response when Bonnie first told Cora she came from a family of Pentecostal missionaries.

"And you made it out of that crap with your brain intact?"

"I take it you're not into religion either," Bonnie said with a sly smile.

"Honey, my firm belief is that religion is the most destructive creation man has come up with yet."

"That's pretty heavy."

"Listen, more wars have been fought and more people have been killed in the name of religion than anything you can think of."

"What about God?" Bonnie asked.

"Religion has nothing to do with God or spirituality; it has to do with man. Man invented religion out of his arrogance and insecurity that this might be all there is."

Bonnie sat looking at Cora with wide-open eyes, in awe that someone felt about religion the same way she did. At the very same instant that she was thrilled, she was terrified that a lightning bolt was going to turn Cora into a large lump of coal in front of her eyes. As much as she thought Cora was right, the old programming was still in the deepest recesses of her mind, ready to overtake her in a moment like this.

Bonnie and her older sister Gail had been raised more by relatives and church members than by their parents. Their parents were always gone on some missionary trek around the world to spread the gospel. They were never without food or clothing, or treated badly, but as they got older, the constant indoctrination of the Pentecostal faith by whoever was keeping them that week or that month, brought the two of them closer together by rebelling against it. A couple of events happened when Bonnie reached high school age that caused her to turn her back on religion and her parents for good. The first was the realization that her parents loved their religion more than they loved her, and secondly, when she discovered the zenith of the Pentecostal faith, which was speaking in tongues (supposedly a gift from God to a chosen few), could be achieved by drinking large quantities of tequila in a short period of time.

Both Gail and Bonnie left home as soon as each turned eighteen. Gail had married and moved to Portland, Oregon, where she resided with her husband and three children. They talked on the phone at least once a week.

Bonnie had chosen education as a way out. After graduating valedictorian and almost acing her SAT test, she had a number of academic scholarships offered to her. She took the one farthest away from Florida, a small school in Texas.

"You're awesome," Bonnie said softly as Cora's statement rolled around her brain.

"I don't know about that, but I am old enough to say what I think and not give a fuck what anyone else thinks about it."

Bonnie had to admit, Cora certainly seemed to lead her life her way. There was only one area of her life where she was dependent on someone else; because of her rare version of motion sickness, she didn't drive. Thus Cora, depended on Harold, friends or the local cab company for transportation.

"Maggie was telling me about Anne Rice's new book. I want to get it." Cora took a sip of her Mimosa. Maggie was one of Cora's many friends whom she talked about, but Bonnie had never met.

"Oh, I can't handle that vampire stuff."

"Bonnie, her sex scenes are the best." Cora laughed.

"Sex, what's that?" They both laughed loud enough to turn a few more heads in the Hotel Galvez dinning room.

Four blocks from the Hotel Galvez, The Recycle Shop was doing a booming business. Collin Ramsey's bicycle and shell shop was overflowing with customers on summer vacation. They were renting three wheeled bicycles and converted golf carts to cruise Galveston's Seawall Boulevard. Even though Collin was in his third year of being Mayor of Galveston, he still liked to come down and work a few hours in one of his businesses on the weekend. He didn't want to lose touch with the man on the street.

"Excuse me, how many hours do we get for $15.00 dollars?"

"I'm sorry?" Collin said, turning away from the TV where he had been watching the latest weather report.

"How long does the fifteen dollars get us?"

"Two hours."

"Okay, thanks." The man turned away and Collin went back to watching the TV. He had been preoccupied all morning worrying about the season's fourth storm. He knew the odds were in his favor of Dolly not coming close to Galveston, but he also knew Lady Luck was still treating him like an ugly stepchild. The knot in his stomach grew tighter with each breath.

Ten miles to the west of The Recycle Shop, Lex Levin was slowly opening one eye. A drum and bugle corps convention was being held inside his head and his mouth tasted like he had sucked on an old sweat sock. He and Sarah had attended a neighbor's birthday party the night before and the celebration had lasted until the wee hours of the morning. He gingerly lifted his head off the pillow and opened his other eye as Sarah came bouncing into the room.

"Well, are we alive after all?"

"I wouldn't call it alive," Lex croaked. "Just breathing."

"You were certainly lively last night. You were all over the place, mostly all over Jane."

Lex acted as if he hadn't heard that last remark. He gingerly sat up and squinted out through the glass doors at the blue waters of the Gulf.

"I'm surprised Sam didn't cut your dick off and hand it to you."

Lex tried to focus his blood shot eyes on Sarah.

"Oh I guess you don't remember."

He ran his hand through his hair, but softly. Even it hurt. He didn't remember fucking up. Hell, he couldn't remember much of anything. He vaguely remembered sitting out on Sam's deck talking about Levin Towers with Jim Winters and Pat Johnson. This wasn't the first time he couldn't recall all of the previous night's events. He felt a stab of panic and anxiety start to drill into his foggy brain. He got up and stumbled toward the bathroom for a shower.

"Looks like Dolly's a full blown hurricane. Maybe she'll visit us."

Oh good, that's what I need, Lex thought as he gently closed the bathroom door. Hurricanes were not in Lex's game plan at any time. He glanced at himself in the mirror. *Shit, I look as bad as I feel.* He stepped into the oversized shower, adjusted the water temperature and turned the massage spray on full. As he showered, he thought about the impending storm out in the Gulf. When Lex was growing up in

66

Iowa, he had seen his share of destruction from tornadoes and had a healthy respect for the havoc that Mother Nature could bestow.

When he had first moved to Galveston, he hadn't worried much about hurricanes because they didn't show up in the middle of the night unannounced, like tornadoes. A person had plenty of warning about a hurricane and Lex felt anyone that was caught in one was an idiot. He would begin making plans to exit the island in plenty of time.

CHAPTER THIRTEEN

Only a few days old, she was already quite organized and was rapidly molding into a recognizable form. She instinctively headed for warmer waters.

Galveston's Emergency Manager, Jason Abernathy, arrived at his office shortly after eight a.m., just as he had for the last twenty years. The sun glistened on the blue waters of the Gulf. It was Monday, August 26, Jason's wedding anniversary. As he climbed out of his county-provided pickup truck, his thoughts were not on Cathy, his wife of twenty-five years, but of Dolly, who had only been in this world a mere three days and counting.

"Roger, anything new with Dolly?" Jason asked his assistant as he unlocked the door to his office.

"She's gettin' it together."

"This could be it; the one we've been dreading." Jason set his briefcase on the small metal desk scrunched into the back of the room. Jason hung his hat on a gray metal coat rack, the only other piece of furniture in the room. He had made this same statement for the eight years he had been Assistant Emergency Manager, and the following twelve years as Manager, for every tropical storm or hurricane that had shown up on the National Weather Service radar screen. Jason wasn't a meteorologist but he probably knew more about hurricanes than some of the weathermen in the area and he was convinced that Galveston was going to take another hit like the big one in 1900. That one killed between six and eight thousand people, depending on which report you read.

Jason's interest in hurricanes began in 1983, his first year in emergency management, which was also the same year that the last hurricane to touch Galveston soil had arrived. Hurricane Alicia was a Category 3 and caused major problems in the Houston/Galveston area. The maximum storm surge was 12.5 feet in the Seabrook area. Alicia got Jason's attention and opened up an insatiable study of hurricanes that continued to this day.

"So far she hasn't made up her mind if she wants to visit the Gulf shores or the Atlantic Coast, but I think she's wobbling a little to the north. We'll see when we get her latest coordinates."

"Let's keep our fingers crossed."

"Hell, I'll take up cross-stitch if it'll help," Roger said as he walked out of the room. Jason watched him leave and nodded his head. *Yeah, let's cross everything* he thought as he made the sign of the cross. *This could be the one.*

This could be it, thought Boone as he sat in the small meeting room with the seven other senior supervisors of International Petroleum. *Just what I've been waiting for.* They were going over stage three of the company's hurricane plan. Stage three was enacted when a hurricane formed that could come into the Gulf of Mexico and possibly strike the Texas coast: primarily it consisted of clean up and securing all buildings. If the hurricane did come into the Gulf, they would go to stage two which would mean shutting down certain processing tanks. It took about eighteen hours to cool down and drain the tanks. If it became a real possibility of the hurricane hitting in the Houston-Galveston area, they would go to stage one which was a complete lock-down of the plant with only a skeleton crew. He knew this would be the best time for his little surprise. If they went to stage one, Boone would make sure he was heading up the crew. The thought crossed his mind that he hoped whoever volunteered for the lock-down crew were people he didn't like. Then he realized it really didn't matter, he didn't care for a living soul in this plant, and that included himself.

Well, this could be it, Collin thought as he slumped down behind his desk and stared out the window at the Gulf. He could see the headline in his mind:

Galveston Mayor Indicted on Embezzlement Charges

This goddamn hurricane was coming to wreck his life; he was sure of it. He punched the button on his intercom.

"Sue."

"Yes sir."

"Has Jason called this morning?"

"No sir. Do you want me to get him on the line for you?"

"No . . . uh, yes, would you?" Collin got up and walked over to the coffee pot sitting on the table by the window and poured his third cup of the morning. He looked out of his third story office window at the blue waters and crystal blue sky. "You're out there somewhere you son-of-a-bitch," he said softly.

"I beg your pardon?" Sue said.

"What?" Collin said, turning around and seeing Sue standing in the doorway. "Nothing, just muttering to myself."

"Jason's on line one." She closed the door. Collin walked over and picked up the phone.

"Jason, anything new on our girl?"

"Actually, she took a little turn to the north this morning."

"Really?" Collin exclaimed.

"Yeah, just a little, but still it's a good sign. If she keeps it up she'll be unpacking her bags in Florida instead of somewhere around here."

"Let's hope so," Collin said, flopping down in his chair. "Keep me up to date."

"Will do." Jason hung up.

Collin set the phone in its cradle and let out a big sigh.

This could be it, thought Sarah as she sat at the bar sipping her coffee and reading the morning paper. She had been waiting for a hurricane ever since they had completed the house. *God, am I sick or what?* She felt a twinge of guilt as the thought crossed her mind. She certainly didn't want anyone to be hurt, but the only way she could prove that her design would stand up against a hurricane was to be in one. And besides, if you live on the coast, you're going to have to deal with a hurricane sooner or later, she told herself. She had been here over five years and the biggest blow to hit this island was Lex.

Maybe that could be it, Jack thought as he pulled into his parking space and turned off the engine. The idea had come to him on the drive to work. It's that invisible line or point that everyone crosses sooner or later. It was that point when you didn't have IT any more, whatever IT was. For an athlete, it was that step or that reaction you didn't have any more. For most people it was simply when you were no longer young but had become old. The problem was you never knew exactly when you crossed that line. IT only came into vision with hindsight. He looked up at his reflection in the rear view mirror. The gray hairs at his temples seemed a little more predominate than he remembered. *She said I had a great sadness about me. Could that be what's wrong with me? I'm sad because I'm*

71

getting old? As he climbed out of his car he had the uneasy feeling it was much more than that.

CHAPTER FOURTEEN

Sue ushered Lex into Collin's office. It was nine o'clock Tuesday morning and Collin was sitting at his desk looking at the latest report on Dolly. She hadn't moved much in the last twelve hours. It was still up in the air, which way she was going to go.

"Mayor," Lex said, extending his hand.

"Lex, good to see you again." Collin stood up from behind his desk and came around to shake his hand. "Have a seat." Collin pointed toward the two chairs beside the small table in front of the window. "Coffee?"

"No thanks." Lex sat down.

"One more for me and I think I'll have my heart started." Collin poured a cup and sat down in the other chair. "I assume you're wanting to talk about the West Beach."

"Beats talking about the weather." Lex smiled.

"That's the damn truth. Here we are almost to Labor Day weekend and a goddamn storm is sitting out there," Collin said, a little more forcefully than he intended.

"I didn't mean to be flippant about it. I know if it heads this way it can be bad for all of us."

"Yeah, some worse than others." Collin gazed out the window, took a sip of coffee and then turned to Lex. "You know you've got an uphill battle with the council on this West Beach project."

Lex nodded. "All I can say is some of the rumors of what I want to do out there are completely false. If the council would give me the opportunity to lay out my complete plan to them, I think they would see this is a great thing for Galveston."

"Well, I think I have an open mind and I could be a big help to you if we can see eye to eye on the details."

Lex analyzed Collin for a second, then leaned forward, but before he could say anything, Sue knocked and came through the door.

"Sorry to bother you Mr. Ramsey, but Jason Abernathy called and wanted to know if he could get with you this afternoon to talk about evacuation procedures if Dolly makes a move today."

Collin sighed and said "Sure, anytime after three. I'm clear aren't I?"

"Yes sir," Sue said, closing the door.

"Why don't we take a drive out to West Beach and you can explain just what you have in mind."

"Great idea." Lex stood up.

Collin and Lex were standing in the middle of the property where Lex wanted to build Galveston's first high rise condominium in nearly a decade. It was a beautiful blue-sky day as they stood looking down the beach.

"It's gonna take some strong convincing that it's not going to become a concrete jungle out here. People are used to the look of beach houses," Collin said. "Not to mention dealing with the environmentalist." Collin wasn't sure how to play this. He had never done anything like this and he didn't want to come on too strong.

"What I have in mind will only enhance the look and add to their property values. I have also commissioned an environmental study that will give a complete approval."

That was a good sign. If Lex had bought himself an environmental study, surely he would be willing to buy some mayoral influence. Collin reached down and picked up a seashell and tossed it into the water that ran toward their feet and then slowly ebbed back to sea. "I think it will take more than that to turn the council around."

"Let's cut to the chase." Lex turned toward Collin. "Just how much is it gonna cost to turn em' around, Mayor?"

"Fifty thousand," Collin spat out, without looking Lex in the eye.

"Fifty thousand," Lex repeated slowly. "That's a nice round number."

Collin kept staring out at the whitecaps of the waves as they fell on the beach. He wanted to act cool, as if this was the way he always did business, but he was wound tight as an eight-day clock. He could feel a thin line of moisture forming on his top lip and just around his hairline, and he knew he had to keep his mouth shut or the price would go down. The first one to speak lost in these negotiations.

"I think we can do that," Lex said after an eternity. Collin unclenched his fists at his side. "But it's going to take a little time to get things arranged." Collin tensed again immediately.

"How much time?" Collin asked, taking every ounce of energy in his body to sound calm and relaxed.

"I can have half of it by the end of the week and the rest in two weeks."

Collin knew he had no alternative but to accept whatever terms Lex wanted. He couldn't let Lex know how desperate he was, so he nodded his head and started to the car.

"Oh Collin," Lex said. "One other thing."

Collin froze, and then slowly turned around.

"Nice doing business with you." Lex had his hand out and was smiling like a hungry cat looking at his dinner.

"Uh, right." Collin shook his hand and turned away as the nausea in his stomach threatened to explode upward.

CHAPTER FIFTEEN

"She's on the move," Roger said as he entered Jason's office.

"It's about time." Jason looked up as Roger came around to his side of the desk.

"Look at this," Roger said, pointing to the coordinates on the paper. "She's in the Gulf."

Dolly had barely moved in the last eighteen hours, but now it looked like she had finally made up her mind which coast she was going to visit.

"They're sending in a plane in the next hour, we'll see if she's changed much."

"I have the feeling she hasn't."

"Me either," Roger said as he left. Jason reached for the telephone.

Jack sat at his desk staring at the blank computer screen. His only accomplishment of the day was winning fourteen straight Free Cell games and two games of Solitaire. He couldn't focus on anything other than the mindless escape of the computer games. It had been like this all week. Nothing interested him. Nothing. And he was tired. He hadn't slept well because of nightmares and night sweats and now all he wanted to do was go to sleep. *That damn woman, who was she?* He was about to try one more game of Solitaire when Donnie Mayes stuck his head through the open door.

"Hey Nolte, Dolly's in the Gulf. Captain wants you start on the work schedules. If it comes this way, we're gonna need everybody." Jack stared up at Donnie like he'd spoken to him in Greek.

"You okay?" Donnie asked, stepping into the room.

"Uh yeah, just had something on my mind. I'll get to work on it."

"We're gonna make a downtown run tonight, hit The Mercury Room, and a couple of others. You wanna come?" Normally Jack would have led the pack, but he shook his head instead.

"Naw, I got some stuff to do." Donnie looked at him in disbelief for a moment, then left. Jack returned his stare to his computer screen. A name was running through his mind, but it wasn't Dolly, it was Molly. *Where in the hell did that come from?* Molly was a name he had buried deep and a long, long time ago.

Molly was a year older than Jack. She was a cheerleader at Bellaire High and possibly the most beautiful girl Jack had ever seen. She was also the deciding factor in his trying out for the football team that year. Jack made the team, although he was never sure why. He barely tipped the scales at a hundred and fifty pounds soaking wet and was just a whisper under five foot eight. He guessed they needed a live blocking dummy or something for practice. He was on the "B" team, of course, but he was a member of the Bellaire High football team with his picture in the school annual and the whole bit. But the real treat of the year was that he ended up in drama class with Molly and they had become friends.

To his surprise, Molly had no clue he was on the football team, in fact she knew very few of the players and had only tried out as cheerleader the year before because her mother had pressured her in to it. Molly liked Jack because he was funny. Humor had been the centerpiece of Jack's personality for most of his young life and he used it to his full advantage.

Jack knew Molly had a boyfriend, and knew him well. Dutch Harris Jr. was in his final year at Bellaire High where he had been the star halfback on the football team for three years. His dad had been an All-State running back at Bellaire thirty years before Junior stepped into a pair of cleats. Most of the kids called him Little Dutch, but never to his face because he was so sensitive about his height. Little Dutch wouldn't know Jack from a hole in the wall; at least that's what Jack thought, until one day just before spring break when Dutch confronted him in the school cafeteria.

Jack had just piled his tray with food and sat down with a couple of his buddies when Dutch came swaggering over to their table. Dutch wasn't much taller than Jack, maybe an inch, but outweighed him by about fifty pounds and was solid as a rock from the workout room. He stopped next to Jack with his arms crossed. Jack looked up at Dutch; his forearms looked the size of Jack's legs.

"I hear you and Molly are quite cozy in class."

Jack stared up at Dutch. He could feel the blood rushing up his neck and into his face.

"I, uh, I don't know . . . "

"Shut up dickhead." Dutch cut him off mid-sentence. "Molly is my girl and if you need someone to work with you in your stupid little plays, find someone else."

Jack's mouth was open but nothing came out. Out of the corner of his eye he saw Molly walk up.

"Dutch quit being an ass," she said. "Jack's a nice guy."

"Well, he's going to be a nice guy with no front teeth."

Jack could picture Dutch's fist knocking his front teeth out with no problem. He also got a clear vision of other maiming that could take place on his body. He still couldn't get his mouth to work and he knew his face must have been beaming like a red exit sign. Dutch stared down at Jack for a few more seconds, then turned and walked off with Molly trailing behind him. Jack slowly let out his breath and faced his buddies. They seemed to be in a state of shock also.

"Have you been fuckin' around with Molly?" Ricky Walton asked.

"No." He looked at Sammy and Will sitting across from him. "I don't know what that was about." Jack got up and walked out of the cafeteria feeling as if every eye in the room was staring at him like he had the world's biggest zit on his forehead. He walked straight down the hall and out the front door. He found a concrete bench under a large oak tree and collapsed on it. He knew exactly what Dutch was talking about.

Two months earlier Jack and Molly were cast as the leads in a one act play for the interscholastic league contest. In the play it called for Jack to kiss Molly, nothing passionate, just a quick good-bye kiss. About a week after they had been cast, Molly asked Jack if he would like to come over to her house after school so they could rehearse. Somehow Jack managed to say, "Yeah, that sounds cool. What time?" without stuttering or jumping up and down with glee.

"How 'bout eight?" Molly blessed him with one of her thousand-watt smiles.

He was at Molly's at eight on the dot. She invited him in and led him through the house to a large den.

"I'm going to meet your dad at the club."

Jack turned to see a pretty woman in her mid-forties standing in the doorway.

"Okay, Mom. Oh, this is Jack. He's in the play with me."

"Nice to meet you, Jack."

"Nice to meet you, Mrs. Ryan."

"Ready to get started?" Molly asked.

An hour later Jack and Molly were locked in a deep kiss. It was only supposed to be a peck on the lips, but the instant his lips touched hers, an electric current ran through his body. Instead of pulling away, Molly kissed him back. He felt her tongue touch his and it sent a jolt that raised goose bumps on his arms. It felt as if the air in the room had gotten lighter. Jack was pretty sure he was dreaming. He really couldn't be standing here kissing the girl he had been secretly in love with for at least a year. But when Molly slid her hand down to his butt and pulled him to her and ground her crotch into his, he knew he was wide-awake. They finally pulled themselves away from each other about ten minutes before her parents were due home.

"I think we might need to work on this again tomorrow night, don't you?" Molly asked, looking up at Jack with the bluest eyes he had ever seen.

"Oh yes, definitely."

They met the next night and quite a few more after that. Each night the period of time of working on their lines prior to the kiss became shorter and shorter. Jack didn't know what to think. He knew he was in love with Molly, hell, he'd been in love with her way before the first kiss, but he still didn't know how she felt about him. She never said anything; they just kissed, hugged and groped each other for an hour or so and then he went home.

And she sure didn't tell Dutch just now in the cafeteria that she was madly in love with Jack. *No, she said I was nice. Nice. What the fuck did that mean? Nice kisser? Had nice hands for feeling her tits?* Jack leaned back against the tall oak tree and let out a big sigh.

Jack saw very little of Molly after the infamous cafeteria incident. There was no more rehearsing. They won second at the interscholastic league contest and he only saw her in class the rest of the year where she would hardly look at him.

That summer Jack hit a growth spurt that was unbelievable. When school started the next August, he was a solid hundred and ninety-five and stood six-foot one. He had worked all summer at a city swimming pool as a lifeguard and his muscles were smooth and slender from swimming a hundred and fifty laps every day. By the second week of football camp, Jack was the starting quarterback. He was the fastest player on the team and could throw a football over sixty yards with deadly accuracy.

The first day of class he saw Molly in the hallway standing by her locker. He hadn't seen Molly all summer and knew that Little Dutch had gotten a full scholarship to TCU. He assumed they were still together. He walked up beside her.

"Hi," Jack said, leaning up against a locker. Molly turned around and looked up at Jack.

"Jack, is that you?" She had a bewildered look on her face.

"Yeah, I ate my vegetables just like my mom told me to." Molly laughed and then they lingered for a moment until the silence became too awkward.

"You taking drama again this year?" Molly asked.

"Yeah, you?"

"Yes, maybe we'll get the same class again."

"I'd like that." Jack smiled down at her.

"Me too. That would be nice."

Nice. The word stung Jack.

"I'd better get to class. See you around." Jack turned and walked away.

Not only did Jack and Molly end up in the same drama class, but also a speech class that Jack wasn't going to take but changed his mind at the last minute. Seeing Molly a minimum of twice a day, it wasn't long before they were eating lunch together in the cafeteria and spending time together at a burger joint down the street from school. One day Jack managed to screw up his courage enough to ask if she and Little Dutch were still together.

"I guess," she said meekly, not looking Jack in the eye. "I write him all the time but he never writes back."

"I can understand that." Molly whipped her head up with a shocked look on her face.

"I doubt if he can write," Jack managed to say before Molly could get her mouth open. She stared at Jack for a moment then they both burst out laughing. It wasn't long until Jack and Molly began officially dating.

Life couldn't get much better as far as Jack was concerned. They were having a great year in football, thanks mostly to Jack, and he was madly in love with the most beautiful girl in the world and she seemed to be in love with him. Molly had written Dutch a long Dear John letter shortly after they began dating. He hadn't written back but then he had never written her since trotting off to TCU to be a big football star like his father. It was during spring break that Dutch popped back into their lives. Jack and Molly were sitting at a table in the food court of Sharpstown Mall when Dutch strutted up to their table.

"Well, look at the cute little high school sweethearts." Molly jumped when she heard his voice. She looked up at Dutch who was standing with his legs apart and his arms crossed like some school principal that had just caught someone cheating on a test.

"Dutch, don't make a . . ."

"Shut up, bitch, I'll get to y . . ." Jack's right hand shot out and grabbed a hand full of Dutch's crotch before he could finish the sentence. In the next instant Jack seized the front of Dutch's shirt with his other hand and jerked his head down on the table. As Jack increased the pressure on Dutch's balls, tears began filling his eyes. The pain was so intense he couldn't open his mouth to speak.

"Now that I've got your attention, *dickhead*, here's the deal. You apologize to Molly, and then you crawl out of here and never let me see you again." Jack squeezed a little harder to get his point across and Dutch began an eerie little whine that escaped between his clinched jaws. "Have you got that?" Jack squeezed some more and Dutch quickly nodded his head in an affirmative manner as if he was afraid to open his mouth or he would begin screaming. Jack then gave a hard shove to Dutch, sending him crashing into the table beside them where he crumpled to the floor and curled up in a fetal position. Jack got up and walked over and stood beside Dutch.

"I didn't hear your apology," Jack said. Dutch, who hadn't seen Jack since his growth spurt had kicked in, looked up at the six-foot one, hundred and ninety pounder staring down at him.

"I'm sorry," he whispered weakly. That was the last time Jack ever saw Dutch.

For the next couple of months Jack was on cloud nine. Jack and Molly had moved from heavy petting to lovemaking and Jack couldn't wait to race to school the next day and see Molly's beautiful smile. But when the month of May rolled around the white elephant that had been sauntering around with them all year finally got too big to ignore. Molly was graduating and was expected to go off to college, and it was TCU of all places because mommy and daddy were both big-time alumni. The fact that Molly was a year older than Jack suddenly loomed larger than life. A couple of nights after Molly walked across the stage and picked up her diploma was the first time she brought it up. They were in a small motel down by the Astrodome that had been their tryst locale for the past year. It was clean, out of the way and cheap. They were in bed after an exhausting session of lovemaking. Jack was lying on his back with Molly snuggled up under one arm.

"Jack, do you want to marry me?"

"Of course. You know that." Jack stroked her hair. Molly sat up on one elbow so she could look at Jack.

"But when?"

Jack scooted up so he could lean against the headboard of the bed.

"Well, I don't know. I have to get out of high school first."

"I know," Molly sighed and laid her head back on Jack's chest. She slid her hand down under the sheets until she found what she was looking for. She took Jack in her hand and felt him start to get hard almost immediately. "You know, the sooner we get married, the sooner we can do this every day," she said as she slowly stroked him.

Jack reached down and turned Molly's chin up and kissed her deeply and then worked his way down to her breast where he ran his tongue around her nipple. Within minutes he had pulled Molly on top of him and they were making love for the third time that night.

She didn't say a thing about getting married for the next couple of weeks and then it seemed to come up almost every time they were together, until it escalated into a huge fight around the Fourth of July. They both said things in the heat of the argument that they regretted later but never apologized for. Jack knew he loved Molly more than anything in the world but he also knew he couldn't get married now. He had another year of high school and he needed to go to college to get a good job to be able to take care of a family. He also knew he had a good shot at getting an athletic scholarship. They just needed to wait. It would be difficult with Molly going off to school, but he was sure they could manage for at least a year. Jack couldn't understand why Molly didn't see this the same way.

Things seem to cool off for a few days, and then after Molly got back from a trip to Fort Worth to enroll at TCU, they had another big fight ending with Molly telling Jack she didn't want to see him anymore. Jack, in all of his wisdom at the age of seventeen, said that suited him fine. He never wanted to see her again, and he didn't. He did, however, see her picture in the Houston paper some six months later announcing her engagement to Dutch Harris, Jr. Jack made a solemn promise to himself that day never to trust women again. So far he had been true to his vow.

Jack got up and walked around his desk to look out the window. It was a beautiful August day. He stopped in front of a hurricane-tracking map of the Gulf of Mexico that covered almost a whole wall. *Dolly.* Then he thought about the girl at the game last Saturday night. *Big fuckin' deal.*

By six that evening, Dolly's progress was well documented by the local radio and television stations. A hurricane was in the Gulf of Mexico. Had it not been for the fact that a hurricane hadn't reached land anywhere in the United States in two years and Galveston hadn't been hit since Alicia in 1983, this might have grabbed the public's attention. Instead, most people's lives were still dominated by traffic, the heat, their mundane jobs and the fact that this weekend was the last holiday for the summer.

Cora watched Dr. Neil Frank, local hurricane authority and television weatherman, tell his viewers that a hurricane had moved into the Gulf of Mexico and it could be headed for Texas. She had an uneasy feeling in her stomach. She had lived in Galveston all of her married life, and wasn't afraid of storms, but for some reason, this time was different.

"Dolly, now that's a scary-sounding storm," Harold said as he flopped into his easy chair in front of the TV, sloshing his drink on the armrest.

"Neil says it's a pretty big one."

"He thinks they're all big. Besides, what the hell does he know, he's just a goddamn TV weatherman." Harold took a sip of his rum and Coke.

"He was head of the hurricane center in Miami. I'd say he knows a little bit about hurricanes."

"Humph, big deal."

Cora rolled her eyes and sighed. They watched in silence until the commercial came on.

"Well if it heads here, I want to leave."

"Leave?" Harold snorted. "And go where?"

"I don't care. Off this island." Cora stared at Harold.

He shook his head and took another drink. "That's stupid, we've been through storms before and you haven't wanted to leave."

"I know."

Harold stood up after a moment.

"Well I've lived here all my life, and I've never left because of some goddamned storm and I'm not going to start now." He stared down at Cora, then turned his glass up and drained it in one big swallow. "Better call a cab or get your walking shoes on." He staggered toward the kitchen to mix another rum and Coke.

"We've been through storms before," J.D. said as he lifted up her hair and gently kissed her on the back of the neck. "It may not even come here."

"Storms yes, but not a hurricane." Beverley turned around to face him.

"I know, but I can get double pay plus a bonus if I work the lock-down. Then I can take off and go check out the Arlington job." He put his arms around her waist and looked deep into her eyes. "If it starts this way, I want you and the kids to go to Mom's."

She studied his face and knew he had made up his mind. She could usually maneuver J.D. around to her way of thinking, but if he set his mind on something, there was no use in trying to change it.

"Okay, but I still don't like it."

"That's my girl, now let's work on our lock-down procedures," he said as he slipped a hand under her blouse and cupped one of her braless breasts.

"That's the first thing you've said all night that I like," she said, reaching down and caressing his crotch while lightly kissing his lips.

The atmosphere in Lex and Sarah's kitchen was the best it had been in months, maybe years. Sarah hummed to herself as she sliced the avocado for their salad and Lex had a big grin on his face as he turned the chicken breast on the grill. Their attitudes had nothing to do with each other; they were way beyond even pretending they liked each other's company, much less loved each other.

Lex was thinking about his meeting with Collin Ramsey and how if he worked it right, he could probably pay Collin only half of what he was asking. He was sure Collin was in dire straits over something and would take whatever he could get. If Lex could string him out, he could get Collin to swing the council before he came up with the other twenty-five thousand, and then what was Collin going to do, tell the world Lex owed him another twenty-five on their original bribe? He would pay Collin half, and then he was taking a little trip north to Chicago. He damn sure wasn't going to wait around to see Dolly up close.

Sarah, on the other hand, had been in a great mood ever since she heard that Dolly was now in the Gulf of Mexico and could possibly make land somewhere around Galveston. Sarah continued humming *Hello Dolly* as she tossed the salad.

Collin was in his study, frowning at the television as if he could simply will Dolly into backing up and vacationing in Florida. He stirred the ice around in his glass and sipped at the scotch. This was his third since he got home and it wasn't helping. They had had their first decision-makers meeting this afternoon. The decision-makers were the emergency managers from a three-county area and the Mayors from the thirteen cities in those counties. They always held a meeting as soon as a hurricane came into the Gulf. This was to make sure everyone was on the same page and to go over standard procedures of evacuation if they needed to call one. Making the call was always a big decision, not only because of the cost to the cities themselves, but due to the tremendous cost to the various refineries and plants in their area. If all the plants went into lock-down, the total loss of revenue could be as high as three hundred million dollars a day.

Collin drained his glass and stood up to make another.

CHAPTER SIXTEEN

Boone peeled the stencil from the door of the truck and stepped back to examine his work. It was just after midnight as he gazed at the International Petroleum name and logo in yellow on the forest green background. He had lifted the stencil and a gallon of green paint from the company body shop earlier in the day. He walked around his forty-foot bomb looking at his handiwork. It had been almost eighteen hours of continuous work and he was still full of energy. He had a new step in his walk ever since he had decided this weekend would be D-Day for IP industries.

For the past year he had gone through the motions of living without feeling alive. Now that he had focus and a deadline, his rage was fueling him to action. When he first thought about his plan for payback almost a year ago, he didn't have a timetable. He just started building his bomb. It was something to do. The weekends he wasn't working for the evil empire he spent traveling the countryside buying sacks of fertilizer.

Boone had no idea of the magnitude of destruction that he was creating inside the tanker of the eighteen-wheeler. When he had begun, his mind had slipped into the realm of someday. Someday in the future, IP would get what it so justly deserved. Someday, the fertilizer that he was buying and dumping into the black belly of the tanker would be enough. He had no concept of tonnage and detonation. He had no sense of the chain reaction he was about to inflict on an unsuspecting population.

Somewhere before the pain and before the madness, he was aware that IP and other chemical plants up and down the Gulf Coast produced and used a variety of toxic and deadly gases such as Phosgene, a lethal gas used in the manufacturing of plastics and pesticides. It was developed during World War I as a choking agent and was responsible for a large number of deaths during that war. Phosgene is a half-brother to mustard gas.

After 9-11, upper management at IP had given a lot of lip service to the Homeland Security mandate that chemical plants and refineries beef up their security because of vulnerability to terrorism. A few improvements had been initiated early on but when lack of federal funding from the highly touted but ineffectual Homeland Security Department never materialized, security was put on the back burner as usual.

If Boone could have articulated what he wanted, it certainly would not have been to instigate a chain of events that could change the course of American history, just as the events of 9-11 had done. What Boone wanted--other than retribution--was for the survivor's guilt to go away which had begun the moment his father and brother had vaporized on that clear day in May. He should have bought it right beside Herman and Charley, but because of a simple change of a dental appointment, all he ended up with was a sore jaw and a numb lip. If International Petroleum had provided professional counseling for their employees after the explosion, the pain might have been redirected before it turned into the all-consuming rage that saturated him now.

He wiped his forehead and threw the empty paint can in the trash barrel in the corner of the barn. He would drive the rig into Texas City tonight and park it in a truck stop on Texas 146 not far from the plant. There was always an IP truck or two sitting there so it would not be noted as anything out of the ordinary. He would cab it back out to the farm to get his Silverado and then home for a few hours' sleep.

By noon Wednesday, the latest coordinates and data were in from the National Hurricane Center in Miami and a second decision-makers meeting was called for that afternoon. Dolly was now officially a Category 2 hurricane with sustained winds between 96 and 110 miles per hour. She was considered a moderate storm and was in the middle of the Gulf and moving very slowly. Evacuation time for the immediate Galveston area for a Category 2 was ten hours, but, depending on what time of the day the hurricane was expected to arrive, you might have to add at least twenty hours to the call. You wouldn't want to make the call in the middle of the night when it would be hard to reach the general public.

Collin studied the latest information on Dolly and paced his office. The odds were still greater for her going somewhere other than Galveston. There was plenty of time for her to take a customary northerly turn and miss them completely or continue westward into Mexico, and yet he had this uneasy feeling in the pit of his stomach that this was not going to be the case.

Lex stared out the window in the general direction where Dolly idled almost stationary some six hundred miles to the southeast, but his mind was not on hurricanes. He had awakened in the middle of the night thinking about the two recent phone calls he had received from long-forgotten associates. If he had heard from only one of them he wouldn't have worried much about it, but to hear from both within days of one another had sent a large red flag flying.

Dennis Johnson and Marcy Tidwell had been the president and vice-president of a savings and loan in Des Moines, Iowa. Together, the three of them had cooked up a project called Haven Estates, a retirement development of condos, patio homes, a fifteen hundred acre man-made stocked lake and an eighteen-hole golf course. Two years later, with the project less than half completed, the money was gone and so were Dennis, Marcy and Lex. The savings and loan had become another statistic in the great S&L crash of the eighties. He had only spoken with Dennis once since leaving Des Moines and that was almost five years ago. He and Marcy had gone their separate ways and Dennis was running a small bank in the Kansas City area.

Lex opened the drawer on his desk and dug out a small phone book. He thumbed through it until he found D. Johnson scribbled under the J's. Picking up the phone, he dialed the number. *I don't know why I'm doing this,* he thought as he listened to the soft ring in his ear. *He's not going to be home this time of day.* Just as he was about to hang up, a voice answered.

"Hello?"

"Dennis?"

"Uh, no, who is this?"

"Lex Le . . . uh, a friend. Who is this?"

"Detective Heath. Can I help?"

Lex slammed the phone on its cradle as if it had turned into a red-hot, smoldering piece of iron. He gaped at the phone. *Detective?* Lex got up and paced in front of his desk rubbing his forehead. *Great reaction, Levin, hanging up the phone. Yeah, they'll never figure out who called, between caller ID and the police checking the phone records. You dumb shit!* He stewed for a moment and then sat back down at his desk. He eyed the phone, picked it up and dialed Dennis's number. Someone answered on the second ring.

"Hello?"

"Yes, is this Detective…?

"Heath. Yes, it is."

"Sorry, I just called a moment ago and we were cut off."

"Oh yes, Mr…?"

"Levin. Lex Levin. Is Dennis available?" Lex concentrated on keeping his breathing slow and easy, his voice calm and matter-of-fact. "Is something wrong?"

"I'm afraid so, Mr. Levin. Were you a close friend of Mr. Johnson's?"

Did he say were? ran through Lex's brain, but out of his mouth, came, "Not really. We haven't actually spoken in years. He had called and I was just now getting around to returning his phone call."

"Oh, when did he call?"

"Last week sometime."

"Did Mr. Johnson leave a message as to why he wanted to speak to you?"

"No."

"Well, I'm sorry to inform you, but Mr. Johnson is dead. He's been murdered."

"Murdered? Oh, my God. How? What happened?" Lex sank back in his chair.

"I'm afraid I can't go into that right now, but Mr. Levin, could I have your phone number, just in case we need to reach you again."

"Uh, sure, but I really don't know that I can be of much help. Like I said, I haven't spoken with Dennis in years."

"You might be able to help us with some background information," the detective responded.

Thanks a lot, Dennis, Lex thought, but said aloud, "Sure, whatever you need."

CHAPTER SEVENTEEN

She didn't feel as strong as she had the day before. Her outer layers were slowing and wanting to separate. Maybe she was dying.

Evacuations are not mandatory in Texas. Jason thought about that every time a storm entered the Gulf. He felt they should be. He looked up as Roger came through the door.

"Here's the latest. Good and bad."

"Give me the good," Jason said, taking the data from Roger.

"She's hardly moved and she doesn't seem quite as organized."

"That is good. What's the bad?"

"She's still headin' right for us, hasn't wobbled a bit."

Jason studied the information. This looked good, damn good. Maybe they had gotten lucky again. If Dolly kept this up, she might not be more than a tropical storm by the time she reached the coast.

"What if she keeps this pace up?" Jason asked, looking up.

"Probably late Saturday or Saturday night."

"Yeah, that's what I was thinking. If we do have to make a call, we can do it for Friday morning. That should give us plenty of time."

By late Thursday afternoon everyone was breathing a little easier. Actually, only Jason and Collin were feeling better. Most of the island hadn't taken much notice of Dolly at all. People were going about their business as usual, no scramble for plywood or other items in preparation for a storm. Almost a third of the residents of Galveston had never been in a hurricane and didn't think they were going to be in one this year, either. Even Dr. Neil Frank said Dolly had weakened and was barely a Category 2 and by morning could be downgraded to a 1 or even a tropical storm.

Collin was still a little antsy but was beginning to think that Lady Luck was turning her smile on him once again. He picked up the phone and dialed Lex's office. He still needed to get some money into the evacuation account.

Bonnie had been thinking about Cora all week. When they had talked on Monday, Cora had dropped a hint that she was worried about the storm in the Gulf. Bonnie had told her she would be glad to come get her and bring her to Houston, that she had plenty of room for Cora to visit for a day or two.

"Hello." Cora, picked up on the first ring.

"Hey, it's me. Whatcha up to?"

"Oh, just listening to the fuckin' freight train in the den."

"What?"

"Harold's passed out in front of the TV. The old fart didn't make it through the six o'clock news."

"Oh," Bonnie said with a laugh. "I was thinking about coming and getting you after I get off work tomorrow. How does that sound?"

"Oh, you don't have to make a trip down here for me; besides it looks like Dolly ain't gonna be much of a blow job anyway."

"I don't mind. It'll be fun. We'll go shopping at the Galleria and maybe take in a movie." Bonnie thought she could actually hear snoring in the background. She would be glad to rescue Cora from the lump of hot air slouched in his easy chair.

"Are you sure? I don't want to be any trouble."

"Yes, I'm sure. I'll be there by noon."

"Ok, I'll see you then."

Bonnie hung up the phone and smiled. This was going to be a fun weekend.

Lex dialed the code on the safe in the closet and popped it open. He counted out twenty-five thousand in cash and put it in the case. "I hope this solves your little problem, Mayor, because this is all you're getting," he said softly and then laughed to himself. He closed the door to the safe and set the briefcase underneath a long rack of tailored suits. *I need a drink.*

As he stepped into the kitchen, the phone rang. He picked up the receiver hanging on the wall.

"Hello," he said as he opened the door to the cabinet to get a tall glass.

"Mr. Levin?"

"Yes," Lex answered as he bent down to open the door to the freezer under the bar to grab a handful of ice.

"This is Detective Heath."

Lex stood up immediately. "Yes?"

"I hate to bother you at home, but I need to ask you a few questions."

"I can't imagine there's anything I could help you with, Detective. Like I said yesterday, Dennis and I haven't spoken in years."

"Do you know a Marcy Tidwell?"

Lex felt like someone had kicked him in the stomach. He was glad this conversation was not taking place face-to-face because all the color had just run out of his.

"Uh, Marcy Tidwell . . . yes, I believe she worked with Dennis at one time. Why?"

"Well, we found her name, along with yours, written on a day calendar in Mr. Johnson's office. The day was last Thursday."

"Last Thursday . . . yes, I believe that's the day Dennis called."

"But you didn't talk to him?"

"No, I was out. He left a message to call him."

Lex slumped down on the barstool. He filled the glass to the rim with scotch.

"Did you contact Miss Tidwell?" Lex tried to sound uninterested.

"Well, we've been trying to, but it seems she's disappeared."

"Disappeared?"

"She was working for a real estate company in a suburb just north of here and hasn't been seen since last Thursday."

What the hell's going on here? Lex's brain screamed as he tried to stay calm.

"So I take it you haven't heard from Miss Tidwell?" Heath inquired after a moment.

"Uh, no, not in years," Lex lied. He thought about the message from her two weeks ago.

"Well, thank you for your time, Mr. Levin."

Heath hung up before he could respond. Lex hung the phone back on the wall and took a drink of scotch. He heard the door swing open and saw Sara walk in. He hadn't even heard her pull into the garage. He stared at her.

"What the hell is wrong with you? You look like shit."

"And a good day to you too." Lex turned the glass up and drained it.

J.D. and Beverly watched the ten o'clock news from bed. The weatherman reported that the information received on Dolly at six that evening indicated she was becoming disorganized and weaker, but was making a beeline for the Houston area. He reminded everyone that Dolly was still considered a moderate storm and would probably make landfall in the Houston-Galveston area sometime Saturday evening. People in low-lying areas, especially around Galveston, should take precautions and evacuate by noon Saturday, just to be on the safe side.

"Are y'all going on lock-down?" Beverly snuggled up close to J.D.

"Yep, soon as we get everything drained and shut down. Why don't you take the kids up to Mom's after school tomorrow and I'll meet you there Sunday."

"Okay, but I don't like being away from you, even if it is a small storm."

J.D. rolled over, gently brushed her hair back and kissed her softly on the mouth. His tongue explored hers. They held each other like that for a moment and then he pulled away.

"I love you so much, I don't like being away from you more than an hour at a time."

Ten minutes later they were making love.

CHAPTER EIGHTEEN

It was a little after ten p.m. when she eased over the massive deep-water eddy floating aimlessly in the Gulf. She instantly began taking the new life into her at an explosive rate. She looked as if she had consumed a billion fireflies as the energy inside her increased by the minute. Within four hours she would be twice as strong, and by daylight tomorrow she would be the most powerful storm of the century.

Jason strolled along the beach as the sun beat down and warmed his skin. His two sons were busy building a large sandcastle while his wife lay under the umbrella reading her newest romance novel. He loved living in Galveston and enjoyed spending time with his family by the water. He had stopped to look out at the waves rolling in when he noticed something on the horizon. At first, it looked like some low-riding clouds were right at the water's edge, but as he stared, the clouds seemed to be getting taller and taller. As he squinted his eyes to get a better look, he had the feeling that something was very wrong. Suddenly, he realized what he was seeing wasn't clouds, but a huge wave forming and growing taller by the second. He began hearing a ringing, soft at first, then becoming louder and louder. He looked all around to see where it was coming from and finally noticed a seashell by his feet. It was vibrating each time it rang. As he gazed down at the seashell, the sunlight began fading and he was soon engulfed in darkness. He bolted up in bed as the telephone continued to ring. Groping in the dark, he fumbled with the receiver and pulled it to his ear.

"Jason, we've got trouble," the voice said.

"Roger, is that you?" Jason tried to shake the sleep from his consciousness.

"Yeah. Sorry to wake you, but it's bad, real bad."

"What's bad?" Jason mumbled.

"Dolly must have found a hot spot. A big one."

"Oh, no." Jason sat up abruptly. "When? What time is it?"

"It's a little after four. The center started seeing movement on the radar sometime after midnight and sent a plane. They just radioed and said she's up to a four and growing."

"Oh, my God," Jason gasped.

"That's not all. She's hauling ass and heading straight for us."

The men inside the aircraft were accustomed to being jerked and jolted on every flight they took. They were hurricane hunters. They were in the Air Force Reserve's 53rd Weather Reconnaissance Squadron based out of Keesler Air Force Base in Biloxi, Mississippi. The four men on this flight had flown over two hundred flights into hurricanes in the last five years. They had been in some bad ones but nothing compared to what they were in now.

"God Almighty! This ain't no two. Look at this," Les Wilks shouted, scanning the readings he was getting back from the GPS dropsondes they had dropped into the storm. "This son-of-a-bitch is a five! Wind speed at a hundred and seventy-five!"

The GPS dropsondes sent back wind speeds, barometric pressure, air temperature and moisture content. The plane rocked and bucked and flew sideways at times. Les pulled his harness tighter.

"Hold on, we're at the wall," Captain Tom Lewis said in a calm voice over the radio. They were about to enter the eye of Dolly.

"Roger that," Les and Billy Siler said in unison.

As the plane entered the eye of Dolly, the wind dropped from a hundred and seventy-miles an hour to fifty. They were immediately caught in an updraft that took them up 1500 feet in a second and then dropped them like a rock. Clipboards, pencils and anything else that wasn't strapped down or fixed in place flew all over the plane. Les held on to his laptop with both hands. He looked out of the window beside him and saw stars sparkling in a clear sky. Below, he could see white splashes of water on a relatively calm sea. The wall of Dolly's forty-mile wide eye was stacks and stacks of white clouds on top of one another.

"Man, I dread going back into that bitch," Les said, looking over at Billy, making eye contact.

"One good thing."

"What's that?" Les asked.

"When we get outta here, we're headin' for Mississippi. I sure feel sorry for those folks in the path of this one," Billy said softly. Les nodded his head and stared back out the window.

CHAPTER NINETEEN

There was a light rain falling as J.D. looked out the window. He closed the blind and pulled the shade down. He slipped on his jeans and sat down on the side of the bed to lace up his steel-toed work boots. Beverly rolled over and rubbed his back.

"Is it raining out?"

"Yep, looks like it's gonna be a wet one today. Why don't you get the kids up and go on to Mom's?" J.D. turned around to look at her. "I don't want to worry about y'all getting off the island."

"Alright, I'll fix some breakfast and we'll load up." Beverly yawned. "Will you meet us as soon as you can?"

"As soon as I can get there. I promise." J.D. brushed her hair back. He leaned over and gave her a kiss, then stood up and glanced at the clock. It read 5:15 a.m.

Jason looked at the clock on the wall. It was 5:15 a.m. He leaned back in his chair and stared at the ceiling. He knew this day was coming, he had known it for as long as he could remember, and now that it was here, he felt unusually calm. It was going to be bad and there was nothing he could do about it.

"God, this is unbelievable!" Roger charged through the door. "She's a five!"

Roger waved the printout in Jason's direction. He grabbed it and scanned hurriedly.

"Bill told me the fly boys said it was the worst they've ever been in." Roger fidgeted in front of Jason's desk.

"First thing we've got to do is stop school. I'll call them and you get hold of the media. Tell 'em its bad, but don't overdo it. We can't afford a panic evacuation. We want an orderly one."

"I'm on it." Roger jumped up and all but ran out of the office. Jason grabbed the phone and punched in Collin's home phone number. The calm that he had been experiencing a few moments earlier had been replaced with pure energy. Jason's job was about to kick into high gear. Collin answered on the second ring.

"Yeah," Collin yawned into the phone.

"It's me. We've got a problem. Dolly got supercharged overnight. She's a five."

"What?" Collin sat up in bed and reached for his glasses on the nightstand. "How the hell did that happen?"

"Probably found a hot spot last night."

"Hot spot? What the hell is that?"

"An area where the warm water goes deeper than normal. It's usually only warm about thirty feet deep, but in a hot spot, the water can be warm down to six hundred feet."

"And?"

"If a hurricane drifts over one of them, it can get super-charged in a hurry. Sorta like a hurricane taking steroids."

"Never heard of such a thing."

"They only discovered them a few years ago. They still don't know what causes them or, for that matter, where they are. Pretty sure that's what happened with Andrew in '92."

"Okay, I'm on my way to the office. Get the wheels rolling and I'll call you as soon as I get there."

By nine that morning most of the Galveston area knew that a bad storm was heading their way. The radio and television stations had gone into over-kill mode immediately. The "Storm of the Century" logo in spinning graphics accompanied every report aired. People began boarding up and making preparations for either leaving or riding it out. Home Depot, Lowe's and the lumberyards had a run on plywood and masking tape. Grocery stores were packed with people buying canned goods and water. There was a sense of urgency in the air, but it was still far from panic status. To some, this was old-hat, to others, although new, not unexpected. This afternoon would see a steady stream of cars, trucks and RV's heading across the bridge on I-45 to Houston and places further north. Dolly's arrival time was estimated for late Saturday afternoon or evening.

Lex heard the change in Dolly's status on the radio as he shaved. He hadn't been too concerned up until this point. He had made plans to leave today as soon as he met with Collin, but now he was wishing he had left yesterday. He felt a twinge of anxiety in the pit of his stomach.

He was about to walk out the door when the phone rang. Ignoring it at first, he shook his head and picked up the phone.

"Hello?"

"Mr. Levin, Detective Heath."

"Yes, Detective, what can I do for you?" Lex said in a monotone voice.

"I was calling about Miss Tidwell."

"Oh. Does she know anything about Dennis?"

There was a pause on the other end of the line.

"She's been murdered." Lex sank down into the large easy chair. The slight anxiety he felt about the storm lurched in a whole new direction. It wasn't that he gave a shit about either Marcy or Dennis, but something was very wrong.

"Can you think of anyone who would want these two people dead?"

"Uh, no, I told you all I know. I don't know what to think." His voice trailed off as he closed his eyes and ran his fingers through his hair. Right now, if he had the opportunity, he'd kill them both himself for getting him involved in this mess. Lex really didn't know of anyone who would want them dead. That was what was eating at him.

"I don't want to alarm you, but since your name was written on the day calendar along with Miss Tidwell's, I would advise you to be aware that someone may be looking for you as well."

"Me? Why would someone be looking for me?"

"I don't know."

Lex heard the unasked question in Detective Heath's tone that suggested he might very well know what was going on. Lex mentally kicked himself for getting involved with those two small-time cheats. More than likely they owed somebody money and were calling him to bail their asses out.

"Is there anything else you would like to tell me, Mr. Levin?"

"I don't know anything," Lex almost shouted.

"You know where I am. Call me if you think of anything."

The phone went dead in Lex's ear. He gripped the receiver tight for a moment, then banged a hole in the elegant faux finished wall with it. Lex's controlled world didn't tolerate surprises. Stunned at his lack of restraint, he caught his breath and thought of Sarah's reaction when she saw it.

The activity at International Petroleum was in high gear. The brass at IP had waited until the last minute to call a lock-down, and now that Dolly was a pretty solid bet to make a visit, they were working overtime to get everything drained, cooled and shut down.

"These assholes have to push everything to the limit, don't they." Carl grunted, as he strained to open the discharge valve on the tank they were working on.

"Hey, they don't want to put a plug in the golden goose's ass any sooner than they have to," J.D. replied.

Carl was about J.D's. age and had come to work for IP a month after he had. He was always telling jokes and kept everyone laughing. J.D. liked working with him. The rain was steady as they worked to get the valve open. It finally gave and turned a quarter of an inch.

"Damn, you'd think that son-of-a-bitch was welded shut." Carl slumped back against the tank.

"Hell, they haven't shut this place down since the last big bang." J.D. was breathing hard as he sat down beside Carl. "I just hope we can get it done before the weather gets really shitty."

"Ain't that the truth?" Carl wiped the water from his face.

J.D. looked up at the gray skies and thought about Beverly. He hadn't turned on his radio this morning until after he had crossed over the inter-coastal bridge and was almost to work. As soon as he heard the update on Dolly, he stopped and called her. She said they were almost packed and as soon as she could herd everybody into the car, they would leave.

"Speaking of shitty weather, that goddamn asshole Boone must like hurricanes," Carl said.

"Why's that?" J.D. asked.

"Today's the first day I've ever seen the man smile. He was walking around the locker room this morning like he'd won the Publishers Clearing House."

The rain ran off of J.D's hardhat down the front of his shirt in a steady stream as he looked at Carl and shook his head. "Who knows? The man's strange."

They rested a bit and then J.D. got to his feet.

"Come on, let's get this thing drained and find a dry spot."

It was getting close to noon and Beverly thought that the rain had increased in the last hour. She looked out the window for the fourteenth time in the last ten minutes. She had gotten the kids up as soon as J.D. left and made everyone breakfast. They were excited about going to grandma's house and not to school. A battle had started almost immediately between Dallas and Austin as to which video games they would take. Beverly told them they had to pick one apiece. Finally sometime after eight o'clock, they had the car loaded, only to find Louise's battery was as dead as her namesake. Beverly had called Maxine and they were now waiting for her to come get them and take them to higher ground.

Bonnie turned the volume up a notch as the sweet harmonies of the "BeGood Tanyas" filled her car. Bonnie was a closet country listener and had discovered this CD at a flea market a couple of months of ago. She patted the steering wheel in time and strained to see what had brought traffic to a stand still on I-45. She had just passed the greyhound racetrack outside of La Marque when the freeway suddenly became a parking lot. She expected traffic to be slow coming out of Galveston but not in this direction. The rain was beating against the windshield and every now and then a gust of wind would nudge her Mazda slightly. She felt uneasy and squirmed in her seat. She had been in a full-fledged hurricane early in her childhood and hadn't cared for the experience.

Collin had been on the phone all morning and everything had been going smoothly. They had gotten word out that school was canceled and the evacuation process was progressing as planned. The Galveston police, county constables, and the Texas Highway Patrol had swung into gear and were monitoring the evacuation routes all the way into Houston. Within a few hours there would be only one way off the island. Every intersection had a policeman to make sure the traffic would continue at a steady pace.

Collin had just set up a meeting with Lex at the West Beach project site when Sue opened the door to his office. Her face was scrunched into a frown.

"Now what?" Collin hung up the phone.

"A tanker truck has overturned on the bridge."

"Shit."

"Its where the bridge meets the mainland, the worst possible place. It was carrying gasoline or something flammable and they're gonna have to do a clean up. Traffic is stopped in both directions."

"How long is that going to take?" Collin asked, softly.

"At least four hours."

CHAPTER TWENTY

Sean Micheals fidgeted in his seat as the Channel 11 News van inched its way across the bridge onto Galveston Island. The rain had been steady all the way from Houston. He doodled on a yellow legal pad as he daydreamed of anchoring the news for a major network. Sean had been with Channel 11 for a little over two years as a street reporter doing mostly fluff pieces and the shit work that the more experienced reporters wouldn't touch with a ten-foot pole. Sean was convinced Dolly was going to be his ticket to the big time. *Just like Dan Rather.* He stared out of the rain-streaked windshield. Forty years ago on this same island, Dan Rather had vaulted into major network television history courtesy of Hurricane Carla.

The reporter who normally would have drawn this assignment was out on vacation. The news director had finally given in to Sean's persistent begging and pleading and sent Sean and twenty-year veteran cameraman, Jim Wells, to cover the story.

"Man, this is gonna be fun," Sean gloated, looking over at Jim behind the wheel. Jim turned to Sean. "Have you ever been in a hurricane?"

"Uh, no."

"I didn't think so," Jim said in a tone of condescension.

"What?" Sean asked wide-eyed.

Jim didn't offer a response and Sean returned to his daydreaming. They had stopped and shot a piece on the overturned tanker truck and sent it back to the station for insert into the afternoon news. Sean thought his opening for the story would please the news director. He had made a remark to the effect that getting off Gilligan's Island was easier than escaping Galveston today.

The pilot Lex had contracted to fly him off the island had called his office first thing that morning and said he was a little concerned about the update on Dolly. Lex didn't want to waste time haggling with him, so he immediately doubled what he had agreed to pay him. It was amazing what people would do for a little money. Actually, in this case it was quite a bit of money, but he felt it was worth every penny. Still, it had taken some persuading on his part, but then Lex was the king of persuasion.

He had learned the art many years ago as a child growing up on a dairy farm in Iowa. He had recognized early on that a farm was not where he intended to spend the rest of his life. He had honed his art on his mother whom he could manipulate into operating out of his perspective of the world. She, in turn, kept dad off his ass and made sure his younger brother Todd did the work of two people. When Lex was a teenager, he began secretly calling himself "The Operator," one who mans the controls. He continued that dialogue within himself to this day. It had served him well.

The pilot had said anything under a steady forty-mile-an-hour wind would be all right. Lex had told him he had a quick meeting and should be able to make it to Galveston airport by four. Sarah had made it clear last night she that wasn't leaving, so he hadn't bothered to tell her his plans.

It was a quarter till three when Lex stepped out of the elevator into the dimly lit parking garage. His heels clicked loudly on the concrete floor and echoed throughout the almost empty cavernous room as he walked briskly toward his parking space with his briefcase in his right hand. A foreboding that he should have left the island earlier had slowly consumed him throughout the day.

As he approached his car, he heard a muted shuffling sound behind him. He turned to see a small man standing in the shadows with a raincoat slung over his right arm and covering his hand. He had a crumpled hat pulled down on his head.

"Hello, Mr. Levin? I was wondering if I could have a moment of your time?"

"I'm sorry, but I have a meeting that I'm already running a little late for," Lex said as he glanced down at his watch. When he looked back at the man, he noticed he had pulled the raincoat up his arm slightly and his hand was exposed. And in his right hand was a large gun.

"I think you're going to be a little later than you think. Now, unlock the doors and get into the car." The man motioned with the gun.

The color slowly ebbed out of Lex's face as he did as he was told. He got into the driver's seat as the man quickly climbed into the passenger's side.

"Look, if this is a robbery, I don't have any money with me," Lex said, holding the briefcase containing twenty-five thousand dollars to his chest.

"It's not a robbery. Now put the briefcase in the back and drive." The man once again motioned with the gun. Lex laid the briefcase on the seat and started the car.

"Where to?"

"Your house. I hear it's the showplace of the island."

There was something familiar about the voice, but Lex couldn't quite get a handle on it. He glanced at the man as he pulled out of the parking garage onto

15th Street and turned right, but he had the hat pulled so low, he couldn't get a good look at his face. As he approached Broadway, the light turned red. Lex came to a stop as a Galveston police car pulled up beside them. He turned and stared over at the police car.

"Don't even think about it. Unless you're betting that cop is Superman in disguise and is faster than a speeding bullet."

Lex gripped the steering wheel until his knuckles turned white.

"Besides, when we get to your house you might convince me to let you live."

What had been mostly irritation swiftly turned to fear. "Who are you?" Lex croaked.

"Richard," the man said with a smile.

A tiny light went on in the room of recognition in Lex's brain, but it was so dim it illuminated no memories.

"I'm Richard Hanson."

Suddenly, the room was bright with light. Richard Hanson was the largest investor in the Haven Estates project, which, of course, made him the largest loser in the Haven Estates project.

Beverly and company piled into Maxine's Suburban as soon as the wheels rolled to a stop beside the doublewide. Beverly and Tyler sat in the front with Maxine. Paris, Dallas and Austin were in the backseat. Dallas and Austin were pushing and poking each other before they got out of the driveway.

"Stop it," Beverly snapped. "It's already been a long day and we don't need this shit. Paris, you sit in the middle. Now move it."

The two boys immediately separated and began looking out their respective windows. Paris shook her head, heaved a long-suffering sigh and buried her head in her book.

"Sorry it took me so long to get here," Maxine apologized, as she drove out of the drive and onto the access road only to immediately stop again behind a long line of cars waiting to enter the ramp and join the outgoing traffic. "There was some kind of wreck on the bridge."

"Oh, I know. It was on TV. Don't worry about it. I'm just glad you got here." Beverly reached over and patted Maxine on her leg.

"Well, we aren't out of the woods, yet." Maxine hunched over the steering wheel peering through the rain. "Not by a long shot."

The digital clock on the dash of Bonnie's Mazda clicked to 4:07 as she stopped in front of Cora's house. It had taken her almost six hours to make a fifty-five minute trip. The rain came down in sheets as Bonnie opened her door and ran for Cora's front porch. As she reached the top step the door opened.

"Ain't this some shit?" Cora waved her in. Bonnie ducked under her arm and came inside, shaking her purple and pink locks like a wet dog.

"Well, that was quite a trip."

"Yeah, the TV people have been yammering about it all day. Some numbnuts in a tanker truck decided to unload a little early." Cora gave Bonnie a hug. "Glad you're here."

"Are you ready?" Bonnie asked, looking around for Cora's bags and signs of Harold. "Where's . . .?"

"Oh, he's over at The Elbow Room with some buddies. They're having a little hurricane party," Cora said over her shoulder as she headed into the bedroom to get her suitcase.

"Cora, this is a really bad storm."

"I know. I tried to get him to listen to reason." Cora fiddled with the handle on her suitcase. "He said he was glad I was going so he wouldn't have to listen to me whine about a pissy little storm." Bonnie stared at Cora for a moment, then shook her head and turned for the door.

They were scrunched in Bonnie's Mazda with Cora holding her bag on her lap and staring at the dashboard.

"We're gonna be in this traffic for quite awhile. Are you going to be okay?"

"No problem. Doesn't look like there's going to be much movement to deal with." Cora laughed.

Collin jerked his cell phone off the dash to call his office for the third time in twenty minutes. He could barely make out the white caps crashing on the beach through the downpour that had been falling for the last half hour. The wind gusts were getting stronger and rocked his Explorer from side to side. His patience was wearing thin as he waited for Lex to show. *The son-of-a-bitch is doing this on purpose just to show me who has the upper hand.* That Lex, a sleazy developer that he could hardly stand to be in the same room with, was in control of his destiny and his only hope of getting out of this jam, infuriated him.

"Mayor Ramsey's office," Sue said as she came on the line.

"It's me. Heard from him?"

"No, I called his office and they said he left a little before three."

"Okay, anyone else looking for me?"

"Jason called. He's afraid everyone's not going to make it off the island because of the tie-up on the bridge today."

"Well, what the hell does he want me to do about it?" Collin yelled.

There was silence on the other end of the phone.

"I'm sorry, I didn't mean to yell at you, I'm just . . . "

"I know, don't worry about it. I think he was just calling to let you know what was going on," Sue said quietly.

Collin looked at his watch. It was almost four-thirty.

"I'll be back in a half hour." Collin punched the off button. He squinted through the windshield at the angry sea. *Levin, you bastard, if you bail on me, I'll kill ya.*

CHAPTER TWENTY-ONE

Sarah stepped out onto the porch of her office. The blowing rain was coming in sideways off the Gulf that was only a few blocks away. As she opened her umbrella, a gust of wind caught it and flipped one side up. The rain stung as it hit her face. She turned her back to the wind and managed to get the umbrella into semi-working order and ran to her car parked in the driveway. As she opened the door, another gust of wind caught her umbrella and jerked it out of her hand. She hurriedly got in and closed the door. She was soaked. She watched her umbrella doing cartwheels down 13th Street. *Damn, and Dolly's not even here yet.* She stared through the rain-drenched windshield of her car. *This is really cool.*

"Come on, Dolly. You're going to make me famous," she said out loud as she started the car, backed out, and headed toward Seawall Boulevard. She pulled her cell phone out of her purse and punched in Lex's office number. Karen answered on the second ring.

"Is Lex there?"

"No, he left here about an hour-and-a-half ago."

"Did he say where he was going?"

"Uh, no, but I think he must have been meeting Collin Ramsey. His office has called a couple of times for him."

"Well, thanks. I'll see him at home." Sarah punched the off button and slipped her phone into her purse. *He and Collin are probably half way out of town by now. It would be just like those two weenies to ride it out in Houston.* She turned onto Seawall Boulevard and headed west toward her house.

Boone looked out the tiny window in his office at the water covering up the sidewalks that wound through the maze of tanks and buildings known as International Petroleum. He glanced at his watch. It was almost 5:30. By his calculations, it was going to be another five hours before they had everything drained and cooled and everyone out except for the lock-down crew. *That should work out about right,* he thought. *I can slip out of here about midnight and get the truck.* According to the latest radio report, Dolly was supposed to make her appearance around six in the morning.

Boone sat back down at his desk in the cramped office and picked up his cup of coffee. *Sorry, Dolly, but there ain't gonna be much to blow on when you get here.* He smiled and leaned back in his chair.

Beverly, Maxine and the kids had been in the car for almost three hours now and had traveled less than two miles. They were almost to the mainland as they inched across the causeway bridge. The rain and wind seemed to be increasing with each passing hour.

"As hard as this rain is now, I'm worried it's going to-- " Maxine caught herself and mouthed the word "flood" as she looked at Beverly.

"You know how high the water can get at Highway 6, right at the turn-off," Beverly whispered.

"I'm scared, Mommy," Dallas said.

"It's gonna be all right, sugar. Mimi will get us there." Beverly turned around and touched Dallas's leg.

"It's just a little rain, darling." Maxine tried to sound upbeat. "Your Grandma Mimi has been through lots of storms. Your mama and I are gonna take good care of you." Beverly and Maxine threw each other a look of concern. Paris caught it, and the knot that had been building in her stomach grew a little larger.

"Yeah, it's just silly old rain," Paris said, looking over at Dallas. "How 'bout a game. Let's play, 'Is This a Word?'"

"Yeah, that's a good game."

CHAPTER TWENTY-TWO

Lex eased the Jaguar inside the garage at about the same time Bonnie and Cora were loading up for their trek off the island. The normal ten-minute drive to his house had taken almost a half-hour. The water in the streets had gotten progressively deeper the closer they came to his house off of San Luis Road on West Beach. They had made the trip without a word between them. Lex had glanced over at Richard a few times only to find him staring intently back at him.

Lex turned the engine off, and after a moment the silence became deafening.

"Let's go inside," Richard said suddenly. Lex jumped and hit the car horn, which made him jump again. As Lex was opening his door, he asked if he could get his briefcase. Richard motioned for him to get it and they both got out of the car.

Once inside the house, Richard walked over to the floor-to-ceiling windows and looked out at the driving rain.

"I thought you might ask me how I've been, but I guess you really couldn't care less, huh, Lex?"

"Well, I, uh, I'm sorry, uh, how . . . ?"

"Shut up," Richard shouted, as he turned and stuck the gun in Lex's face. "You didn't give a fuck about me or my family then and you damn sure don't now."

120

Lex jumped back and clutched the briefcase to his chest as if it might provide some sort of protection.

"I'm going to tell you how I am . . . and my family." Richard slowly walked around Lex, still pointing the gun at his head.

"You know, we trusted you. We believed you. I, more than anybody. It took a lot of convincing for me to talk my brother into investing in your little project, but I stayed on him because I trusted you . . . and Dennis and Marcy. Yeah, I convinced him, or wore him down, that Haven Estates was a good solid deal. When he finally came around, he really came around. Most of that money was his."

Lex opened his mouth to say something.

"Just shut up and listen . . . you know, he had owned that little chain of department stores for over thirty years, had about fifty people working for him. Some of them had been with him the whole time, depended on him for their family's welfare. Yeah, you didn't screw up just a few people's lives, you got a whole bunch of 'em."

Lex clutched the briefcase tighter to his chest.

"He felt responsible for all those people. I'm sure you wouldn't know what that feeling is like. And when the business went under, it killed him. All those families out of work. You probably didn't know that, you were long gone by then . . . Oh, he pulled the trigger, but you put the gun in his mouth . . . you, Dennis and Marcy."

Lex was truly terrified now. His mouth was as dry as if he had walked across Death Valley. He was so weak; he wasn't sure how much longer he could even stand before collapsing on the floor in a blubbering heap.

"And, of course, his wife blames me for the whole thing and I can understand that. I haven't had a nickel since then, and I've felt guilty for so long that I'm not much good to anyone. My wife left me two years ago and our son, who had to drop out of college, won't speak to me. So you see, Lex, you've touched a lot of people in your short life. A lot of good people."

Tears were streaming down Lex's face. Not tears of remorse, simply tears of unadulterated fear. As he held the briefcase in a stranglehold, he remembered the money inside.

"Richard, I have money," he whispered. "I have money and I can get you more." Lex slowly released the grip on the briefcase and opened it. Richard looked at the briefcase full of money being held in front of him. A tiny glimmer of hope crept through Lex's brain. A voice that had retreated to the farthest corners of his mind when Richard had first stuck the gun in his face now spoke up. *You're The Operator; you're the one in control.* Lex took a deep breath.

"See, I have twenty-five thousand here, and I can get more . . . lots more," Lex said in a buttery smooth voice. *You can do this.*

Richard reached out and took hold of the briefcase. He stared at it for a long time and then looked up at Lex. Lex gave Richard his best smile.

"I can get you lots of money, Richard. Whatever you want." Lex felt his old confidence slowly returning to his body. He stood a little straighter.

"Money. Do you think money can bring my brother back . . . or get my family back?" Richard said in low dangerous voice. "This is what I think about your fucking money," he shouted. He quickly opened the sliding glass door onto the deck and held the open briefcase up to the thirty-mile-an-hour wind coming off of the Gulf. The money flew in all directions at once and was gone within a matter of seconds with the exception of the few bills that stuck to the window and wrapped around the legs of the patio furniture.

Suddenly, everything in Lex's vision went into slow motion. The money wasn't blowing madly out the door and away; it was floating very slowly like leaves on a fall day. He saw Richard drop the briefcase. It seemed to take forever for it to hit the floor. He then watched as Richard turned toward him, raising the gun level with his face. The action now slowed to the point that Lex saw a tiny puff of blue smoke and the bullet exit the barrel of the gun.

Jason had just received the latest information from the hurricane center in Miami. He picked up the phone to call Collin for the second time in an hour. He absent-mindedly circled the data on the paper in front of him as he listened to the ringing in his ear.

"Mayor Ramsey's office."

"Sue, it's Jason."

"He just walked in. Hold on." Jason quit circling and began underlining.

"Whatcha got?" Collin asked after a moment.

"It keeps getting worse," Jason said with a sigh. "Shows no signs of turning and she isn't slowing down. She could get here sometime after midnight."

Collin leaned back in his chair and looked out at the darkening skies. He ran his fingers through his thinning hair.

"It's gonna be bad, isn't it?" Collin sighed after a moment.

"Terrible is more like it. We need to start urging everyone to get to shelter. We're not going to get everyone off. With the evacuation expanded, the routes are already at a standstill."

"Okay, I'll contact the media."

"Good. I'll fax you the locations of the shelters that are set up now."

Collin hung up the phone and walked over to look out his third-story window. He had been entertaining thoughts of getting in his car and leaving all afternoon. Especially after Lex was a no-show, but now that was out of the question and, deep in his heart, he knew he couldn't do that anyway. He was glad Joan and their ten-year-old daughter, Melissa, had left yesterday to visit Joan's sister in Huntsville.

He walked out into the outer office to where Sue sat at her desk trying to look calm.

"Jason's faxing some stuff over. We need to contact all the media when it gets here."

"Okay."

"Where's Robert and the boys?" Collin asked.

"They're at home." Sue looked worried.

"Why don't you call and tell them to come on down here. I think this is going to be one of the safest places to ride this out."

"Thanks, Collin."

CHAPTER TWENTY-THREE

She was stronger than ever now. Her eyewall was the tightest of her short life and her reach was over three hundred miles wide. She was the most powerful force on the planet. And she was still hungry.

It was dark as Maxine's Suburban inched along the highway. They had finally made it to Highway 6 and were creeping through Buena Vista, a tiny bedroom community located on the shores of Highland Bayou. Highland Bayou was a small bay adjoining Galveston Bay. Each row of houses had a street in front and a canal in back, lined with sailboats and powerboats secured to their respective docks.

As Dolly's headwinds increased, Galveston Bay began slowly oozing over Highway 6 into Highland Bayou. The occasional flash of lightning revealed how deep the water was getting on the road.

"See if you can get KTRH on the radio, they should have the latest weather information," Maxine said as she massaged the back of her neck. Her head hurt and her shoulders ached from the non-stop tension.

Beverly played with the radio dial until she found what she was looking for.

"Latest word now is Dolly is expected to come ashore sometime around midnight," the voice said crackling through the static. "All residents of Galveston and the surrounding counties are urged to seek shelter as soon as possible. There is a flash flood warning out for the entire Houston-Galveston area until further notice." Maxine and Beverly glanced at each other. A sudden flash of lightning accompanied by a loud crack of thunder made everyone in the ten-year-old Suburban jump. Paris let out a yell and Tyler began to cry. Beverly held Tyler close to her chest. She turned around.

"I'm sorry, Mom," Paris murmured.

"It's okay, sugar, it scared me too." Beverly looked into the wide-eyed faces of Dallas and Austin.

"What if the water gets too deep to go on?" Austin asked quietly.

"We don't have too much farther, honey. We'll make it."

Beverly turned back around and looked out the windshield. There was only the briefest glimpse of the road between the swipe of the wipers and the drenching rain.

"We need to find shelter," Maxine muttered under her breath.

"Got anything in mind?"

"Maybe."

As Sarah turned into her driveway, the sight of the open door to her empty garage disrupted the interview with Katy Couric that she had running in her head. *That's strange.* She pulled into the garage, closed the garage door, and went into the house. As she came into the kitchen, she pulled her jacket off and tossed it on a bar stool along with her purse. She walked over to the wet bar and took a bottle of Bombay out of the cabinet and mixed herself a gin and tonic.

It was quiet in the house as she sipped her drink. She remembered how loud the wind had been howling on her way home. *This place does feel solid.* She leaned against the large wooden island in the middle of the kitchen and took another drink. She smiled as she imagined herself sitting with Oprah discussing her hurricane-proof house.

She decided a long, hot, bubble bath was in order. As she walked out of the kitchen, she glanced out toward the deck and noticed some paper or trash stuck to the sliding glass doors and on the deck furniture. She slipped her shoes off and walked over to the window. She stared at a slip of the paper and realized it was a hundred-dollar bill. Sarah slid the door open and pulled the bill off of the glass. The wind was really gusting now and she quickly closed the door. She studied the wet bill in her hand. It looked real.

Sarah turned around to go to her bedroom, still looking at the bill, when something caught in her peripheral vision. She turned her head slightly, then screamed and fell back against the glass doors. Lex was slumped back in the overstuffed easy chair. His arms were hanging loosely over the arms of the chair and his head was back against the headrest. Where his left eye should have been, there was a large bloody hole that opened to his left ear. His white shirt and jacket were covered in blood and gray matter. The eye on the right side of Lex's face seemed to be staring right at her. Sarah knew she was screaming, but she couldn't stop.

After a long moment, she quickly crawled on all fours away from the door to the other side of the room. She pulled herself up to the bar beside the kitchen door and stood on wobbly legs. She wasn't sure what to do. Spying the phone on the wall beside her, *Call the police,* flashed through her mind, but before she could pick up the phone, another thought appeared. *What if someone is still in the house?* She grabbed for her purse and knocked it off the bar with the contents scattering across the tile floor. She fell to her knees and frantically crammed everything back inside, then scooped up the keys to her car and ran barefoot through the kitchen and down to the garage. Sarah fumbled with her keys and, after dropping them twice, realized she still had the hundred-dollar bill in her hand. Finally, she managed to get her car started and backed quickly out onto the water-filled street.

Cora had not had a bit of trouble with her motion sickness. After three hours, she and Bonnie were just coming up on 61st. Street. They had traveled less than fifty city blocks. Bonnie had called the station on her cell phone to get the latest weather information.

"It isn't good," Bonnie told Cora. "They're saying Dolly could be here in less than five hours."

"Oh shit, even if we get off the island, we're gonna be up to our tits in water somewhere out on I-45. We need to go to Plan B."

"Any suggestions?"

"I think our best bet is to try to get to Ball High School. See if you can turn left up here at the next intersection," Cora suggested, squinting to see through the windshield.

As they approached the red light at 61st, it was obvious that turning wasn't going to be easy. The traffic was in a logjam as everyone tried to get onto Broadway to exit the island. After fifteen minutes of creeping forward through the honking of many horns and hurled curses, they managed to turn left onto 61st.

"I think we're going to have to go down to Avenue Q or R to find a street that will take us back to 41st." Between the slapping of the windshield wipers, Cora tried to get a glimpse of the street signs. The water was getting deeper as they drove back toward the seawall. After twelve hours of steady rain and the tide running a good three to four feet above normal, Galveston Island was slowing sinking.

Jack squinted his eyes to see through the rain as he made his way down Loop 610 on the west side of Houston. The wind had picked up in the last hour and Jack could feel the gusts rock his Navigator every so often. The gravity of the situation that Dolly was creating had finally pulled Jack out of the self-pity pit he had been wallowing in for the past week and he had thrown himself into his work. His mom had called yesterday from New Mexico after hearing about Dolly on the national news. She had asked Jack to check on her sister who still lived in their old neighborhood in Bellaire.

He had monitored the conditions around town all day and knew that some areas were approaching flood stage. The rain hadn't let up since starting early that morning and Bellaire was certainly prone to flooding.

He had stopped by his condo after work, changed clothes and headed for the west side of town. A trip that should have taken about thirty minutes was now approaching two hours. *What the hell was I thinking? I should have taken off earlier.* He was worried now that Braes Bayou might already be out of its banks and flooding the neighborhood. It hadn't been when Jack left, but that was two hours ago. He picked up the walkie-talkie lying on the passengers seat.

"This is Unit 7," Jack said.

"Go ahead, 7. This is Command."

"What's the latest on Braes Bayou?" Houston had one hundred and twenty-six flood sensors on bayous, creeks and rivers around the city and sensors on twenty-seven different roadways. The Emergency Management Center monitored these at all times during flood situations.

"Hold on . . . not out of its banks yet, but could be within the hour."

"Thanks, Unit 7 out." Jack let out a sigh as he laid the walkie-talkie on the seat.

Thirty minutes later Jack was in the driveway of his Aunt Nita's large, two-story house. The water in the street was curb-to-curb and creeping its way up the drive toward the front door. Jack pulled on a rain slicker and headed for the porch. It opened before he could punch the doorbell.

"Jack." Aunt Nita said. "You're a sight for sore eyes." She reached out and pulled him to her. They hugged tightly.

"You're looking good, Aunt Nita," Jack said, pulling away. "How's Harry?"

"Ornery as ever. He's in the den." Aunt Nita turned and Jack followed her down the hall toward the back of the house. Aunt Nita and Uncle Harry were Jack's favorite relatives. He had spent many a night at sleepovers with his cousin Bret who had been two years older than Jack. They were best friends and Jack had spent as much time at this house as his own. Bret had been involved in a terrible car wreck five years ago that killed a mother and her six-month-old son. He had survived the accident with barely a scratch, due mainly to the fact that he was only semi-conscious at the instant of collision, from the ten Johnny Walker Blacks he had consumed shortly before running the red light where he broadsided the young mother. He had committed suicide three months later. Jack had only seen his Aunt and Uncle a few times since then. As he walked past the familiar pictures on the walls, he felt bad that he had not checked up on them more often in the past few years.

As they stepped down into the large den that ran almost the length of the back of their house, Uncle Harry looked up from his recliner in the far corner of the room situated in front of the large screen TV.

"Jack." Harry struggled to get out of the chair. After a moment of straining, he slumped back. "To hell with it. How are you?" he said with a laugh.

"Fine, Uncle Harry." Jack went over and shook his hand. "You ready for a little ride in the rain?"

130

"If I can get out of this damn chair." Harry gave a little chuckle.

Jack reached out a hand and helped Uncle Harry out of the recliner.

"Let me pee and I'm ready," he said, shuffling out of the room.

Jack walked over to a long bookcase in the back of the room. The top two shelves were filled with dozens of pictures. He scanned through them as he walked along the bookcase. His eyes stopped on a rectangular picture frame on the back of the second shelf against the wall. He reached in and picked it up. It was a picture that had been taken after a football game. Jack had his uniform on and was holding his helmet in his left hand and had his arm around a beautiful young girl in a cheerleader outfit. On the other side of her was Bret.

"I always loved that picture."

Jack jumped slightly. He hadn't heard Aunt Nita come up behind him.

"Y'all were the cutest couple I ever saw."

"It was a long time ago." Jack stared at the picture.

"You know, Mrs. Ryan still lives right down the street. I hope she's okay. I've heard she's bedridden now. Diabetes, I think."

Jack set the picture back down.

"I feel bad. I haven't been down there to see how she's doing since Bill died."

"Who's taking care of her?"

"Well, I'm not sure."

Jack loaded Aunt Nita and Uncle Harry, a suitcase that weighed a ton, and a pan of brownies fresh out of the oven into his Navigator. The water was slowly creeping up the drive and was hubcap deep in the street. As Jack backed out of the drive, he looked down toward the Ryan's one story, rambling ranch house that sat at the end of the street. He could see a light on in a front window.

"Maybe I ought to check on Mrs. Ryan before we get out of here. That water is coming up pretty fast," Jack said, turning around to look at Uncle Harry.

"Yeah, that house sits right on the bayou. They're always the first to get water."

The rain was coming down in sheets now and the water was almost up to the running boards on the Navigator. He eased into the driveway.

"Y'all wait here. I'll check it out." Jack climbed out of the Navigator and stepped into water almost up to his knees. He pulled the hood of his slicker over his head and made his way to the front door. He rang the doorbell just as a blinding flash of lightning lit up the sky. Jack jumped at the booming clap of thunder and glanced out into the street. When the front door opened, he turned and saw Molly's beautiful blue eyes staring up at him.

"Let's take the shot right over there with me standing on the seawall." Sean demanded as he and Jim stood on the front steps of the Hotel Galvez. They had decided this would be a good location to work out of and ride out the storm. Jim looked down at Sean as if to say something, then pulled the hood from his raincoat up over his head and walked toward the seawall lugging his camera on his shoulder. He leaned into the wind now, as the gusts were getting near the sixty-mph range. Sean struggled to stay up with Jim as they crossed the street. The station had pre-empted the regular shows and were covering the weather full-time. It was time for a live report from Sean.

The swells were running four to five feet high and the waves were crashing loudly on the rocks as they reached the seawall. Huge sprays of water were shooting over the seawall and on to the street. Sean clung to a light pole while Jim checked his camera and batteries. After a moment, Jim held his hand up to his ear and turned the volume up on his two-way radio.

"One minute," he shouted to Sean, holding up one finger. After what seemed like ten minutes to Sean, Jim held up his hand with his palm facing Sean, counted to five and then pointed to Sean.

"Thank you, Greg. As you can see from the angry sea behind me, Galveston's in for . . . " suddenly a gust of wind and a giant splash of water knocked Sean off the seawall on to the sidewalk. Jim leaned into the wind and kept the camera pointed at Sean as he clumsily tried to get up only to fall again on his back like a large turtle in a slicker suit. Jim wasn't sure when they cut the feed and took it back to the station. He was laughing too hard to notice.

CHAPTER TWENTY-FOUR

Sarah quit crying and caught her breath some twenty minutes after running out of her house. *I have to call the police,* was the only thought she could hold on to. It made her feel like she was taking some kind of action and it kept her from thinking about the scene her eyes had documented in her living room.

The water was getting deeper as she slowly made her way down Seawall Boulevard. She wasn't sure where she was and she appeared to be alone on the street. There had been a car in front of her a moment ago, but its taillights faded into blackness in the pounding rain.

None of the stores were open and it was dark except for the lightning that seemed to be getting more intense with each passing moment. She felt her high anxiety transforming into uncontrolled panic and knew she needed to find someone or someplace soon. A bright array of lightning lit up what looked like a small strip center or convenience store on her left that was built on higher ground. She pulled into the parking lot and began searching through her purse for her cell phone. After dumping the contents out on the seat with no results, she decided it must have fallen out at the house. She looked up and spotted a pay phone on the wall beside the store. Sarah opened the door and got out only to be thrown up against the side of her car by a strong gust of wind. The fear that had been running through her, the fear that there was a murderer somewhere about, morphed into another fear. She was completely alone and out in the middle of a terrible storm. *This is not cool*, rattled around somewhere in the back of her mind.

She held on the side of the car and made her way to the phone. As she was taking the last step to the wall, she stepped on a piece of broken glass. It was the first time she realized she was barefoot. The cut was deep; putting her off balance and in the same instant, the wind slammed her headfirst into the wall. Sarah's world went black.

Everything in the plant was cooled, drained and shut down. The lock-down crew was gathered in the break room downing coffee and swapping their usual lies while trying to get dried out. The rest of the shift had already headed for home or higher ground. Boone stole out of his office looking both ways before slipping into the darkness. It wasn't hard concealing himself once out in the torrential downpour. Visibility was no more than ten feet in front of him. Boone climbed into his truck and drove out of the parking lot to the waiting nightmare sitting quietly at the Chevron truck stop up the road.

They were the only car traveling in the direction of the seawall and had passed the last car waiting in line to get on Broadway two blocks ago at the intersection of Stewart Road and 61st. As Bonnie started across Avenue T, she saw the water splash up over the headlights.

"Uh oh." She put the car in reverse. The engine hesitated. She mashed on the gas pedal and felt the car shake and die. She quickly tried to restart it, but to no avail. They listened to the hammering rain beat up the little car. Finally Cora sighed loudly, "I think its time to abandon ship."

The water was high enough that it took some effort to get the doors open, and when they did, the water began filling up the floorboard of the car.

"Hope you have insurance," Cora said as she struggled to get out.

"Fuck the insurance. I wish I had a raft." Bonnie stepped out in the knee-deep water. The lightning was like giant strobe lights in the sky making movement look erratic.

"We should try to make it up to Galveston College. It's a lot closer than the high school," Cora shouted. Bonnie nodded, and they began wading up the street holding on to each other. There was not a house in sight, since this part of 61st was retail stores long boarded up.

The water wasn't too cold, but it was dirty and filled with debris. Each step into the wind was beginning to be a struggle. As they approached Seawall Boulevard, Cora saw a group of buildings off to their right that were on higher ground.

"Let's see if we can get out of the water for minute," Cora shouted in Bonnie's ear as she pointed to the buildings. That was fine with Bonnie; she jumped every time something bumped into her legs. She nodded, and they struggled in the direction of the buildings with Cora in the lead. Almost immediately, Bonnie noticed the water getting deeper. She was about to grab hold of Cora's jacket when suddenly Cora was completely gone. As Bonnie's hand grabbed wet air, her feet began to slip, and in an instant she was under water. She didn't panic as her reflexes automatically took over. She did a hard scissor kick and her head burst above the water line. While in school at Southwest Texas University, she had gotten a job at Aquarena Springs working in the underwater show. She had become an excellent swimmer and had learned to hold her breath for long periods of time.

She heard a scream and saw Cora frantically splashing in the water to her right. She swam over and got Cora under her arm.

136

"I have you. Don't fight me." Bonnie yelled, as she began pulling her toward the building. Thankfully, Cora reacted to what she said. Bonnie felt something solid under her foot.

"I think we can stand up here," she yelled, over the howling wind. They both stood holding each other tightly. Bonnie could see the relief in Cora's face.

"I think we stepped into a fucking ditch." Cora wiped her sleeve across her face. The water was deep, but wasn't rushing, as they slowly crawled up the embankment on to higher ground.

When they were out of the water, they collapsed on a nearby concrete curb, exhausted, and soaked to the bone. The rain pounded them, stinging their skin as they huddled with their backs to the wind, trying to catch their breath. Bonnie knew they were in serious trouble. She had no idea where they were and she could barely open her eyes under the assault of the wind and rain. The noise frightened her too. She had heard of a roaring wind, but this was ridiculous. Above the howling, she could hear metal scraping against metal, and thunder, and maybe her heart pounding in her ears.

Bonnie looked over at the building before them. A flash of light lit up the parking lot and they could see a car or truck of some kind with its door open.

"Maybe we can get in with those people," Bonnie said at the top of her voice.

They tried to stand and found it easier to move through the wind on their all fours. They were almost to the car when Cora heard Bonnie cry out. She looked around and saw Bonnie pointing toward someone lying on the ground by the wall of the building. They both crawled over to the figure under the pay phone.

"Is she alive?"

"Yes," Bonnie said, feeling her pulse.

"Do you think we ought to move her?"

Bonnie saw the blood and the slash on her forehead. "Probably hit this wall." Bonnie looked down at the woman as the rain beat down on her face. "I don't think we have any choice. Let's get her into the car."

They dragged her close to the car and after a short struggle, they managed to have her stretched out in the back. They crawled in, shut the doors and collapsed in the front seat exhausted. It felt good to be out of the unforgiving rain. Bonnie leaned her head back on the headrest, the relief so great she could feel the tears stinging her eyes. Before she dissolved into a blubbering mass of hysteria, she turned her attention to the purse and its contents strewn in the floorboard and seat.

"Wonder who she is?"

"Sarah Levin." Cora held up a driver's license.

CHAPTER TWENTY-FIVE

Maxine and Beverly had made it almost to Hitchcock, a small community on Highway 6, about six miles past Bayou Vista, when the old Suburban began to stammer.

"Uh, oh." Maxine stopped, put it neutral, and pumped the gas pedal to rev the engine.

"Is it the water?"

"No, I think we're running out of gas." Maxine frowned at Beverly.

Immediately the car behind them began honking its horn. Maxine rolled down her window and waved for them to come around. She thought they might stop and ask if they needed help, but they just drove on by, splashing water into the window. Maxine and Beverly watched car after car creep past them without giving them a look.

"Too scared to stop, and too embarrassed to look," Maxine grumbled.

"Well unless a bus comes by, I doubt if anyone has room for six more passengers." They watched as the parade of detachment and non-involvement became fewer and fewer, until there were none at all.

"Well, we can't stay here."

"Yeah, and just our luck, we forgot to bring our life raft and scuba gear." Beverly strained to see out the window.

Lightning lit up the sky like a continual fireworks show and the thunder was so loud it sounded like cannons were being fired right outside their Suburban. The wind shook the old truck with increasingly stronger gusts. During a particularly bright flash, Maxine saw a building off to the right with a familiar logo on the sign, flapping in the wind.

"Okay. You guys wait here. I have an idea." Maxine was out of the door before Beverly could say a word.

"Mommy, where is Mimi going?" Dallas looked terrified.

"I'm not sure honey, but she'll be back." Beverly tried to show as much calmness as possible. They had been great little troupers up until now, but she could see the fear in their faces, and she knew she needed to try to get their minds focused on something else.

"Did I ever tell you about the time Mimi walked eight miles in the snow, uphill both ways, just to save me and your dad?"

"Save you?" Austin asked wide-eyed.

"Yeah, it was before we had you guys, and we were just on the verge of dying of boredom, and she brought us batteries."

The three kids looked at Beverly liked she had two heads.

"Just like these." She handed Dallas and Austin each two batteries. The boys had been playing their video games for hours, until the batteries had run down. Beverly had cherished the non-beeping in her ears for the last hour, but she knew it would be good to get their minds off what was happening. For the next ten minutes, the only sound inside the Suburban was the beeping of the furiously played video games, while Mother Nature played outside.

Suddenly Paris pointed excitedly toward the front of the Suburban. They all strained to look through the rain-streaked windshield to see Maxine struggling toward them, carrying something orange in her arms. Beverly pushed her door open and jumped out to help her. Soon Maxine and Beverly were back inside, wrestling with a bundle of sopping wet life jackets.

"Where did you get these, Mimi?" Austin asked, as she cinched him into his life jacket.

"There's a boat store just across the road. I didn't think they would mind if we borrowed these for a while. I also borrowed this." She held up a new ski rope still enclosed in a plastic bag.

"Are we going skiing?" Dallas wanted to know.

"No, but we're going for a boat ride."

"Boat ride?" everyone chimed in unison.

"But first, we have to get to the boat." Maxine ripped the plastic bag open that contained the ski rope. "Now, I want you to loop this around you." She handed the rope to Austin. "And we'll tie a knot in front so you can't get loose."

She did this with each one until everyone was tied together with about five feet of rope between him or her. Then she tied the ends to herself and Beverly.

"I'll lead because I know the way and your mom will bring up the rear." She checked the knots to make sure they were tight. "Ready?" She looked at the kids. They all nodded their heads, not sure what was happening.

"Now, I know the water is getting pretty deep out there, but these life jackets will keep you afloat, and you can't go anywhere because we're all tied together." Seeing the apprehension in their eyes, she continued, "Your mom and I are going to take care of you, I promise."

"That's right," Beverly said with as much conviction as she could muster.

Maxine got out first with Austin behind her, then Dallas and Paris, and Beverly followed with Tyler on her hip. The water was about thigh deep on Maxine, but up to Dallas' chest. His life jacket floated in the water and made him walk on his tiptoes. The lightning flashed and Beverly could see the boat dealership about thirty yards away. As they trudged through the water with their heads down against the raging wind, they struggled to find solid footing. They were only a few yards from the Suburban when Paris cried out as her feet slipped out from under her. Beverly stopped immediately and jerked on the rope. Paris went under, but popped back to the surface in an instant, bobbing up and down in the water as the life jacket did its job.

"You okay?" Beverly shouted.

Paris nodded her head and wiped the water from her eyes. The others had stopped and were looking back at Paris and Beverly.

"She's alright," Beverly yelled through the howling wind. Maxine turned and began walking toward the boat store.

They were almost to the front of the store when a streak of lightning struck nearby and lit up the sky as if it were high noon. Beverly froze in mid-step. She threw her hand to her mouth to stifle the scream that was flying up from deep in her chest and desperately trying to escape through her open lips. Hanging from the back of Dallas' life jacket was a large brown snake. Apparently, it struck at Dallas and had only gotten a mouth full of canvas-covered cork. Beverly couldn't get her legs to move. Paris stopped when she felt the rope tug on her back and looked around at Beverly. When she saw the terror written all over her mother's face, she yelled, "What's wrong?"

Everyone looked back at Beverly as she continued to stare straight ahead. Paris turned to see what was wrong and at first couldn't see what it was. Then as another flash of lightning hit, she saw the snake hanging from Dallas's life jacket four feet in front of her. When she screamed, Dallas turned to see what was wrong and Beverly could see the white puffy insides of the snake's mouth with its glistening fang stuck in the orange jacket. She knew it was a cottonmouth water moccasin, a very poisonous snake. Its flat black eye seemed to be glaring right at her.

Instantly, her panic changed into something much more powerful than the hurricane that was bearing down upon them: a mother's need to protect her children. In the eerie strobe light effect of the lightning, Beverly was standing next to Paris, and in a second, next to Dallas. Clutching Tyler tightly to her chest with her left hand she reached out with her right and grabbed the snake by the tail. The tension of the last eight hours and the rage at the thing that threatened her son came together in one swift movement, as she ripped it from his life jacket and slung it as far as she could out into the rising water. She reached down, pulled Dallas to her and squeezed him till he cried out. Paris came slogging up behind her and hugged both of them.

"What happened Mommy?" Dallas asked, looking bewildered.

"Nothing, you just had some trash hanging on your jacket."

J.D. and the rest of the lock-down crew were camped around the small TV sitting on the counter in the back of the break room. Some were standing and a few were sitting in chairs pulled up close to the counter. The reporter was giving the latest coordinates of Dolly and said the barometric pressure of 26.23 was the lowest ever recorded for a hurricane. He said it was still a Category 5, and reminded viewers that the last hurricane of this magnitude to make landfall in the United States, was Camille, which roared into Mississippi in 1969 killing 256 people. They were projecting landfall sometime after midnight, which was a little more than an hour from now.

God I'm glad Bev and the kids got off the island this morning. J.D. stared blankly at the TV. The thought didn't completely comfort him, since he hadn't talked to them since early this morning. He had gotten a, "Sorry, the circuits are busy at this time," message, every time he had tried to call this afternoon.

"Damn, this son-of-a-bitch is gonna be rough," Carl said nervously to J.D. "You think this is the safest place to be?"

"No, the safest place would be somewhere close to Oklahoma, but I think we'll be all right," J.D. grinned. "This building is built like a bunker." J.D. wasn't sure he believed that, but he didn't want to spread any more fear than what was already in the room.

"Y'all seen Boone?" Roy Huggins asked.

"No, not in the last thirty minutes or so. You check his office?" J.D. asked.

"Yeah, I just came from there. No sign of him." Roy pulled some change from his pocket for the coffee machine.

"Who?" Sam Jenkings asked, walking up beside Roy.

"Boone." Roy punched the buttons on the machine.

"Knowing that grouchy bastard, he's probably sitting out in the rain wondering why it's picking on him," Sam chuckled.

"No shit," Carl said. Nobody said anything for a moment as they drank their coffee and watched the portable TV.

"I hate to say this, but we'd better go look for him." J.D. pushed his chair back from the table. "He might be in trouble and need some help."

"Oh he needs help alright, but not any kind we can give him," Sam answered.

"I know he's an asshole, but I'm gonna go look for him." J.D. slipped his hardhat on. As he was opening the door Roy called out to him. "Hold on, I'll come with ya."

Carl and Sam frowned at each other and then Carl said, "Might as well, beats watching it on the tube." They all stepped out into the blowing rain.

"Let's fan out," J.D. called. "I'll go north." They nodded and each headed in a different direction.

Jack and Molly stared at each other until the silence was broken by another large boom of thunder. Finally, Molly invited Jack in out of the rain.

"This is unbelievable," Molly said, shaking her head.

"You're right." Jack shuffled uncomfortably from one foot to the other. " I came over to get my aunt and uncle, and she told me your mom wasn't doing so well."

"Yeah, she's diabetic, but mostly I think she has just given up since dad died." Molly didn't look at him directly.

"Well you can't stay here, the bayou is coming up pretty fast."

"I don't know what I was thinking. I knew there was a storm coming, but I've hardly paid attention to the news. The last I'd heard it wasn't going to be much, then all of sudden; it's the storm of the century. I feel like such an idiot."

"Well don't. It caught everybody off guard."

"I've only been here a week and I've been so distracted, finding her this way."

"What do you mean?"

"The last time I was home was at Dad's funeral last year. I talk with Mom every week and she always assures me she is doing fine. She has a home care group that comes by with meals and looks in on her every day. Then one day a couple of weeks ago, a cousin of mine called and told me how she really is. I came home immediately and found her unable to get around by herself." Molly crossed her arms and held herself for a moment.

Jack started to reach out and touch her, but instead said, "Where is she? We don't have much time."

"Back here." Molly led Jack down a hallway to the master bedroom. Jack looked down at the frail woman lying in bed. Molly's mom had always been a strong, striking woman. He knew she was close to the same age as his mom, yet she appeared to be twenty years older. He wouldn't have recognized her had he not known who she was.

"Do you remember Jack?" Molly asked her mother. Mrs. Ryan had a befuddled look on her face. "Jack is going to take us to higher ground. You know how the bayou can get out of its banks."

"Hello Mrs. Ryan. Don't worry, we're just going to go for a little ride." Mrs. Ryan looked confused, and then a smile of recognition crept onto her face.

"Are you my knight in shinning armor?"

"Complete with floaties." Jack smiled down at her. "Is she on insulin?"

"Yes, it's in the fridge."

"You grab that and whatever you can carry. I'll get your mom. We need to get out of here now." Molly wheeled and left the room. Jack pulled the sheet and bedspread around Mrs. Ryan, wrapping her in it like a cocoon. He lifted the feeble woman as gently as possible and started toward the living room.

Molly opened the front door and Jack stepped onto the porch with Mrs. Ryan in his arms. The rain was coming down in sheets and the sky crackled with electricity. Jack reached up and covered her head with the bedspread.

"Hold on Mrs. Ryan," he said as he headed for the Navigator. Uncle Harry opened the back door as he approached and Jack slid Mrs. Ryan into the seat beside them. Molly climbed into the front seat as Jack came around and jumped in behind the wheel.

146

"Eileen, I just feel terrible that it takes a storm to bring neighbors together," Aunt Nita said as she pulled the blanket tight around Mrs. Ryan.

"Don't feel bad, Nita, the street runs both ways. I'm just glad to be here."

"Yes, Mrs. Cook, thank you for thinking of us. " Molly turned around in her seat. "I don't know what we would have done."

Jack began backing out of the drive and into the street. The water was up to the running boards of the Navigator. He was shocked at how fast the water was rising.

"We're a long way from being out of this. I'm not sure we can get through to Loop 610." Jack eased the Navigator down the street.

Within moments, the water was almost up to the headlights.

Uncle Harry leaned forward and said, "Jack, I think our best bet is back to our house. We've ridden out a couple of floods on the second floor."

"I think you're right. I just hope we can get back there before this thing drowns out." A big gust of wind rocked the Navigator as Jack felt the engine miss.

CHAPTER TWENTY-SIX

"Do you know her?" Bonnie was surprised.

"I don't know her, but I know who she is." Cora looked at the woman lying on the backseat. "She's the hurricane lady."

"Hurricane lady?"

"That's what people were calling her. She claimed to have built a hurricane-proof house. It was in the papers a couple of years ago. I think she's married to some big developer." They looked at each other and then back at the woman. The wind was rocking the Lexus with a steady rhythm now.

"Maybe we ought to go to her house. Is it far?" Bonnie asked.

"Let's see." Cora looked at Sarah's drivers license. "I don't think so."

A gust of wind suddenly hit and it felt as if the Lexus actually moved in the parking lot.

"We sure as hell need to be somewhere other than here." Bonnie reached for the keys that were still in the ignition and started the car. "Which way?"

"That way." Cora pointed west down Seawall Boulevard.

They were about to turn back because the water in the street was getting too deep, when they spotted the house. It sat off to the left on the beach side of the street. Bonnie caught a glimpse of it as she turned into the long driveway. From this side it looked like a huge bird sitting with its back to them with its wings semi-extended. The view of the house from an airplane overhead would resemble a large boomerang. As Bonnie followed the drive, she saw the garage door was open. She pulled the Lexus inside, and after a quick look, found the remote over the visor and closed the door behind them.

Good or bad, Bonnie knew this was where she was going to ride out the storm or die in it. She was weary of inching her way down Galveston Island in a car that could get you just so far. After sloshing down streets, falling in ditches and crawling through parking lots on her hands and knees, she was grateful to be out of the relentless wind and rain. Being in the garage with the door closed was such a relief that she could have passed out right behind the wheel of the car. After a long silence, Cora seemed to come alive.

"I guess we can't leave her here in the car."

"You're probably right. I guess if we're going to stay in her house, we ought to invite her along."

"Let's get her inside to a bed and see if we can find something for this cut on her forehead." Cora opened her door and got out. "Looks like her foot is bleeding as well."

After laboring up the stairs, they stood inside the kitchen, holding Sarah between them. Bonnie spotted a hallway off to her left.

"I'll go find a bedroom. You rest a minute." They laid Sarah gently onto the floor.

Ten minutes later they collapsed on the plush carpet beside the bed that Sarah lay on.

"Goddamn, you'd think in a house this big, they'd have a fuckin' elevator. Those stairs almost got me," Cora said, wheezing.

"Cora, are you saying you're out of shape?"

149

"Look at you. Hey, when I was your age, I could screw all night and not even loose my breath." Cora grinned as Bonnie shook her head. "Oops, didn't mean to hit a nerve. I know your love life is in time out."

"And yours?"

"Touché. Help me up." Cora held up a hand. "Let's see if we can find anything in the bathroom for Mrs. Levin's head."

They rummaged through the medicine cabinet in Sarah's large bathroom and found iodine, swabs, bandages and aloe vera gel. Bonnie cleaned the cut on Sarah's foot and forehead and then they wrapped her head with the bandages. Sarah moaned a few times, but remained unconscious.

"Do you think we need to call EMS or somebody?" Bonnie thought of the large gash on Sarah's forehead was serious.

"I doubt if they're even coming out. You saw the street out there."

"Maybe we should have gone to the college. There might have been somebody there who would know what to do." Bonnie had a worried look on her face.

"Well, unless there was a doctor there, I don't think she would get any more care than what we're giving her. Besides, we weren't having much luck getting to the college." Cora placed a wet cloth across Sarah's forehead.

"It does feel safe here." Bonnie crossed her arms and looked around the room. Cora said, "It makes you wonder what the hell she was doing out there. I mean she was fucking barefoot."

"Yeah, and where's her husband?" Bonnie picked up a picture of Sarah and Lex.

"Maybe he's at a bar having a hurricane party," Cora said sarcastically as she looked up at Bonnie. They eyed each other for a moment.

"I think I'm gonna go check out the rest of the house." Bonnie headed for the door. Cora smoothed Sarah's hair back and held her hand.

"Mrs. Levin, can you hear me?" she asked in a kind voice. Sarah made no sound and continued her deep sleep. Cora looked around at the massive bedroom. *You could probably put most of my house in these two rooms.*

She got up from the bed to explore and opened a door beside the bathroom door. It was the biggest walk-in closet she had ever seen. *Hell I could live in here.* She eyeballed the rows of dresses down one side, and suits and pants on the other. It would be good to get out of the wet clothes she was in, and a hot shower wasn't such a bad idea either. At the end of the closet was a shoe rack that was about five feet wide, and went from the floor to above Cora's head. It was filled with every kind of shoe imaginable. She was about to try on a pair of red heels when she heard something behind her. Cora jumped, mortified that Sarah Levin was about to catch her nosing around and playing dress up in her closet.

"Jesus, you scared the shit out of me. I thought you were Mrs. Levin."

She sagged with relief. "That's what I get for thinking my size tens will fit in a size seven "

Bonnie was standing there with her mouth open, but no words were coming out. The color had drained from her face and she was white as the wall beside her.

"Good God, you look like you've just seen a ghost."

"No, just a dead man," Bonnie stammered.

Maxine and Beverly dried off the kids with paper towels they found in a small bathroom. They were all huddled together on a dingy sofa in the manager's office. The electricity was still working and they turned on a lamp on the manager's desk, which barely lit the room.

"I'm going to see if I can find us some transportation." Maxine headed for the door.

"Why don't we just get some gas for the truck?" Beverly shrugged. Maxine motioned for Beverly to follow her. They walked over to the door away from the kids.

"Because, even if we got it running, it's soon going to be too deep to go anywhere, and we need to get to shelter fast," Maxine murmured.

"What's wrong with this place?" Beverly asked.

"Honey, we need some place a lot stronger and bigger than this." She lowered her voice even more and said, "If this really is a Category five storm, we are in deep trouble."

Beverly could see the concern in Maxine's eyes, but the idea of going back outside made her whole body tense. "Where are we going to go?"

"You'll see. First we need a boat."

"You were serious about a boat?" Beverly knew she didn't want to hear a plan that had anything to do with taking her kids back out into the water. Maxine saw the look on her face and grabbed Beverly by the shoulders.

"Trust me Beverly, I know what I'm doing."

Beverly stared at Maxine intently. After a moment, a tiny smile inched into one corner of her face.

"Never a salesman around when you need one," Beverly cracked. "You guys stay right here. We'll be back in a minute," she said to the kids and followed Maxine out the door. They walked through the showroom of the dealership studying the boats on display.

"These are too big," Maxine said. "We need something big enough but able to run in shallow water." Beverly spied a wall filled with brochures. She picked some up and scanned through them.

"This one looks about right." She held up the brochure.

"Yeah, I wonder if they have something like this?" Maxine read the description of the boat.

"I have an idea." Beverly headed back toward the manger's office. "I worked at a car dealership one time, and we kept a file on all the cars ready for delivery, you know, all checked out and ready to drive away. Maybe they do that here too."

After shuffling through drawers, Beverly held up a piece of paper from the file she had been looking through. They were sitting at the manager's desk. The drawers on the filing cabinet behind were standing open.

"Look at this." she handed the paper to Maxine.

"Perfect. If we're lucky, it might be inside somewhere."

Jack nursed the Navigator to within a half a block of his aunt and uncle's house before it gave up and came to a halt.

"Uncle Harry, give me the keys to the house. I'm gonna take Mrs. Ryan in first and then I'll come back and get the rest of you."

"I'll go with you." Molly started to open her door.

"No, I want you to stay here with them, in case they need you before I get back."

Molly nodded and closed the door. Jack stuck the walkie-talkie into his pocket, climbed out of the Navigator into water above his knees, and waded around to the passenger's side. He picked up Mrs. Ryan and began wading toward his aunt's house. Small tree limbs and other debris were starting to clog the water-filled street as he ducked his head into the wind and continued sloshing through the water. He turned in front of the house and almost fell when his foot struck the curb unexpectedly. Mrs. Ryan let out a yelp.

"Sorry." Jack looked down at her as he regained his footing. He reached the porch, holding Mrs. Ryan in one arm, and unlocked the front door.

Jack quickly took her upstairs to a bedroom and laid her on the bed. Then he sprinted back downstairs and out the doorway into the pouring rain.

Aunt Nita retrieved some towels and passed them all around. "We look like a bunch of drowned rats."

Uncle Harry flopped down in a chair.

"If anyone's hungry, I've got plenty of snacks. Can I make anyone a sandwich?" Aunt Nita was always the perfect hostess for any occasion. She didn't wait for anyone to answer and headed for the kitchen. "I can at least make us a pot of coffee before the bayou runs us upstairs."

"Better hurry." Uncle Harry pointed to the water seeping under the front door.

"I'm gonna check on my mom." Molly handed the towel to Jack and headed up the stairs.

"You wouldn't happen to have a little something to put in that coffee for a hot toddy?" Jack asked.

"Sure do." Uncle Harry got up and followed Aunt Nita. "Good call, Jack," he said over his shoulder as he hurried off to the kitchen. Jack squished through the wet carpet over to the front window and peered out. He could just make out his Navigator, sitting in the middle of the street, with water almost up to the windows.

The second floor of City Hall had been turned into Command Central. Collin walked down the hall and stuck his head in the door of the EMS unit. The men were all engaged in conversation of some kind as the phones constantly rang and two-way radios crackled with static and concerned voices. There were five TV monitors lined up on one wall, each carrying a different station.

"How we doing, Ralph?" Collin asked.

Ralph set the phone in its cradle and turned around. Collin could see the sadness saturating his features.

"That was a woman with three kids. She's stranded in a house over by Schreiber Park and there's nothing I can do."

He listened as Ralph took a few more calls. Collin knew the storm had reached the point where emergency vehicles could no longer operate without risking the lives of the first responders, but he was glad he wasn't the one having to tell the people on the other end of the line that no help would be coming. He saw Jason come out of the door at the end of the hall, and was relieved that he had an excuse to leave Ralph to his duty. Jason was reading a computer printout. He looked up as Collin approached.

"I know I sound like a broken record, but it's even worse than I thought. This is one fast-moving storm." Jason read the printout for a moment, then handed it Collin.

"What's this?" Collin asked.

"The latest data." Jason pulled a small calculator out of his pocket and punched in a few numbers. He scratched his head.

"What?" Collin asked.

"I'm thinking about how much wind pressure this building can take."

"How do you calculate that?"

"Well, pressure against a wall mounts with the square of the wind speed, so that a threefold increase in wind speed gives a nine-fold increase in pressure." Jason gestured with his hands. Collin wasn't completely slack-jawed, but his eyes were glazed over as if Jason had just explained Einstein's theory of relativity.

"A twenty-five mile-per-hour wind causes about one point six pounds of pressure per square foot."

"Uh huh." Collin was still in the dark.

"And, in a hundred and twenty-five mile-per-hour wind, it becomes twelve hundred and fifty pounds."

"Damn," Collin said, as the light bulb came on.

"And, the lower the barometric pressure, the higher the winds." Jason handed the printout to Collin.

"That's low, I take it." Collin read the figures.

"The lowest I've ever heard of. The one that hit here in 1900 was 27.49." Collin's shoulders slumped and he let out a long sigh.

"Wait, it gets worse. It also affects how high the storm surge is," Jason explained. Collin stared at Jason as if it was way more information than he wanted to hear, but Jason continued anyway. "I think the winds could be close to two hundred miles per hour and the surge could be as much as eighteen or twenty feet high when it hits the island, because it's coming in at high tide. And, if the surge goes up the bay into the ship channel, it could be a thirty foot wall of water, fifty miles wide, by the time it hits Houston."

Collin's knees were weak and he needed a place to sit down. He spotted a wooden chair against the wall, and shuffled toward it. Jason followed and stood beside Collin as he melted into the chair.

"We're gonna lose a lot of people, aren't we?" Collin stared down at the floor, not wanting to hear the answer.

"The last Category 5 was Mitch, which hit Central America in '98." Jason stood with his head leaned back against the wall.

"And?"

Jason was quiet for a long time. "It killed nine thousand," he said quietly.

The statement took the breath out of Collin's lungs. He had only been concerned about one death up until that moment. The death of his political career. Now the true reality of the situation screamed in his mind. *Nine thousand.* The nausea in his stomach hit with amazing speed. He managed to stand up on weak, shaky legs.

"Excuse me, I need to hit the men's room," he said, hoping not to throw up before he got there.

CHAPTER TWENTY-SEVEN

J.D. squinted his eyes to keep the water from blurring his vision. Rain poured off the bill of his hardhat like a waterfall, and he felt like he was walking directly into the force of a fire hose aimed in his direction. He came to the end of the property line so he headed back. If Boone was smart, he was holed up somewhere dry, probably having a swig from that little flask he kept hidden inside his boot. J.D. had more than once seen him take a hit when he thought no one was looking. He wondered again why he'd never reported him. Drinking on the job was grounds for dismissal. The safety of everyone involved depended on each man at IP acting responsibly. But Boone never once acted the least bit out of control. That was just it. Boone was wound tight, ready to spring. There was a line that you knew you should never cross with him. If the truth were told, he didn't want to be in Boone's crosshairs. So, J.D. avoided him and gave him the nod to isolation that he seemed to require.

He'd probably intentionally set out to get away from them all. It would be like Boone to go off somewhere and sulk. J.D. had had about enough of him anyway and here he was out in this shit looking for the bastard. Beverly would be pissed if she knew that he was dodging debris and bolts of lightning, risking his life to find Boone. He wished he hadn't volunteered for this gig. He was soaked to the bone and was growing a bruise on his right shoulder thanks to a collision with a five-gallon bucket that hit him from behind. There wasn't enough overtime in the world worth this. He never guessed at five this morning this day would turn into a walking nightmare.

The nagging worry of not knowing for sure that Beverly and the kids were safe at his mom's house wouldn't go away. He would try to phone his mom's house again as soon as he got back to the break room. At the thought of the break room, he picked up his pace a little. There was hot coffee waiting and a place to dry out.

As he worked his way back toward the center of the plant, the more pissed off he got. *That bastard sure as hell wouldn't be out looking for one of us.* The wind and rain were blowing so hard he was almost crawling between tanks to keep from being picked up and blown away. He would scramble a few feet and then get behind a tank and rest. The air was filled with debris, trash and continuous lightning flashes. He felt like a target in a shooting gallery.

He spotted a small maintenance shed off to his left and angled over to it. He wrestled the door open, which was no small task, until the wind took hold and ripped the door off its hinges. In an instant, it sailed off into the night. Out of the battering rain and wind, he was able to get his breath and rest for a minute. He slumped down against a wall and shined his flashlight around the small room. It was filled with wrenches and tools, and on one wall hung a number of oxygen backpacks with their masks hanging from them. These were used when workmen had go down inside some of the tanks for maintenance. He was glad he had never had to do that in his few years at IP. He wasn't sure if he could handle that gig. J.D. spotted a couple of heavy rain slickers hanging on a peg. He pulled one on and headed out the door.

Boone eased his forty-foot annihilation creation out of the deserted truck stop, and on to the highway toward IP. He gripped the steering wheel tightly, as he struggled to see the road through the pounding rain. He knew Dolly must be getting close to landfall and he wanted to get this done before she got to him first. He was lightheaded with the adrenaline rush surging through his veins. *Ain't nuthin or nobody gonna stop me now.* He reached under his jacket to his shirt pocket for Libby's ring. A cold shock ran through him. It wasn't there. He patted his pocket frantically, then dug in his pants pocket. Nothing. He switched hands on the steering wheel and searched his other pocket.

"Where the fuck is it?" he screamed. He beat the steering wheel, and then slugged the dash. *Okay, think. When did you have it last?* He took some deep breaths, calmed down and remembered. It was lying on his desk. He was sitting at his desk, holding it in his hand, looking at Libby's picture, when Sam Lovett came bursting through the door to tell him everything was shut down. He had laid the picture down on the desk with the ring on top of it.

No problem. I'll run into the office soon as I get there and then give IP their little present. A crooked smile returned to his face. Boone reached down and slipped the Beretta out of his boot, and laid it on the seat beside him. Then he reached down with his other hand, and grabbed the flask.

J.D. was at one of the main walkways through the plant where he was able to hold on to the metal guardrail that ran along the sidewalk. He was splashing around a large cooling tank when he saw an IP tanker truck coming up the entrance road. *What the hell?* He rested under a concrete pillar that sheltered him from the direct force of the wind. The truck came to stop and J.D. saw the door open. A man climbed down from the cab. *Goddamn, it's Boone!* J.D. wiped the rain from his eyes and squinted to make sure he was seeing what he was seeing.

At that moment, Carl came out from behind a building to his right and fought his way through the wind toward Boone. J.D. headed toward the two men. He was about to wave his arms and yell at them, when he saw Boone raise his arm toward Carl. He was holding something in his hand, and a flash of fire came out of it. Carl suddenly reeled backwards as if he had been hit in the chest with a baseball bat, and crumbled to the ground on his back. J.D. froze in his tracks as he watched Boone walk up to Carl and point down at him. Another flash emerged from his hand. Instantly J.D. splashed to the ground beside the tank. Boone looked all around, and then reached down and began dragging Carl over by the tanker. He pushed his body up under the truck and headed off in the direction of the break room.

As soon as Boone was out of sight, J.D. hurried over to where Carl's lifeless body lay. His mind was racing as he tried to comprehend what his eyes had just taken in. He inched up to Carl, who was spread-eagled on his back with his arms above his head. Water splashed up against his body. His shirt was covered in blood and most of his face was gone. J.D. turned and threw up.

After a moment, he wiped his sleeve across his mouth and looked around. *What the fuck is going on?* He was shaking all over. He needed to get out of the wind and rain for a minute to think. He looked up at the truck, checked to see if anyone was around, and then began climbing into the cab. He was so weak he could barely pull himself up.

Once inside he grabbed hold of the wheel to stop his shaking hands. His mind replayed the scene he had just witnessed. He looked down and saw some of Carl's blood on his hands. He quickly wiped them off on his jeans. He took a couple of deep breaths and scanned the interior of the cab. He saw a small metal box with three toggle switches on top, lying on the passenger's seat. With trembling hands, he reached over and picked it up. *What the hell is this?* There were six wires coming out of one side of the box. He took his hand and followed them up to the small back window in the cab where the glass had been removed, and noticed they continued onto the top of the tanker. J.D. stared at the wires and the box.

He whispered softly to himself, as the reality of what he'd just seen and what he knew about Boone clicked into place. "I'm sittin' in a bomb."

Boone slipped into the little outer room outside the break room. The noise of the wind and rain outside was a dull roar in the background as he tried to listen for voices coming from inside the next room. He stepped to one side of the door and peered through the small glass window. He could see Wendell Hinson, a huge black man, who had worked for IP as long as he could remember, and Lupe Romero, who had come to work there sometime in the past year, sitting at a table in the far end of the room playing cards. He strained to get a look toward the other end of the room where the men's lockers were located. He could see only two rows of lockers, but he couldn't hear any voices coming from there. He listened for a moment and decided these were the only two people in the room. *Where is everybody?* Boone thought this was odd, but he was on a mission and wasn't going to be distracted. He took a deep breath and continued down the hallway toward his office. He was about to open his door when he heard something behind him. He turned and saw Wendell and Lupe coming out of the break room.

"Hey there you are. Everybody's out looking for you." Wendell was holding the door open for the man behind him when he spotted Boone.

"Yeah, everybody was afraid something happened to you," Lupe said with a goofy grin on his face.

"Here I am." Boone raised the gun and shot both of them before they could move. He looked down at the two men lying on the floor. He had hit Lupe in the middle of his Adam's apple. His neck had a gaping hole where blood was pouring out onto his chest. Wendell had fallen in an upright position by the door. The bullet had entered his chest just above the heart but Boone could see that he was still breathing. Wendell looked up at Boone, disbelief on his face.

"You wouldn't understand," Boone muttered as he shot him again between the eyes. *God, let's get this over with.* All that was left was to get Libby's ring and he could finish the job he started. Boone was about to retire.

J.D. saw Boone come out of the building. He slid over to the passenger's side of the cab and opened the door. He set the small metal box on the seat where he found it, and slipped down to the ground. He crawled on all fours toward the loading dock located about fifty feet from the parked truck. J.D. was almost to the wooden steps on the side of the dock, when something nicked his right ear, and he saw chips of wood fly up from the top step. His ear felt as if someone had stuck a lit cigarette to it. He grabbed the side of his head and spun around to see Boone standing in front of the truck with his arm extended, holding a gun. J.D. reacted instantly. He flattened himself on the ground with a big splash and crawled furiously around the side of the loading dock.

As soon as he was around the dock, he stood and ran. The wind was at his back now as he splashed toward the machine shop. It was a large metal building sitting at a ninety-degree angle from the loading dock. He skidded to a stop and jerked the door open. Once inside, he darted and dodged around the large machines and workbenches until he reached the back of the building. He squatted down behind a large drill press to catch his breath. *I've got to find some place to hide.* He tensed as he waited for the front door to fly open and Boone to come in with guns blazing. *The bastard's trying to kill everybody.* J.D.'s heart was pounding as he tried to get his breath under control.

He scanned the room and saw another door a few feet from where he was hiding. He quickly crawled over to it and eased it open. The building was blocking the wind and rain on this side. He stepped out the door and stood with his back to the wall. *I need somewhere he would never look.* He stared out into the darkness. When the place came to him, he shuddered all over as if he had stepped into a pool of ice water.

CHAPTER TWENTY-EIGHT

At about the time J.D. began his search for Boone, Beverly and Maxine were loading up their new ride with life jackets, two small paddles, a reel of anchor rope and flashlights. They had discovered the boat in the back of the second building of the dealership. It was an eighteen-foot Blazer bay boat, with a one hundred and fifteen-horse-power Yamaha engine. It was a wide boat with a ninety-one inch beam so it would ride shallow in the water. There was a tunnel hull for the prop and it could operate in less than two feet of water. Maxine climbed into the boat, turned the key on the console and watched the gas gauge register full.

"Why don't we just wait in that one for the water to rise?" Beverly shined her flashlight onto the huge fifty-footer, sitting in the corner of the building. Maxine shot her a no-nonsense look.

"Ooh look at this." Beverly picked up a large searchlight sitting on a workbench. She flipped the switch and a wide beam of light lit up a corner of the building.

"Perfect, let's get the kids and get out of here." Maxine climbed down from the boat.

"Okay. I saw a candy machine by the front. I know they have got to be starving."

"Good idea." Maxine sloshed through the water that was already invading the building.

The kids were still clumped together on the couch when Beverly and Maxine got to the office.

"Treats." Beverly held out the candy bars and small sacks of chips.

"All right," Austin said. "Have you got Reese's?"

"You bet." Beverly handed Austin two Reese's peanut butter cup candies.

"I want M&M's," Dallas said.

"Here you go. And Paris, I got you some potato chips."

"Thanks, Mom." Paris took the bag of chips. Tyler who was sitting in her lap reached for it. "Okay, you can have some."

Everybody eagerly tore their candy bars open.

"Okay gang, we've got an adventure ahead of us." Maxine kneeled down in front of them.

"Where're we going?" Paris looked scared.

"Yeah, where are we going?" Beverly glanced over at Maxine.

"To the dog track. It's the biggest building around here that I can think of." All the kids looked at Maxine with shocked expressions.

"Highway 2004 runs right beside this building and all the way up to the track."

"How far is it?" Dallas asked.

"Not far, about three miles."

They ate the rest of their candy bars in silence as the wind roared and the thunder boomed overhead.

The kids were crowded together under the snap-on canvas cover that enclosed the front half of the boat, with Paris in the middle holding Tyler, and Dallas and

166

Austin on either side of her. Beverly had given them a couple of flashlights so they weren't completely in the dark.

"Y'all okay?" Beverly leaned down under the cover.

"We're fine, mom," Paris said. The boys nodded in unison.

"Now, it's going to be really loud and windy when we get outside, but Mimi and I are gonna take care of you. Okay?" Beverly put her arms around them. Tyler began to cry and reached out for his mother.

"It's okay sweetie, Paris has got you." She kissed him on the cheek.

Maxine and Beverly opened the large sliding door. The main building offered some resistance to the wind as the second building sat catty-cornered to the one in front. The water outside was rising rapidly now, and was about four to five feet deep. The building's foundation was a little over three feet off the ground, so the driveway out the door had a slight decline to it. The water was lapping up to the middle of the wheels on the trailer.

"Okay, let me get in and you push us out." Maxine stepped up on the fender of the wheel and climbed into the boat. They had found the four-wheeler the dealership used to move the boats around in the yard and had it hooked to the trailer. Beverly got on the small tractor and started the engine. Slowly she pushed the trailer out of the door and into the rising water. Soon the boat was floating on the trailer.

"Let me get the motor started, and then you unhook us from the trailer and get in," Maxine shouted. Beverly nodded and got off the tractor and waded up to the front of the boat. Maxine sat down at the console and turned the key. The starter turned over three or four times before the engine sputtered and came to life. Beverly unhooked the boat from the trailer, climbed in and stood in front of Maxine.

"Turn the spotlight on," Maxine yelled. Beverly flipped the switch and a wide beam of light cut through the darkness.

"Is everybody's jacket on tight?" Beverly shouted over the howling wind. They nodded and slunk lower into the boat. Maxine slowly pushed the throttle forward and they began moving through the water.

The lot was filled with all sizes of boats and some were bumping against one another as the water rose. The farther they moved from the building the more they felt the wind to their backs. The gusts were getting close to hurricane range now. They were about fifty yards from the building, when in between lightning flashes, Beverly's light caught the chain link fence directly in front of them.

"Stop," Beverly shouted. Maxine immediately pulled the throttle back and put the boat into neutral.

"What is it?" Maxine stood up so she could see. In the next instant, they bumped into the fence, throwing Maxine into the console. Beverly lost her balance and fell forward on the canvas cover and the kids. They all began yelling and crying.

"It's okay," Beverly shouted. "It's okay."

Beverly quickly moved to help Maxine. Paris stuck her head out from the cover. "What happened?"

"We just bumped into a fence," Beverly yelled. "Stay under there." She looked up at Maxine. "Are you all right?"

Maxine nodded as she sat back in the seat. "Damn, should've known. Do you see a gate anywhere?"

Beverly kept shining the light up and down the fence line.

"I think there's something over there," she yelled, pointing the light to her left. They grabbed hold of the fence and began pulling the boat along beside it toward the gate.

Beverly groaned, as she shone the light on the gate. "It's chained."

They stared at the chain in frustration, and then Maxine yelled, "Back to the shop." She put the boat in gear and turned around

Back at the trailer, Maxine searched the shop for something they could use to get the gate open, while Beverly stood in waist deep water and kept the boat from floating away. Her arms ached and the calves of her legs were beginning to cramp as she strained to hold the boat against the wind. Remembering the earlier incident with Dallas, Beverly tried to keep her breathing calm to suppress the fear that threatened to overwhelm her. Her eyes constantly darted all around watching for snakes as she held the boat with one hand and swept the light back and forth with the other.

"This ought to do it," Maxine yelled as she approached the boat.

"What is it?"

"A propane torch and some bolt cutters."

They made their way down FM 2004 through the choppy water with Beverly crouched down in the bow, lighting the way and Maxine at the wheel. It had taken them about fifteen minutes to cut through the chain that held the gate closed to the boat yard. The wind roared like two freight trains running side by side and the air was filled with electricity from the continuous light show. Every once in a while a piece of debris would come flying pass them like a piece of shrapnel from an exploding bomb and Beverly would crouch a little lower in the boat.

Beverly swept the light back and forth, looking for road signs and fence post to keep them on track. The going was slow because about every fifty yards or so they would come upon an abandoned car or truck, and they would have to maneuver around it. Some of the cars had only the rooftops sticking out of the water. Beverly wondered where the people were. She would shine the light cautiously in the windows; always afraid she was going to see a body floating inside. On one SUV, a nasty looking water moccasin was curled on the roof. Her light caught his flat black eyes as he stared at them. She shuddered and turned away.

There were also lots of tree limbs and other trash in the water to watch out for. Something caught Beverly's eye off to her left and she swung the bright beam around. It was a fifty-five gallon drum. Probably gas for some farmer's tractor. It crashed into the side of the boat with a loud bang. The kids all screamed as the boat rocked back and forth in a jerky motion.

"It's okay," Beverly yelled as she grabbed one of the small paddles beside her and pushed the barrel away from the boat. Soon it was out of sight.

"Everybody all right?" Beverly asked as she stuck her head under the canvas cover. The wide-eyed kids nodded with tears running down their faces.

"It was just a speed bump," Beverly said with a grin.

"When are we gonna get there Mommy?" Dallas cried.

"Soon sugar, soon." Beverly rose back up and turned to look at Maxine.

"You okay?" she shouted.

"Yeah," Maxine yelled back.

Beverly turned and continued sweeping the light back and forth in front of the boat. She was soaked to the bone now and she could feel the cold creeping into her body. She was growing wearier by the minute; the strain of trying to maintain control and not panic was exhausting. A couple of times when she thought she was going to lose it altogether, she would catch one of the kids staring at her and she knew she had to keep up a good front for them.

She crouched lower in the boat trying to get a little protection from the penetrating rain. The stinging on the back of her neck reminded her of when she had gotten her one and only tattoo. It was a tiny dragonfly below her waistline and just above her right hip. She and J.D. and gotten them together on their third date, his over the left hip. She smiled and wished he were there with them. J.D. had assured her the break room was built to withstand hurricane winds, that he would be safe and sound. *Maybe we ought to be with him.*

"We're getting close now," Maxine shouted over the roaring wind. "That looks like the dog kennels."

A giant bolt of lightning streaked across the sky and they could see the outline of the Gulf Greyhound Park directly in front of them.

Jack had put Mrs. Ryan in the middle upstairs bedroom because he felt it was the most secure room in the house. He had huffed and puffed and manhandled Uncle Harry's recliner up the stairs and put it in the room for him. Aunt Nita was lying down on the other twin bed across from Mrs. Ryan. Uncle Harry had found his old Coleman lantern, which had been used on many a camping trip, and a couple of flashlights, while Aunt Nita had gathered up a handful of candles, so they could find their way around.

Jack and Molly were sitting opposite each other in the hallway outside of the bedroom with a couple of candles lit between them. The water downstairs was almost a foot deep and the electricity had gone out within the last hour. The storm was increasing and the hallway constantly flashed with light, which cast weird shadows on the walls.

"So where's Little Dutch?" Jack tried to sound as casual as possible.

"What?" Molly had a perplexed look on her face. "Oh my God, you think I'm married to Dutch." Jack shrugged his shoulders with a confirmation.

"Jack, I was never married to Dutch. I broke up with him two months after we got engaged. I knew I didn't love him . . . I didn't even like him." Molly stared back at Jack. "I was so upset after we broke up. I was pretty crazy for a while."

"I didn't know. I uh, I guess I was pretty crazy, too."

Neither one said anything for a moment as Jack stared at the flickering flame of the candle and Molly looked at her hands in her lap.

"I guess I blew it huh? . . . I just couldn't . . . hell, I was a kid."

"Jack, we were both kids." Molly leaned forward and took his hand.

"Why did you want to get married right then? Why couldn't you wait?"

Molly leaned back against the wall and looked away.

"I was pregnant."

"What?" Jack said wide-eyed. "Why didn't you tell me?"

"Because you would have done the right thing. You would have married me, but I would have always worried that it would have been for the wrong reason. I wanted you to marry me because you loved me."

"I did love you."

"I know, but that would have changed things. I-- I'm sorry, Jack. I screwed up." Her voice trailed off as tears welled up in her eyes and spilled onto the face that he thought he would never see again. He could feel a release of all the tenderness he'd felt for her come back in that instant. Jack stared at her for a moment longer, then pulled her to him.

"What did you do?"

"A friend of mine knew a doctor in Dallas who took care of everything."

They held each other tightly.

"I'm sorry, Jack. I should have told you."

Jack pulled back and looked deep into her eyes. He brushed a tear from her cheek.

"You know, I never got over you," he said softly.

"Me either."

He leaned forward and kissed her. Her lips parted slightly and he felt her tongue touch his. A small charge surged through his body and twenty years disappeared in an instant. He was seventeen years old and consumed with lust and love. A particularly loud clap of thunder brought him back to the present. They both jumped, and then giggled like two teenagers. Jack leaned back against the wall.

"So, you didn't marry the prince of shortness."

"No." She smiled. "I met someone the next semester, and we dated until he graduated and then we got married." Molly straightened and leaned back. "We moved to New York where Robert's family was in the import/export business. He was quite successful and we got to travel the world."

"Sounds like a good marriage."

"Yes, it was . . . for quite a few years." Molly looked off again. "And then Robert decided he needed to trade me in for a younger model."

"I'm sorry."

"Oh, it worked out okay. I caught him test-driving the new prototype."

Jack raised his eyebrows and started to say something, but didn't.

"I got half the business, which I sold."

"Those paybacks are hell." Jack nodded.

"Sounds like you know about paybacks?"

"Let's just say I've seen that movie."

"Wendy?"

Jack gave her a surprised look.

"My mom wrote me."

"And you remembered her name?"

Molly gave a little shrug.

"Actually, Wendy was a really good person. I'm the one who screwed that one up."

"That one?"

Jack held up two fingers. "Two time loser. Wendy and I were married about four years. I had just gotten on with the fire department when I met this . . . girl. I don't know what it was about her. I just flipped. I met her on the job. At a fire, of all places."

"A fire?"

"Yeah, her car had caught on fire."

"Let me guess, it was the back seat," Molly said with a twinkle in her eye. "I'm sorry, go on." Jack shook his head and continued.

"Anyway, she was grateful and I let my ego get in the way, and the next thing I know, I'm sneaking around all over the place with her until Wendy catches me red-handed."

"I see."

"Oh, that's not the worse part. I marry her, and then six months later I catch her with this cop, who I thought was a friend of mine." Molly winced as they stared at each other for a moment. "After that, I decided marriage wasn't for me." Jack looked down at his hands. "We're quite a pair, aren't we?"

"We used to be." Molly leaned over and kissed him. They slid over onto the floor. Jack kissed both of her closed eyes and worked his way down her neck and then up to nibble on her ear. The lightning cracked and they both could feel the house shudder slightly under the howling wind.

CHAPTER TWENTY-NINE

J.D. found the maintenance shed. He had constantly glanced over his shoulder for Boone since he left the machine shop, but hadn't seen him. Once inside the shed he squatted down and rested. He wrapped his arms around his knees and buried his face against them. He couldn't remember ever being this frightened. J.D. reached up and felt his throbbing ear. There wasn't much blood, but plenty of pain. He looked around at the oxygen packs hanging on the wall and pulled one down. He checked the gauge to make sure it was full. It would give him an hour and a half of air.

As he was about to leave the shed, he spotted a safety harness lying on the floor. He picked it up and slipped it on. It fit like a parachute harness. He put his arms through the shoulder straps and then brought the leg straps up under each leg and clipped them onto the belt that went around his waist. A large metal hook hung from the belt.

J.D. peeked out around the door to see if he could spot Boone anywhere. After a quick scan he darted out in search of the tank he and Carl had drained earlier in the evening.

After a short slog through torrents of rain and debris, he stood looking up at the curved metal stairway that wound around the side of the large round tank. The tank looked like a giant ten-story softball sitting atop an eight-pronged holder. After a short debate with himself as to whether he could do this or not, he started up the winding stairway. By the time he had made it to the platform at the top of the tank, the wind was blowing so hard he had to grip the railing with both hands. The platform floor was see-through iron mesh. J.D. looked at the hatch, which hit him about mid-chest, as he held onto the railing on either side of him. He cranked it open, took the flashlight out of his pocket and shined it down into the tank. A metal ladder disappeared into the depths. *Goddamn I don't want to do this.* He looked down into the black abyss. Carl's bloody face flashed through his mind. *But I sure as hell don't like the alternative.*

After a moment he swung a leg up to climb into the tank. A gust of wind caught him at the same instant and flipped him over the rail of the stairway. In a desperate flailing grab he managed to get a hand on the railing as he went over and hung by one arm. He quickly reached down with his other hand and hooked the safety harness back on the rail. *At least I'm not going to fall to my death. I'll just hang up here and drown.* He looked down at the ground some ninety feet below him.

He caught his breath and began to pull himself up onto the platform. Slowly he got a knee up on the metal floor. At this point he was going to have to unhook the harness to be able to pull himself all the way onto the platform. He reached out with his left hand and got a firm grip on the mesh metal floor by sticking his fingers and thumb through the diamond-shaped holes. He unhooked the safety hook and quickly grabbed the rain-slickened railing before falling back. After straining every muscle he had plus a few he didn't know about, he lay on the floor of the platform.

J.D. inched his way down the small ladder inside the tank after his second attempt to climb into the hatch proved successful. He adjusted the mask on his face and turned on the valve to the oxygen tank. He breathed in the fresh air and shined his light down the curved ladder below him. He clamped the hook from his harness onto a rung of the ladder and reached up and pulled the hatch closed, then turned his flashlight off to conserve the batteries, and wrapped his arms around the ladder. Instantly the darkness was so black he had an attack of vertigo.

He squeezed his eyes shut and worried about Beverly and the kids and hoped they would be safe and sound at his mother's house. Alvin wasn't that much farther north than where he was right now and it was obvious this storm was going to do a lot of damage over a wide area. J.D. wished he hadn't volunteered for this shift. *Damnit, I should be with my family.* The knot tightened in J.D.'s stomach but he knew his mother would know what to do. He had no choice but to trust that they were all right.

CHAPTER THIRTY

Suddenly her powerful winds encountered solid matter. She had never experienced resistance of any kind in her short life span. She spun faster and gave birth to a dozen tornadoes in less than four minutes.

Dolly officially made landfall on Galveston Island's East Beach at 12:47 Saturday morning. Her winds were clocked at one hundred and seventy-five miles per hour and the storm surge was gauged at twenty-one feet, but that would increase as she moved inland. Palm trees were bent flat to the ground and many were uprooted and sent flying like huge darts to be impaled in buildings and houses.

Most of the island was already under almost four feet of water by the time Dolly officially dragged herself ashore. When the storm surge rolled in, the fun really began.

The two high-rise condos on East Beach were damaged beyond repair in the first half-hour of Dolly's siege. Windows were blown out and rising water did such damage to the bottom four floors of both buildings that they completely collapsed. Pieces of the partially finished Levin Towers were scattered like Legos across the island. The huge UT Medical Center located on the east end of Galveston had been evacuated except for a skeleton crew and they were huddled in the darkness of a second-story cafeteria in the center of the complex. A roof torn from a building five blocks away slammed into the windows of the cafeteria at a little after one a.m., killing all seven people in the room.

At the Galveston Yacht Club a few blocks north of the Medical Center, sixty- and seventy-foot boats were being stacked on top of one another like bathtub toys and some would eventually be found over ten miles away, shipwrecked in front yards or run aground in the produce section of the local Randall's supermarket. Telephone poles were being snapped like toothpicks all over the island. These deadly missiles filled the air like arrows in a John Wayne movie. Cars and trucks were swept along streets and into houses and buildings. Smaller houses were imploding as if made from straw and larger ones were being dismantled piece by piece.

The Elbow Room was in the middle of the block of Avenue N just off 21st and had been a mainstay of the neighborhood since the mid-fifties. It had been Harold's favorite hangout for the last four or five years because it was only a few blocks from his house. He could always stagger home if he'd had too much rum to drive, or as he often told Cora the next morning, "Well, I got over-served again. You'd think as much as I go there, that asshole bartender would learn how much I can drink."

The room sported a large horseshoe bar in the middle with three pool tables off to one side. There was no ambience, no class, and nothing hanging on the walls except old beer signs and two racks of pool cues. It simply was a place to sit and drink. The clientele consisted of white men of various ages who knew very little of each other. The number-one unstated rule in the Elbow Room was no deep discussions. Everything was kept on a superficial level at all times and every situation was black and white, literally and figuratively.

Even though the Elbow Room was built up off the street some five or six feet, the water had been creeping in the front door for the last hour and the roar of the wind had become so loud they had to shout at one another even sitting side by side. Most everyone had gathered at the bar in the middle of the room.

"I think we ought to have one on the house, except I don't know if there's gonna be a house left to have it on," Harold slurred as loud as he could. Mike, the owner and bartender, gave a nervous nod and laughed. The other three men sitting at the bar looked around at Harold.

"Maybe we ought to put Harold up on the house to be our lookout," squeaked Tim Hilbers, a tall, lanky redhead with Alfred E. Neuman ears.

"Yeah, I thought you said this wasn't gonna be much of a blow, Harold." croaked Randy Everett, a middle-aged man sitting next to Tim. Harold looked around at Randy and Tim with glassy red eyes.

"You wouldn't know a good blow job from a bad blow job, Randy."

"Now that's where you're wrong, Harold. There are no bad blow jobs."

The men all laughed and took another drink. They were all trying to act like it was another night at the Elbow Room, but the room was crackling with tension. One of the two men playing pool walked over to peer out the window. Just as he pressed his face up against the pane, a huge crack of thunder hit with a blinding flash of lightning. He jumped back automatically and everyone laughed nervously again. The lights blinked twice and the building went dark. For a moment the place was silent but for the roaring wind outside.

"Better get a candle, Mike. Harold might be afraid of the dark," Tim said amid more nervous laughter. There was a crash of glass breaking behind the counter.

"I've got a lantern down here somewhere," Mike said. "Somebody light a fuckin' match or something."

"Here you go." Randy flicked his lighter and walked around behind the bar.

"A goddamn hurricane outside and you don't even have a fuckin' lantern ready?" Earl Swinson, the man at the window snorted.

"Look, I got plenty of booze, what the hell else do you need in a crisis?"

"Man's got a point," the other man playing pool said.

Mike stood up and set the lantern on the bar. The men gathered around to light it.

The continuous lightning outside gave off an eerie effect in the darkened room. It reminded Randy of a haunted house he had taken his cousin to last Halloween. Something banged against the front door and everyone jumped.

"Goddamn, this shit's getting spooky." Randy looked around sheepishly.

"Whatsamatter, 'fraid of a little storm?" Harold slurred.

Randy was about to answer Harold when a loud crash turned everyone's head toward the front door. A twenty-five gallon drum of oil, which previously resided at the Jiffy Lube three blocks down the street, screamed through the double window by the front door. If Gene Harvey, an Elbow Room regular and local Galveston cop, had been sitting at his usual stool with his trusty radar gun, he would have clocked it at approximately one hundred and fifty-three miles an hour. It caught Mike full in the chest and knocked him over the bar and onto a pool table some thirty feet away. By the time he landed on the table, both lungs were punctured, his spinal cord was broken, and a rib had pierced his heart. A split second later a second gust of wind hit, flinging the door wide open and sending pool cues flying that had been resting in the rack beside the now-broken window. The first of these cues caught Harold in his open mouth, passing completely through him like a hurled spear and out a window on the back wall. As the cue tore through the back of Harold's throat, it broke his neck. His head fell forward limply on his chest and he crumpled to the floor.

As the other men scrambled for shelter the roof began tearing away from the walls of the building. Randy and Tim were sucked completely out of the room, never to be found, and the three remaining men were crushed by the eight hundred pound pool table, which pinned them to the back wall.

CHAPTER THIRTY-ONE

Beverly's arm ached as she swept the light along the fence trying to locate the entrance to Gulf Greyhound Raceway. She thought about J.D. and wished they were all warm and dry and somewhere together. Through the relentless downpour she could see lights moving around inside the giant four-story building.

"Looks like we're not the only ones to think of this place," Beverly shouted.

Maxine nodded and pointed up ahead. Beverly turned and saw a gate standing open in the distance. She shined the light on the gate and was about to stick her head under the tarp and tell the kids they were almost there when suddenly the boat leapt forward at full speed. She was thrown backward into the stern of the boat. As her head smashed into the engine covering, she lost her grip on the light and it flipped into the water.

Dazed and confused, she tried to see what happened. Maxine was slumped over the console and her arm had pushed the throttle wide open. Before Beverly could move, the boat hit the fence at full force. Fortunately, it hit at an angle and glanced off, but not before it tipped perilously over on the right side. Beverly froze in stark terror as she watched the tarp rip off the front of the boat and her six-year old go flying overboard. In a single instant, the living nightmare of being in a boat with four kids in the middle of a hurricane just turned into Beverly's own personal horror movie.

The sound of the kids screaming over the roar of the wind jolted her out of her paralysis. She frantically clawed her way to Maxine who was crumpled down between the console and seat. She desperately had to get the boat stopped and find Austin. Beverly reached up and pulled the throttle all the way back. The boat almost stood on its nose as it abruptly slowed and threw Beverly into the bow on top of the kids. She felt a shot of pain rip through her right arm as she hit the metal railing. Everyone was screaming hysterically now, including Beverly.

"What happened?" Paris yelled.

"I don't know," Beverly screamed back. "We have to find Austin!" She pulled herself up with her good arm and grabbed Dallas, who was sobbing uncontrollably.

"It's alright, Dallas, I have you."

Paris struggled to sit up, still holding Tyler, who was screaming at the top of his lungs.

"Is he okay?" Beverly shouted. Paris held him out and looked at him.

"I think he's just scared. What about Mimi?"

"She's hurt."

Beverly sat Dallas down beside Paris and turned to pull Maxine out from under the console. There was a deep, ugly gash across the back of her neck where something had obviously hit her from behind and her shirt was soaked with blood. A bloody hubcap lay in the seat.

She wrenched Maxine out of the way and laid her on her back. Her dead eyes stared straight up into the relentless downpour.

"Oh God, please no," Beverly gasped and turned away. It was too painful to think about Maxine at this moment. Her mind could only take in one disaster at a time and her first priority had to be finding Austin. She knew what little courage she had left would go pouring out of her if she focused on the lifeless face of the person she was depending on to get them to safety.

"Paris gimme a flashlight!"

Paris scrambled to find one. "Here."

Beverly took it and searched the water behind the boat.

"Let Dallas hold Tyler and you get up in front with the light," Beverly shouted, giving the light back to Paris.

"Austin, " she screamed as loud as she could. "Austin, where are you?" Beverly was once again bordering on hysteria. She knew in her heart if Austin were crying for help, she wouldn't be able to hear him. She quickly moved to the console, slowly pushed the throttle forward and turned the boat into the powerful wind.

The wind gusts were so strong; they couldn't make any headway and were pushed back into the fence. Beverly struggled to get control of the boat. She gave it more gas and they began moving away from the racetrack.

"Anything yet?" she yelled.

"No," Paris shouted back. Tyler was still screaming.

Beverly could barely think. Tyler's screams, the thunder, the lightning, Maxine lying dead in the bottom of the boat, all threatened to take her mind away from what she needed to concentrate on: Austin out there somewhere in the water. She knew she had to get control of her emotions first. She focused on Austin wearing a life jacket and the many hours he had spent in the water at the beach. He would at least know how to paddle to something he could hang on to, but when she got that far, all she could think about was what was out there in the water with him.

When the boat reached a billboard advertising a disc jockey for Rock 105, she realized that they had passed it way before Maxine lost control. It occurred to her that she had come back too far and was in fact going in the wrong direction. She turned around and headed back toward the racetrack, again having to fight to control the boat. It now made sense to her that when Austin fell out of the boat, the wind would push him in the direction of the racetrack.

A big flash of lightning illuminated the area and Beverly caught sight of several vehicles right in front of them.

"Hold on," she yelled. Paris braced herself as the boat clipped the back fender of a partially submerged SUV. Beverly heard something crack from the impact. She pulled the throttle back and the boat slowed. She scrambled to the front to check on everybody. She took the flashlight from Paris and examined the bow of the boat. Water was rushing in at her feet.

"Shit! Now what do I do?"

"I think if we keep moving, the water won't come in so fast." Paris looked up. "I read about it in some of those old Nancy Drew books you have at the house."

Beverly gaped at her daughter.

"For real Mom." Beverly turned and went to the console.

As she reached for the throttle, she realized the wind had blown them up against the fence once again. If Paris and Nancy Drew were right, she needed to keep the boat moving at a steady speed or it was going to sink, along with their hopes of getting to the racetrack at all. She gassed the boat and began following the fence line where she knew there was less chance of submerged debris and it would take her closer to the racetrack.

The sinking feeling in Beverly's stomach was expanding rapidly. She knew the storm was getting stronger and now that the boat was damaged, she would have to think of getting the rest of her family to safety. They couldn't look for Austin much longer. It was not a decision she wanted to make. She had read *Sophie's Choice.*

"Mom! There he is." Paris shouted, pointing the light.

Beverly saw Austin bobbing upright in the choppy water next to the fence. She pulled as close as she could and then put the gear in neutral. She jumped into the water and found it was about waist deep. She grabbed Austin and began wading back to the boat, which was rapidly floating away. Paris saw what was happening and jumped behind the wheel. She put it gear and gave it enough gas to hold it steady until Beverly could grab hold of it.

"Is he okay? Paris shouted.

"I don't know." Beverly hoisted him up into the boat. "I think he's knocked out," she yelled, as she climbed in. Paris shined the light on Austin's face. There didn't appear to be any cuts or bruises on him. Beverly felt for his pulse and checked his breathing. She hugged him to her tightly with tears streaming down her face.

"Austin, honey. Are you all right?" As she rocked back and forth he slowly opened his eyes.

"What happened, Mom?"

"Oh baby, you're okay," she cried. She hugged him tighter, oblivious to the pain in her right arm.

"My head hurts." Austin rubbed his eyes with a fist.

"Where, sugar? Show me." Beverly held Austin away from her so she could look at him. She felt his head for a cut or blood.

"I have a headache." Austin rubbed his forehead.

"I'll get you something as soon as I can, but first we have to get to that building."

"Mommy, what's wrong with Mimi?" Austin spotted his grandmother on the bottom of the boat.

"She's hurt, sugar. We have to get her inside."

187

"Mom, there's more water coming in the boat."

"Austin, sit here by me. We have to hurry."

The boys crowded around the console as Beverly steered toward the racetrack. She found the gate and speeded toward the entrance. As she got closer, she saw cars partially under water and a number of boats gathered by the front doors. She took her small flashlight and began waving it back and forth. After a moment a light waved back at her from the front of the building. When she got close enough she noticed that the large glass doors had been broken out and some men were standing there. They waded out to grab the boat.

"Please help us. I have children in here," Beverly shouted, "and a woman who's injured." Two of the men held the boat as two others held out their arms for the children. Beverly handed them Dallas and Austin, then she held Tyler while Paris climbed out. Beverly handed Tyler back to Paris.

"I need some help with my mother-in-law." One of the men who had been holding the boat climbed inside.

"How bad is she?" he said, kneeling down.

"I think she's dead, but I don't want the kids to know yet." Tears poured down Beverly's face. She reached down and gently closed Maxine's eyes. "Thanks for watching over us. I could feel you with us."

The man stood up. "George, I need some help up here."

After a few minutes, George and another man carried Maxine inside the building.

"We have some other injured folks upstairs. Y'all follow us."

Boone wasn't sure how long he had been sitting in the truck staring at the small metal box in his hand. It could have been a minute, or it could have been much longer. He had followed J.D. into the machine shop and after not finding him with a cursory search, had returned to the truck to find Roy and Sam kneeling over Carl's body. He had shot both of them in the back of the head before they could turn around.

As he ran his fingers over the three switches on the metal box, a tiny sliver of memory tried to come to the front of his mind. He blinked a couple of times as fleeting visions raced in front of his eyes. He could see a dark cloud belching fire like a volcano erupting, and felt the overpowering feeling of mass destruction, but he couldn't quite bring them into focus. It was as if he was trying to remember some tiny bit of knowledge, but it remained too abstract to see clearly. It was like trying to hold on to smoke.

Boone knew it wasn't about his death. Living through this was never an option in his plan. A bolt of lightning lit up the cab of the truck and he caught his reflection in the large side mirror. The person staring back at him had been dead for a long time. He reached up and wiped his face with the sleeve of his shirt. His face was wet, but not from crying. Now the absence of feelings and the ache in his heart were unbearable. He felt no remorse for the things he had done this evening. He only felt empty and devoid of life. *I'll bet I won't even feel this.* He gripped Libby's ring tightly in his fist, took a deep breath, and flipped the switches.

CHAPTER THIRTY-TWO

Collin's secretary, Sue, her husband and children, and most of the EMS staff and patrolmen who were on shift were sitting or milling around in the cafeteria. It was located on the third floor of the large four-story, T-shaped building that was City Hall and the Galveston Police Department. The rest were clustered in the hallways as far away from the windows as possible. There were ten men down on the second floor manning the EMS command center.

Jason poured himself a fresh cup of coffee and wandered out into the hallway. He walked past patrolmen standing in groups trying to look unconcerned. He smiled gratefully to himself as he thought about Cathy and the boys, safe and sound at his brother's house outside of Brenham, a small community about sixty miles northwest of Houston. He got them up and on their way shortly after receiving the phone call at four a.m. from Roger about Dolly's newfound strength. They had called around noon to say they had made the trip with no problems.

Cathy had burst into tears over the phone. She had been upbeat this morning for the children, not wanting to scare them and wanting to be stoic for him, knowing he had a job to do. She had six hours of listening to media reports about the destruction Dolly was about to deliver and she was afraid for him. He tried to reassure her that City Hall had endured many storms and that he was safe.

In the back of his mind, he found himself wishing the new multi-million dollar emergency center that would house fire, police and emergency personal in the future was completed instead of simply an approved plan.

He found an empty space about mid-way down the hall, just past the door to the men's room, and squatted down with his back to the wall. He listened to the sounds of Dolly's ranting and raging outside, shouting to the world that she was Mother Nature's most powerful force. The noise was deafening. Windows were breaking all over the building and it sounded like an enemy army was using a battering ram on every outside door. *I always knew this hurricane was going to arrive someday, but I don't think I ever really thought about what it was going to be like to be in it.* He leaned his head back against the wall and could feel the vibrations of the building. Suddenly, it hit him. *Funny, I sure as hell never thought about if I was going to be around when it was all over.*

He looked up to see Roger coming out of the door from the stairwell, followed by a patrolman who looked barely old enough to shave. Roger spotted Jason and flopped down on the floor beside him. The patrolman leaned up against the wall.

"Anything new down stairs?" Jason shouted.

"Nah, now that she's here. Just got to ride it out," Roger yelled.

"I know. That's why I decided it was coffee break time." Jason held his cup up.

"How are you doing, Kent?" Jason looked up at the patrolman.

"Hangin' in there. First one of these I've ever been through. We don't have many hurricanes in San Angelo," he said with an uneasy laugh.

"Hell, y'all don't have much weather of any kind out there." Roger smiled. Jason agreed and took a sip of his coffee. Suddenly the building seemed to groan like a wounded animal and swayed like a boat on water. Everyone looked around nervously and flattened themselves to the walls.

"I think the roof's going," Jason shouted. There was a loud whoosh as all the air was abruptly sucked out of the hallway. Jason clutched his chest as if he had been kicked in the stomach. There was no air in his lungs. As he turned to look to see what had happened, his eyes grew wide as he saw the end of the building being ripped away as one of Dolly's twister offspring ripped into City Hall. Automatically he grabbed the doorframe beside him and held on. Out of the corner of his eye he saw two blurred shapes go flying past him. Roger and Kent disappeared into the darkness. The wounded building was now shrieking in its final violent death throes. Jason clung to the doorframe with all the strength he could muster. Torn pieces of sheetrock and splinters of lumber filled the air along with the screams of grown men reduced to frightened children. The floor beneath him shuddered, then suddenly gave way. He was suspended for a moment in mid-air and then fell, doing a slow backward flip. His arm caught a jagged stud sticking out of a wall and he felt his forearm snap in two. In the next instant he slammed headfirst into the concrete floor of the level below him, breaking his neck instantly.

Collin was in the stairwell between the second and third floors when the tornado struck. He had just stepped onto the small four-by-four-foot landing to take the next flight of stairs up to the third floor when he felt the building move. He pushed himself into the corner of the stairwell and held his arms out to each wall for support, then he gradually slid down to a sitting position and put his arms over his head. It sounded like a large wrecking ball had just rammed into the front of the building. He glanced up to see the metal door with *FLOOR 3* stenciled on it flying directly toward him. Instinctively, he threw his arms out in front of his face. The top of the door landed with an ear shattering crunch about eight inches above his head at a thirty-degree angle. The bottom of the door hit the second of the steps in front of him and stopped. Collin opened his eyes and saw the door about three inches from his hands, jammed at an angle between the wall and the stairs.

He peeked out around the side of the door, but could only see darkness. He pushed himself further into the corner and pulled his knees up to his chest with his arms. He could hear the crack of wooden studs snapping and the crashing of the concrete walls as they fell. But mostly he could hear the screams of people dying.

Less than twenty blocks from City Hall the Hotel Galvez was taking the worse beating in its ninety-one year history. There were thirty people sheltered inside. The hotel staff consisted of Jeff Hankins, the night manager who had been at the hotel for over twenty years, and his all-volunteer staff for the evening, which included Rick Mays, the doorman and valet, and Lonnie Brewster, bellhop. They were roommates who had worked at the hotel for about two years. Lily Shanks, bar and restaurant manager, who was only into her third week at the hotel, cook Jose Lopez and Maria and Silvia Martinez, two sisters who had been maids at the Galvez for over ten years, rounded out the staff.

The paying guests included Sean Micheals, the overly ambitious reporter, cameraman Jim Wells from Channel 11, and Gavin and Martha Vance, a couple from Fort Worth who had been celebrating their wedding anniversary at the Galvez for forty-two years. This year they had brought their daughter Pam and son-in-law Frank Grisham and three grandchildren, Missy, Will, and Frank Jr. They had checked out earlier in the day only to make their way back to the Galvez four hours later, after realizing they were not going to make it off the island.

Also registered at the Galvez were four college students from SMU in Dallas who had come down for a Labor Day holiday in the sun and weren't going to let some little old storm ruin their weekend, and a middle-aged man whom nobody seemed to know and who kept to himself.

Then there were the people who had simply ended up at the Galvez in the past few hours seeking shelter from the storm. Gene and Joan Cockrell, an elderly couple who lived only a few blocks down the street from the Galvez and were friends of Jeff the night manager, the Hunts, a family of five whose car had stalled on the seawall and a woman who had arrived at the doors on the backside of the Galvez, less than an hour earlier screaming that her children were trapped inside of her car and were about to drown.

The middle-aged stranger had rushed out into the storm and rescued all three children. Jim videotaped the whole heroic episode, including the man's demise as he pushed the last child to the waiting arms of Jamie, one of the students from SMU. The man had made three separate trips out to the woman's car, which was caught between a streetlight and an abandoned truck. By the third trip, the water running down the street behind the Galvez was a raging river. As the exhausted hero pushed the girl to safety a large wooden bus bench rammed into the man. He went under water and never reappeared.

Rick and Lonnie were busy moving the heavy, expensive furniture from the elegant lobby up to the second floor. Jamie, an athletic-looking kid, and Mark, a suntanned blonde who stood about six-three, were stacking sandbags along the front wall under the oval windows. The other two, Len and Joe, who looked like they spent more time in front of a computer than in a workout gym, were supervising the process from a distance.

"Don't ya think that one could be a little straighter," Len cracked, trying to keep from laughing.

"I'll tell you what's going to be straighter. You, after I stick this floor lamp up your ass," Mark replied with a grin.

Sean was interviewing Jeff for additional footage of the rescue of the three children. They were standing by the long wooden front desk that resided to the left and ran perpendicular to the beautiful stained-glass front doors. Everybody else was holed up in a large conference room down the hall from the lobby. It was located in the interior of the building and considered one of the safest places in the hotel.

Rick and Lonnie were loading the elevator at the back of the lobby when something crashed into the front of the building. Sean stopped mid-sentence and Jim swung his camera toward the sound. For a moment everyone was frozen in time. Suddenly a seventy-foot palm tree blasted through the front doors. It roared between Jamie and Mark like a brown rocket leaving a large red gash on Mark's arm. The tree crashed into a long velvet couch bulldozing it into Rick and Lonnie before they could move. The momentum carried them into the semi-full elevator, crushing them into the stacked tables and chairs with so much force that it ruptured the back metal wall.

Sean fainted on the spot. Jim dropped his camera and raced to the elevator. Jeff leaped over the desk and followed. Len and Joe stood as if both their feet were nailed to the floor while Mark and Jamie stared at each other in disbelief. Jim climbed over the shattered palm tree and into the open elevator where the crumpled bodies lay. It took only a glance to tell that they were both dead.

It sounded like a freight train was running through the lobby. Jim could literally see the wind and rolling sheets of rain coming through the gaping hole where the front doors used to be. It played havoc with anything that wasn't nailed down. Paintings from the walls, small tables and lamps and debris from the outside soon flew around the room like a scene from a horror movie.

"We can't do anything for them," Jim shouted.

"Come on, let's get the hell out of here," Jeff yelled. He motioned for the students to follow him. Jim fought through the wind back to the front desk and slapped Sean into consciousness. He pulled him up off the floor and they followed Jeff and the students down the hallway toward the conference room.

Gavin Vance and his son-in-law Frank heard the commotion and came out into the hallway.

"What happened?" Gavin asked.

"A palm tree decided to come in out of the weather," Mark said, holding his hand over the cut on his right arm.

CHAPTER THIRTY-THREE

Sarah and Lex's house stood eighteen feet above the sandy beach and some fifty yards beyond high tides. If they had been among the living or the conscious, they would have been astounded to see water crashing a good two feet over the large wooden deck extending out from their living room. Bonnie and Cora would have too, but they were sitting inside what Sarah called her safe room. They had discovered it after Cora had found a copy of *Architectural Digest* on a nightstand beside Sarah's bed. The cover had a picture of Sarah and Lex standing on the deck. Inside was an interview with Sarah where she had divulged some of the aspects of her hurricane-proof house.

She pointed out that the weakest links in any house in the path of a hurricane are the windows, the gable end of the roof and the garage door, if there was one. She attached two two-by-fours to every other stud on one side of the gable and then secured the other end to the top of a load-bearing wall. She also attached another two-by-four over the first, forming a T. For the windows she installed automatic metal shutters that could be closed with the touch of a button. The interviewer said it sounded like Batman's car.

Sarah also described how she had installed four-foot high metal rails on the front and back of the roof that could be raised and lowered automatically. She got the idea from how race drivers use spoilers on the back of their car to give it down draft, to make it stick to the race track at high speeds. The higher the wind the harder it would push down on the house, rather than lifting the roof off. When she was asked why they were on the front and back of the house and why they weren't permanently left up, she explained that when the eye passes over and the backside of the hurricane hits, the winds will be coming from the opposite direction. She also said she took a number of ideas from the designers of earthquake-proof buildings so that the house had some flexibility to it. But the part of the article that really caught their eye was the description of Sarah's safe room, located in the middle of the house with access through the pantry. It was a circular room built with concrete block and had a thirty-foot diameter. It was stocked with food, a small wet bar and an emergency generator. The control panel for the shutters and roof railings were located there.

Bonnie was sitting in one of the two large easy chairs in the room. Cora was in the other and Sarah was lying on a small double bed off to one side. There was a TV set and stereo in the room along with extra clothing. They had found some cheese, a roll of summer sausage and a box of crackers. They were spread on a plate between the two of them.

"I didn't know I was hungry until took a bite," Bonnie said as she put another slice of cheese and sausage on a cracker.

"Me either."

"Boy you sure can't hear anything in here."

"Yeah, it's quiet as a fuckin' tomb." Cora got up and walked over to the bed. She bent down and felt Sarah's forehead. Sarah's breathing was soft and shallow.

"You think she's gonna come out of it?"

"I don't know." Cora stared down at Sarah for a moment then returned to her chair where she picked up a slice of cheese.

198

"Think she killed him?" Bonnie asked.

"Who knows? I do know the police usually look at the spouse first." Cora put the cheese on a cracker and took a bite.

"Maybe they had a fight?"

"Yeah, there are times you want to kill 'em." Cora nodded. They stared at one another for a moment. Bonnie started to say something and changed her mind. Cora let out a big sigh.

"I know you don't believe me, but Harold really was a good husband for a lot of years. Hey, don't get me wrong, he's always had a big mouth, but he isn't mean, and that big mouth helped him as a salesman. That man can talk to anyone at any time about anything."

Bonnie pulled her feet up under her and settled back in her chair.

"It was only after he retired that things started changing. I think he lost his self-esteem or something. That and the drinking really kicked in. He was a social drinker for a long time. I probably only saw him drunk a few times in thirty years." Cora had a faraway look in her eyes, as though she were remembering something long ago.

"What is it?"

"I was just wondering where he is right now and if he's okay."

Bonnie shifted uncomfortably in her chair, then got up and walked over to the small wet bar. "You thirsty?"

"Yeah, and I could use something stiff."

Bonnie mixed the drinks and handed one to Cora.

"Can I ask you something personal?"

"Why hell yes." Cora took a drink.

"Do you ever, uh, do you regret your life, I mean do you ever wish you had done something else with your life?"

"That's what I like about you, you don't beat around the fucking bush about anything." Cora laughed. "So what's on your mind?"

Bonnie blushed and took a drink.

"Well, I'm just not sure what I want to do with my life and I don't want to get down the road a piece and think, 'damn I wish I'd done that,' or whatever."

"So what is it you want to do?"

."I'm thinking about trying stand-up comedy or maybe even acting."

"Bonnie, I think that is a terrific idea. You'd be great."

"And another thing, I want to do some traveling. My parents traveled all over the world and they never took me and my sister anywhere and I'm still pissed off about that."

"I support you a hundred percent on making a change. And to answer your question, I think I've had a pretty good life."

Bonnie smiled at her.

"So you haven't thought about leaving Harold?"

"I'd be a liar to say I haven't thought about it, but you know, Harold and I don't have a hell of lot. We've got a forty-year old house . . . Ha, I should probably say we had a forty-year old house," Cora chuckled. "And we haven't got much in savings, so if I up and leave him, I don't get shit."

Bonnie sighed and gave Cora an understanding nod.

"And there's something else I've never said anything about. A little over a year ago, in fact just about the time you and I met, he was diagnosed with lung cancer. They say he's in the latter stages."

"Oh Cora, why didn't you ever say anything? Especially when I was hammering on you about what a jerk he was."

"I don't know, probably because I was as pissed off at him as much as you were most of the time."

Bonnie moved her chair over in front of Cora. She reached out and held her hand.

"I'm sorry," Bonnie said softly.

"Me too." Tears formed at the edges of Cora's eyes and began a slow path down her cheeks. Bonnie pulled Cora to her and could feel her soft sobs. After Cora stopped crying she pulled back and asked tenderly, "Is he in treatment of some kind? Chemo?"

"He was, but he quit going. Said it wasn't helping. He said he was already sick and tired and didn't need some asshole doctor to make him more sick and tired." Cora wiped the tears from her eyes with her sleeve.

"I think I can understand that."

"Me too. I think that's why he's not sitting here with us right now."

"You think he wanted this storm to blow him away?" Bonnie was stunned. Some of the things about Harold and Cora's relationship were starting to make sense.

"I believe he would prefer it to rotting to death in his easy chair. Tell you the truth, I think that's why he picked a fight with me this morning. He wanted me off the island."

Bonnie processed this for a while, "If that's the case, I guess we didn't hold up our end of the bargain."

"We may get off this island yet, but it ain't gonna be until after Dolly blows her guts out."

"You think Sarah knew what she was doing? About this house, I mean," Bonnie said looking around the room uneasily.

"All I know is, we're sitting here and Dolly's out there and before I got here, I was soaking wet and scared shitless. Now I'm just scared."

"I need another drink."

201

Cora held her glass out. "Me too. Maybe hurricane parties aren't such a bad idea after all."

CHAPTER THIRTY-FOUR

Boone was right. He didn't feel anything. He opened his eyes. Nothing had happened. *What the hell?* He looked down at the metal box in his hand. He jiggled the switches back and forth. Nothing. Boone looked at the wires going into the back of the box and pulled on them. Everything seemed to be hooked up. He followed the wires up and over the seat and through the open back window. He reached up and pulled on the wires again. Instead of going taut, they limply fell though the window into his lap. All six had been cut in two. Boone stared at the severed wires in his lap.

"J.D.," he said out loud. "That son-of-a . . . " All of a sudden the truck started shaking. He dropped the box and grabbed hold the steering wheel. A noise was overriding the howl of the wind outside. It was a deep intense rumbling, a sound he couldn't place, and one he'd never heard before. The truck vibrated faster. Lightning struck close by and Boone leaned over to look out of the passenger side window, but couldn't see anything.

The storm surge, which had struck the eastern end of Galveston Island approximately forty-five minutes earlier at a little over twenty-one feet, had now risen to over thirty feet high and was roaring up Galveston bay at twenty-five miles per hour. The towering wave struck Boone's truck broadside with such force that it catapulted him through the passenger side window with the same velocity as an ejection seat from a jet fighter plane. This he did feel, but for only a split second, as his skull cracked open like a cow at a slaughterhouse being hit with a twelve-pound sledgehammer when his head caught the metal window frame. What he didn't feel were his shoulders being crushed, as his large body was jammed through the too-small window of the truck. His left leg, which had become entangled with the steering wheel and gearshift, was torn from his torso.

The wave, carrying the truck in front of it like an errant surfboard, engulfed the concrete-block building that housed the break room and other IP offices with such power that it simply dissolved them like a giant sandcastle. The turbulent water destroyed, mangled, or carried with it everything in its forty-mile wide path.

J.D. clung to the ladder with a death grip. He was soaked to the bone and scared beyond reason. The blackness was so thick, he could almost feel it on his skin and it was eerily quiet inside the round tank, which made everything worse. He felt like he was suffocating and he knew he was breathing too hard. He would use up his oxygen too fast if he couldn't get a grip on the claustrophobic panic that was consuming him. He tried thinking about Beverly and the kids. He imagined himself with Beverly, lying on the beach on a perfect summer's day, watching the kids play in the cool Gulf waters.

Something crashed into the tank with great force. It snapped his head forward and the metal rung of the ladder caught him in the center of his forehead. A brilliant bright flash went off in his brain and his arms turned to rubber. He hung limply in his safety harness clamped to the ladder. In his last second of consciousness, he felt the tank give way and begin to roll.

Beverly and the kids were on the second level of Gulf Greyhound Raceway. There was no electricity in the cavernous building, but of the over two hundred people who had sought shelter there, many had flashlights. Beams of light cut through the darkness at odd angles like a laser show.

"Where did they take Mimi?" Austin asked.

"Someplace they can look after her, honey. She's hurt bad." Beverly kneeled down in front of Austin. She caught Paris giving her a look. She kissed him on the cheek, and stood up next to Paris.

"She's dead, isn't she?" Paris asked in a soft voice so that the others couldn't hear.

"Yes, but I don't want them to know yet."

Paris's eyes filled with tears and she hugged her mom. Beverly held her close for a moment and then stepped back.

"Let's find a corner or somewhere we can sit down." Beverly didn't know if she could stand up much longer. Her arm was throbbing and the adrenalin that had been helping her hold it all together was deserting her. She shined the light back toward Austin who stood off by himself.

"Where's Dallas?"

"He was right here." Austin looked around.

"DALLAS," Beverly yelled. "Y'all stay right here. Don't move." She handed Tyler to Paris. Beverly had been so relieved when they found Austin that she vowed that no harm would ever come to another child of hers. She now realized just how unrealistic that was. She had not yet had time to collapse into a heap in a corner somewhere before son number two was lost in this big black cavern.

"DALLAS!" Flashlights turned her way as she moved through the crowd.

The second level of the racetrack where the Simulcast betting took place was a large area with a few smaller rooms off to one side. On the left side, there was a long bar that ran halfway down the room. On the right were the betting windows running the length of the space. In the middle were small cubicles, each with a chair and TV. There were probably forty of them. Up ahead she could see a large opening to her left where flashes of lightning lit up that section. As she got closer she could see Dallas watching the lightning.

"Dallas, what are you doing? You scared the hell out of me."

Dallas turned when he heard his mother.

"Look." He pointed toward the lightning.

Beverly walked up to the opening where she could see tiers of seats laid out on either side, above and below her. The seats were at an angle in stadium seating covering three stories. In front of her was an enormous glass wall four stories high. There were maybe a hundred people scattered around in the seats watching the lightning like it was an IMAX movie. Lightning flashed, revealing a lake where the racetrack was supposed to be. In the distance you could just barely make out the silhouettes of abandoned cars along I-45, which ran parallel to the racetrack.

Beverly was mesmerized at the sight. The trembling of the building brought her back to her senses. She had never been in an earthquake, but for an insane moment she imagined that was exactly what was happening. She could feel the vibration coming up through her feet. She reached down and grabbed Dallas by his hand. She turned for one last look. The lightning was continuous now; it was bright as mid-day outside. Beverly's heart almost stopped when she saw the black churning wall of water coming toward them. The roar was above the other sounds and it sounded like a squadron of jet planes was heading right for them. The wave wasn't like water anymore; it had the density of gumbo soup with okra and shrimp being replaced with cars, pick-up trucks and the remains of large and small buildings.

She turned and raced toward the kids. By this time others had seen what was coming and had started scrambling from their front-row seats to find shelter. Within seconds, panic flew through the crowd.

"PARIS," Beverly screamed as she ran. She saw Paris jump out of the way of a man running past her.

"Here Mom," Paris yelled, holding Tyler and dragging Austin with her. Now there was confusion all around them as people tried to get as far away from the glass side of the building as possible. Beverly shined her flashlight around and spotted a restroom sign on the wall behind them.

"This way," she shouted, and herded them down a small hallway to the restrooms. She opened the door and found four other people huddled in the back of the room. As they ran inside she could hear glass shattering and people screaming.

"Under the counter." Beverly pushed the kids under the lavatories running the length of room. She lay down in front of them, trying to shield them with her body from the carnage outside.

The first thing through the four-story glass wall was a fully loaded 1997 Ford Explorer complete with a family of four, followed by an intact seventy-foot Shell service station sign and about a million gallons of water. There were a few people who were so paralyzed by fear that they were still sitting in their seats. They were crushed to death by the weight of the water before they had time to drown.

Giant pieces of broken glass sailed through the air severing arms, torsos, and screaming heads. The lower level, which already had about four feet of water, filled to the ceiling in a few seconds. People were pummeled into walls, into gaming machines and through the glass windows on the north side of the building. The sounds of dying were deafening.

J.D. was riding in the front car of the Texas Cyclone at Astro World. He was being jerked and wrenched from side to side as the car screamed around a curve and tilted to a forty-five degree angle. His head was suddenly thrown forward and he hit the front of the car. Pain shot through him. *This is no dream.* J.D.'s eyes opened. At least he thought his eyes opened, but everything was still pitch black. *My God, am I blind?* Panic began surging through his body. Suddenly the tank lurched again. *Where am I?* His panic level was increasing rapidly. He reached up to wipe his face and his hand hit the oxygen mask. He let out a small cry and even though the mask muffled the sound, it seemed to reverberate around him. A tiny light went on in his memory banks and the image of the tank came to him. A screeching sound made him jump as something banged into the tank. *Or did we run into something?*

Now he remembered where he was and the movement was no dream. *How can this be? Surely the wind couldn't have blown the tank off its stand. An explosion?* His terror was bordering on crisis stage. He reached into his coat pocket, pulled the flashlight out and turned it on. He realized the only thing preventing him from falling into the eternal black hole was the hook from the safety harness. If he didn't clamp his arms and legs around the metal ladder, he was as vulnerable to the wrenching movement of the tank as a rag doll. *Goddamn, we are moving.*

The thought sent more fear through his body and he grabbed hold of the ladder with both arms and pulled himself as close to it as he could. Another loud crash and he was abruptly tilted over backwards. His body was now in a horizontal position. J.D. held on with all the strength he had. Even though he knew he wasn't going to plunge flailing and screaming into the darkness below because of the safety harness, he couldn't grip the ladder tight enough. He turned off the flashlight and carefully slid it back into his pocket so he wouldn't drop it. Vertigo hit him immediately as the blackness engulfed him once again. J.D. felt like he was on the verge of screaming hysterically. He squeezed his eyes shut and willed himself to close his mind just as tight. Every time a jarring noise reverberated through the tank like a bell, he would force his eyes a little tighter.

After what seemed like an eternity, it felt as if the movement was slowing a bit. It didn't feel as jerky. Nothing happened for a while, although it could have been only a few minutes. J.D ached from clutching the ladder so tightly. He relaxed his grip to try to rest his arms and hands for moment. At that instant the tank abruptly rolled forward and J.D.'s head smacked the ladder rung. Blackness swept over him for the second time.

CHAPTER THIRTY-FIVE

Racing up Galveston Bay, the storm surge destroyed most of Texas City, Dickinson and League City. Kemah, Seabrook and La Porte were physically wiped off the map. The surge, almost fifty miles wide, demolished most of Baytown, Highlands and Channelview, located on the other side of the bay. The eastern edge of the storm surge reached a height of thirty-five feet as it came to the end of the Houston Ship Channel.

One of the largest operations on the Ship Channel is Volkswagen Inc. Houston is the port for all incoming Beetles for the southwest and southeastern part of the United States. At any given time, there are thousands of oval vehicles in various shades of yellow, red, green and blue lined up in rows, door handle to door handle and nose to tail. In a matter of minutes, these little German marvels, which could float, were being delivered all over the south side of Houston. They crashed through houses and buildings like huge marbles shot from a slingshot. A bird's eye view in the early morning light would look like Mother Nature had ripped open a giant bag of M & M's and spread them around the city.

Dolly's hundred-and-seventy mile an hour winds carried enormous amounts of debris that knocked large sections of glass out of Houston's skyscrapers. When the lightning reflected off the millions of pieces of falling shards of glass it looked like a massive ice storm was hitting the Bayou City. Tornadoes were attacking like angry hornets out of a disrupted nest. Trees and telephones were uprooted and rooftops were pried off with ease in neighborhoods all over the city.

Rain fell so hard and so concentrated; it was like a large, slow moving waterfall dumping billions of gallons of water onto an already over-saturated landscape. Within an hour of her official arrival, water was eight feet deep downtown. Freeways turned into swollen rivers out of their banks and underpasses became death traps. The Medical Center, which is a small city in itself, was also experiencing the worst flooding in its history.

Jack had been in constant contact with the Emergency Command Center for the last hour. He knew from the scattered reports they were getting from Galveston and other cities to the south of Houston that Dolly was doing tremendous damage. He could tell from the roar outside that Dolly was now on their doorstep.

"I want to move everyone into the middle bathroom. Ask Aunt Nita for some quilts and blankets." Molly nodded and went into the bedroom. Jack ran down the hall to the bedroom on the north end of the house and pulled a mattress off one of the twin beds. He walked it to the middle bathroom. Molly followed with an arm full of blankets and quilts.

"Line the bathtub with them. I'm going to put your mom in there," Jack yelled. Molly quickly unfolded the blankets and laid them in the tub. Jack leaned the mattress against the wall and went into the bedroom to get Mrs. Ryan. In a moment he returned carrying her in his arms and laid her gently in the tub.

"It's going to be all right Mrs. Ryan. Don't be frightened; I'm just going to cover you. Okay?"

"It's getting worse out, isn't it."

"Yes ma'am, but we're going to be all right."

Jack pulled the mattress into the room and laid it over the tub.

"Bring Aunt Nita and Uncle Harry in here," Jack shouted as he went to retrieve the other twin mattress. Jack could feel movement as the winds beat against the house. The lightning outside was non-stop and the hallway was lit up bright as day.

Soon Aunt Nita and Uncle Harry were sitting on the floor next to the tub with the other mattress leaned up against them.

"I'm going to put the box springs up against the window in the hallway."

"I'll help you," Molly shouted. As they hurried into the bedroom they heard glass breaking downstairs.

Jack turned back toward the door. "Sounds like Dolly's trying to come in through a window. We've got to hurry."

Suddenly a deafening crash and a blast of wind threw Jack out into the hallway. He heard Molly's scream above the chaos. He scrambled to his feet and fought his way back into the room. At first he couldn't see her. Sheets of rain were coming through the gaping hole where the window and part of the wall had been moments ago. He fell to his knees and crawled toward the bed through a tangle of branches and leaves. A huge tree limb lay across the bed and up against the far wall. Jack froze as he saw one of Molly's legs sticking out from under the broken tree.

"Molly!" He pulled himself alongside the bed and saw that she was pinned under the limb. Jack struggled to pick it up. He got both arms underneath it and with all the strength he could muster, pushed it away. As he looked down at Molly's crumpled body, he saw that a jagged piece of window glass was sticking out of the calf of her right leg and blood was spurting out like a geyser. He immediately jerked his belt off and wound it around her thigh and pulled it tight. He then pulled the glass from her leg. The cut was deep and nasty. He felt a small twinge of relief as he saw the tourniquet was stopping most of the bleeding. He quickly took his shirt off and took out his pocketknife. He cut the shirt into strips and wrapped them around her leg in a makeshift bandage.

"Molly, can you hear me?" Her eyes were open but seemed unfocused.

"I'm here. You're going to be just fine." He saw that she had multiple cuts and bruises on her arms and other leg but they didn't look deep. He also knew she could have a serious head injury or internal problems that wouldn't be immediately noticeable. He put his hand under her head and lifted her face up slightly. Her right eye was starting to swell and there was a cut across her forehead. She stared at Jack with a vacant look. He picked her up and carried her to the bathroom.

"Oh my God," Aunt Nita said as he laid Molly on the floor. "What happened?"

"A tree limb came through the window and she caught a good-sized piece of glass in her leg." Jack picked some leaves and twigs out of Molly's hair. She stared up at him with emotionless eyes as shock set in.

"You're gonna be all right," he said, not knowing if he was trying to convince himself or Molly. He checked the makeshift bandage around the gash in her leg. Jack knew he couldn't leave the tourniquet on for very long without causing major damage. If the blood were cut off for too long the cells would die and she would lose her leg, yet if he took it off now, she could bleed to death in a short time. He also knew they were hours away from outside help, maybe days.

"Is she alright?" Uncle Harry asked.

"For the moment. She's going into shock though and I have to stop this bleeding somehow."

"What can we do?" Aunt Nita looked like she was going to cry. Jack shook his head and ran his fingers though his hair as they both stared at him. Dolly roared outside but the room filled with a deathly silence. Jack leaped to his feet.

"The bandages."

"Bandages?" Uncle Harry and Aunt Nita said in unison.

"Be right back." Jack hurried out of the room closing the door behind him.

Jack took the stairs two at a time as he raced down to the rising water in the living room. He had remembered the bandages he and the chief had been given last month at a firefighters' conference in Chicago. These particular bandages had been developed after the first Gulf War and they would soon be available for cities to buy for their EMS services. Uncontrolled bleeding is a major cause of death in combat. Two new bandages had been developed, one by the Army and American Red Cross researchers, which used a human clotting agent called fibrin; and one developed at the Oregon Medical Laser Center in Portland, using a clotting agent derived from shrimp shells. Jack had samples of both in his briefcase.

He waded across the living room and looked out the window to the street. He pressed his face up close but couldn't see anything in the dark. A flash of lightning lit up the sky and the street was illuminated. His breath caught in his chest. The street was empty. His Navigator was nowhere to be seen. *Shit.* Jack waded over to the next window and strained to see through the rain as he searched the street for his truck. He was about to turn away when a series of lightning bolts lit up the neighborhood and something caught in his peripheral vision. He quickly moved to a window on the other side of the front door and jerked the blinds down to get a better look. The lightning flashed again and there was his truck, across the street, in a neighbor's yard, up against a couple of trees.

He opened the front door and stepped out into a small alcove, which protected him from the howling wind. He stood with his back to the closed door and watched broken tree limbs, shingles and other pieces of debris shoot past him like shrapnel from an exploding grenade. *I think I need to stay as low as possible.* He kneeled down so that only his neck and head were above water and moved out away from the porch. Immediately he was swept up in the current and before he could get his bearings he was hurled into something immovable.

It was a large pine tree. He wrapped his arms around its trunk and held on. The bark from the tree dug into his bare chest. He stood up, cautiously holding on to the tree. He inched around to get as much protection as he could from the roaring wind. *This ain't gonna work.* He squinted into the downpour toward the Navigator. *I'll never get back, even if I can make it over there.* Jack looked around and spotted a water hose flopping up and down on top of the rushing water. It was connected to a faucet by the front door. He grabbed hold of the hose and began pulling himself against the current and back toward the house.

A few minutes later he was once again standing in the small alcove at the front of the house. He was surprised at the swiftness of the water, but then he remembered that the land dipped considerably at the end of Uncle Harry's street. He and his cousin Bret used to slip off down there and sit on the bank of a gully and tell lies and drink cans of beer they'd stolen from Uncle Harry's supply he kept in the old refrigerator in the garage. The gully meandered its way around until it eventually turned into a creek that ultimately emptied into the bayou. All this water was rushing downhill while it still had a destination. If the water continued to come down at its present rate, there was no guessing how high the water would rise as the bayou filled up. He needed to get to his truck before he had to dive down for it. He paused to rest briefly and then opened the door and went inside. He waded across the living room and climbed the stairs.

"Uncle Harry," he said, opening the bathroom door, "have you got any rope or maybe some cable, or wire?"

"Rope?" Harry struggled to get to his feet. "I don't think so, what do you need rope for?"

"I need to get to my truck to get some bandages for Molly's leg."

"I can't think of any rope, Jack, but we might have something around here you can use," Aunt Nita said, looking up at Jack. She got to her feet and stood beside the two men.

"The street's like a river out there and I need some sort of life line I can use to make it back once I get across." Jack wiped the water from his eyes and face.

"Let me go look in the garage." Uncle Harry moved past them to the open door. Jack knelt down beside Molly and held her hand in his. Her eyes opened slightly. She started to say something but Jack put his fingers to her lips.

"Just rest. I'm going to get some bandages for your leg."

Jack and Uncle Harry sloshed through the garage with their flashlights cutting through the darkness in search of something for Jack to use, but to no avail.

"I don't have anything long enough to reach across the street," Uncle Harry said, holding up a twenty-foot coil of water hose. Jack shook his head and let out a long sigh.

"How about sheets?" Aunt Nita splashed into the garage with an arm full.

Twenty minutes later, Aunt Nita had cut the sheets into long foot-wide strips and Uncle Harry and Jack had tied them together. Jack stood with the long rope of sheets coiled around his shoulders.

"You think that's going to be long enough?" Uncle Harry asked Jack.

"It has to be. That's all the sheets we've got," Aunt Nita replied.

"I think it'll work. I figure it's about sixty yards over to my truck."

Uncle Harry handed Jack a pair of rubber hip waders he used for wade fishing and a heavy-duty rain slicker with a hood. The waders came almost to Jack's armpits. He drew the slicker's hood tight around his face.

"Be careful, Jack." Aunt Nita stood on her tiptoes and kissed him on the cheek. He opened the door and stepped out into the alcove. He tied one end of the sheet around a porch column by the front door and then began letting the rope of cloth out as he stepped out into the rushing water. This time he was ready for the strength of the current and he leaned into it. The rubber waders helped him keep solid footing and he began to slowly move down the flooded sidewalk toward the street.

It took him a while to reach where he thought the curb would be. He stretched the rope tight and then holding it with both hands unlooped another coil from around his shoulder. Jack could feel small limbs, twigs, and rocks hitting the slicker but so far nothing had penetrated it. He couldn't do much about the water pounding him in the face. He slipped a couple of times, but so far remained upright. He scooted his foot forward and felt the edge of the curb. Once in the street he seemed to make better time. He wasn't sure if it was easier or if he was getting accustomed to wading against the current. He inched along with his head down. As he looked up to see where he was, he realized he had been letting the water move him farther down the street than across it. Jack was startled to see he was almost even with the Navigator, but about ten yards away. His legs were getting tired and he knew he needed to get to the truck as quickly as possible. It felt like he had been fighting the wind and water forever.

What Jack had been avoiding from the time he scooped Molly into his arms and placed her on the bathroom floor was the knowledge that she might die. He was no doctor, but he'd been in the trenches at the fire department long enough to know serious injury when he saw it. The other nagging thing he hadn't been able to admit was that seeing Molly again, kissing her, touching her, had sent his heart soaring and given him hope he hadn't experienced in years. Molly was a precious part of his past that he had somehow turned into a reason to be bitter, and all of a sudden in the midst of the violence and destruction of Dolly, he had found her again. And she was hurt and he was the only one who could help her. Even if she decided they weren't to be together, she needed him. He was terrified that he

217

couldn't help her fast enough. He knew that every minute he took was putting Molly's life in danger.

He leaned into the wind and fought the current with everything he had to keep it from sweeping him down the street and out of the neighborhood completely. Fortunately the Navigator had turned when the rising water moved it out of the street and into the yard. Once he was even with the truck, Jack let the water push him into the side of it. He grabbed the door handle and tried to get his breath as the water kept him pinned to the side of the truck. He reached inside his slicker for Uncle Harry's hammer, which he had stuck in his pants. He had to hold onto the door handle of the truck with one hand while he swung the hammer as hard as he could to smash the window. On his first swing, the glass shattered into a million pieces. *Good old Uncle Harry, I would have never made it inside if he hadn't thought of this.*

He reached inside for something to hold on to. He hooked both arms over the windowsill and pulled himself against the door. *Jesus, I'm whipped.* His briefcase floated in the floorboard of the passenger's side. He reached into the pocket of his slicker and pulled out a length of sheet Aunt Nita had cut. Holding onto the inside of the door with one hand he leaned in as far as he could and grabbed the handle of his briefcase. *This is gonna be tricky.* He held himself halfway into the window. After a small struggle he managed to get hold of the piece of cloth around his waist. He then ran it though the handle of the briefcase and tied a knot. Now the briefcase was bound to him so he could use both hands to pull himself back across the street to safety.

Jack could feel fatigue settling into the deepest recesses of his muscles. His legs and arms were aching and cramping from the constant strain against the never-ending pressure of the driving wind and constantly assaulting water. He took some deep breaths and the vision of Molly lying on the bathroom floor with his belt and bloody bandages wrapped around her leg was uppermost in his mind. A surge of adrenalin replaced the aches in his body.

He gripped the sheet looped around his shoulder and tensed. *Time to go, Jack.* He pulled on the sheet as if he were climbing up the side of a building and took a step against the turbulent water. One hand over the other and one short, sliding step at a time, he moved toward the house at a snail's pace.

He was in the middle of the street, about half way home when out of the corner of his eye he saw movement coming toward him. Jack's reflexes took over. He bent his knees slightly and braced himself automatically to receive a blow to the body. Something black and hairy plowed into him. Jack gripped the sheet with both hands to keep from going down and being swept away in the runaway current. He clenched his jaw and strained with every ounce of energy he had in him to keep from going down.

Whatever hit him was alive. Something was attacking him. Jack fought to stay on his feet and to keep the mounting fear from overtaking him. He looked down to see a pair of wild, yellow eyes staring back at him. It took him a second to realize he had a half-grown black Lab crawling up his chest. The minute their eyes met the dog seemed to sense that he was in a safer place and went limp in his arms. Jack was relieved that he wasn't about to be eaten alive.

Jack regained his balance and held the dog close to his chest. The dog, either out of exhaustion or a sense that he was being saved, didn't move. Jack looked down at his new best friend. *God, I'm glad you weren't a St. Bernard.* He began pulling them both toward the house.

Just when he felt he couldn't take another step, the current didn't feel quite as strong. Jack tilted his head upward slightly and was surprised to see that he was almost to the front porch. The water was a little shallower here and the house blocked a tiny bit of the wind. He heaved one last time on the sheet and he and his newfound pet fell into the alcove of the front porch. The door open immediately and Jack felt hands on him pulling him inside. The dog splashed into the living room like he was home.

The beeping sound made Cora and Bonnie jump. They looked around to see if a garbage truck was going to back into the room, then they realized the sound was coming from the control panel on the wall by the door.

"What the hell is that?" They both got up and walked over to the panel. A green light was blinking in time with the sound.

"I think we must be in the eye. The panels on the roof are changing."

"Changing?"

"Yeah, sensors pick up the sudden drop in wind speed." Bonnie stared at the control panel. "You think we ought to check to see what's happening?"

"I'm game if you are."

Bonnie opened the door and they stepped into the darkened pantry. She turned on the flashlight and shined the small beam on the pantry door. They opened it and stepped out into the kitchen. It looked exactly as it had an hour and half ago. They walked out into the living room. It was quiet. They glanced over at the chair that held the lifeless body of Lex Levin, one hand hung out from under the sheet. They gave wide berth to the chair as if the hand might reach out and grab them.

"Open the door," Cora said. They both jumped a little as frothy white water splashed over their feet. The ocean was at their doorstep.

Bonnie leaned out the door surveying the vastness before her. "Surf's up."

Collin wasn't sure how long he had been huddled behind the door with his face buried in his knees and his arms over his head, but it seemed like hours. His bones ached from the cold and he couldn't stop shaking. When the roar of the storm suddenly stopped his head popped up with an involuntary jerk. He peeked out from behind the door, unsettled by the eerie quiet.

He stood on trembling legs and looked up to the opening where the door that had been protecting him should have been. If he had been positioned in either direction other than exactly where he was when the door had fallen, it would have been the thing that killed him, not the thing that shielded him from Dolly. He was disoriented and in shock. He tried to think where he had been going when the door came crashing down. He had some more questions he wanted to ask Jason. He wanted to know if the storm was over. Jason would know. He knew everything about hurricanes.

He cautiously made his way up the steps holding on to the metal handrail. When he got to the open doorway, he peered anxiously inside squinting his eyes until they adjusted to the dark. He could only see a few feet. To his left was some debris and what looked like a broken chair. He turned to his right and started in the direction that he had last seen Jason. He took a few steps and felt the floor give way underneath him. He lurched to a stop, afraid to move. He stood there, expecting to fall, staring down the hallway and it hit him. There was no hallway. There was no Jason. There was no south end of the building. He looked straight down until a huge pile of broken concrete and twisted steel slowly came into his vision. The sight that his eyes were sending to his brain paralyzed his whole body. The reality of what had happened was creeping into his consciousness. Jason had told him it was going to be bad and he had been right.

He inched his way sideways from the damage, his hands out in front of him. A wire hanging down from what was left of the ceiling slapped him in the face. He jumped as if he had been hot and brushed it out of his way. *Where is everybody? Am I the only one left?* The only sound was his heavy breathing. He stood there for a moment then took a step and stumbled and fell. His head landed on something soft and squishy. He immediately put a hand down to push himself up and felt fabric. *What the hell?* He reached out with his other hand and touched something and knew instantly what it was. *Hair.* Collin let out a moan and flung himself backwards. He squinted his eyes to see what he had fallen on but it was too dark. He tentatively stuck a shaking hand out into the darkness. Once again he felt something warm and wet. It took all the will power he could summon to keep from jerking his hand back. When his fingers came across what could only be teeth, he recoiled in horror with a loud gasp. He pulled himself up on a crooked doorframe to his right. Feeling his way around in the dark was much more frightening than hiding from Dolly in the corner.

The cry brought him out of his trance. It sounded like a small child and it was coming from somewhere in the pile of rubble. He had to get down there. If there was someone alive, he had to find them. He didn't relish the idea of spending the rest of the night alone with what he had just found. He returned to the place where the floor had given way, edged his way by it out the stairwell door. He carefully maneuvered down the stairs to the floor below him, stepping over soggy sheetrock and fragmented cinder blocks. There had to be an exit to the outdoors at the bottom. Before he could find a way out he crashed into a pile of twisted metal, which clanged on the concrete. The sound jangled his already frayed nerves and caused him to cry out.

"Hello?" a weak voice called from somewhere in the darkness.

"Anybody there?" He stopped and waited in the silence.

"Over here," the voice said a little louder. "I can't move. My legs are trapped."

Collin made his way through the rubble. A faint glow of moonlight was coming in through a broken window off to his right. His eyes adjusted enough so he could make out some of the room.

"I'm here. Where are you?"

"In the back of the room I think. Something is on top of me."

Collin pushed desks and chairs out of his way. The sound of another human voice picked his spirits up. He came to a large filing cabinet that had fallen over. It lay at an angle halfway across the back of the room.

"Are you under here?" Collin got down on his knees.

"Yes. I don't think my legs are broken but I'm pinned down."

"Okay, hold on. I'm gonna see if I can find something I can move this with." He felt around in the dark for something he could wedge under the cabinet to get some leverage.

"Is there anyone else in here?" Collin asked.

"I don't know . . . there was." The voice trailed off. Collin thought about his grisly discovery in the hallway and he became more tentative about where he put his hands. Finally, he came across something that felt like a two-by-four. He grasped it and pulled. At first it didn't move and then he felt it give a little. He sat down and pulled with both hands. Finally it came loose. He pulled it into his lap. It was probably a stud out of the wall. It was about four and a half feet long. He crawled back over to the fallen filing cabinet and wedged it under the end about two feet.

"I'm gonna see if I can raise it a little." Collin pulled up with all his strength. It felt like it moved about an inch.

"There. A little more," the voice shouted excitedly. Collin grunted and groaned and pulled with all he had. It moved another inch.

"That's it. Hold it just a second longer."

Collin could hear the man sliding along the floor.

"Yes!" the man said.

Collin dropped the stud and collapsed on the floor. He felt movement beside him and he turned to see a man pull himself up to a sitting position.

"Collin, I thought that was your voice. Thanks," the man said, holding out his hand.

He wanted to grab the man in a bear hug, but instead he wiped the wetness from his face and shook his hand. "Ralph, you all right?"

"I think so."

They sat in the darkness without saying anything for a long moment. Collin was bordering on bawling like a baby. He wasn't sure why it was so important for him not to be the only one left. Why had he made it when others didn't? He was a lowly public servant who hadn't served his public very well. He had scammed and gambled and manipulated. Hell, the day when he should have been taking care of his constituency, he was pissed off because Lex Levin hadn't shown up on time with his bribe.

"You know if anybody else made it?" Ralph asked.

"I thought I heard something earlier and I was on my way to see about it when I heard you."

"Where?"

"It was coming from the south end of the building except there's not much of a building left." Collin helped Ralph to his feet. "I don't suppose you would know where we could find some flashlights."

"Well, I know where they used to keep them," he said, scratching his head. "Let's look over here." They moved an upside-down desk out of the way and piles of books that had been dumped in the floor. Ralph found a small metal cabinet that was turned on its side. They wrestled it around until they had it lying on its back. Ralph opened the door and reached inside.

"Here we go." He handed a flashlight to Collin, who flicked it on.

224

"Let there be light."

They made their way out the front door and waded through waist-deep water around to the huge pile of rubble that up until an hour ago had been the south end of City Hall.

"Can anybody hear me?" Collin yelled. They both stood still and listened.

"If anybody is in here we need to find them fast. The backside of Dolly is gonna show up anytime." Ralph was shining the light down in the mass of ruins.

"I didn't think about that. I thought the storm was over. When it got quiet, all I could think about was finding someone."

"Or them finding you." Ralph agreed.

"Hello, can anybody hear me?" Collin shouted again. A small cry came from their left. "Over here." They both shined their flashlights in the direction of the sound, sweeping their lights back and forth.

"What's that?" Ralph stopped his light. They stared at where the beam illuminated a small circle in the rubble. A bloody hand was poking through the ruins. They both hurried over to it.

"We're here. Can you move your hand?" Silence. The hand didn't move.

Ralph checked the pulse of the hand. He shook his head. As they stood there deciding what to do next they heard the voice again.

"Mommy." A small weak voice came from farther away.

They scrambled in its direction. Collin light caught something as they crawled through the wreckage. There was a small opening between two large pieces of concrete tilted together. He shined the light into the opening and saw a small boy looking back at him. It was Sue's youngest son, Tommy. A pang of guilt shot through him. *My God, I told Sue to bring her family down here. Maybe they would have been safer somewhere else.*

"Mommy," the boy whispered. Collin stared down at the boy and wanted to weep in fear. He was wedged inside a hole not eighteen inches across. Wreckage was laced around him as if he had been standing and the storm had bricked him in. The problem was that where mortar would have been, water flowed in and out and it was almost up to the little boy's waist. Tommy was down inside a well and the water was on the rise.

"Hold on, we're gonna get you out," Collin said. "Let's see if we can move this piece here." They both pulled on the concrete but it wouldn't budge.

"Are you hurt, Tommy?" Collin reached in to touch the boy.

"My foot hurts," he said, wiping his eyes. "Where's my mommy?"

"Let's get you out of here first." Collin stood up and shined his light around to see if he could find something they could use to wedge the concrete out of the way.

"Collin, over here." Ralph was on his knees pulling pieces of debris away from the pile.

"I think we can get to him from this side."

Collin hurried over to where Ralph was digging and began to pull small pieces of concrete and other debris out. They worked frantically side by side digging through the mound of rubble. Within a few minutes they had dug an opening large enough to see Tommy. The water seemed to be rising even faster. Collin soon realized the more debris they moved, the faster the water was able to flow into where he was trapped.

"Hurry," Collin shouted. He reached in to see if he could pull him out. "Give me your hand, Tommy."

Tommy stuck his hand out and Collin grabbed hold of him and gently pulled.

"Oww," Tommy screamed. "My foot's stuck."

Collin let go and began pulling more debris away to make the opening larger. After a few minutes of non-stop work, they had the opening big enough so that Collin could move closer to Tommy. The water was now almost up to the little boy's shoulders. Collin reached under the cold, murky water and felt around for Tommy's foot. Once he found it, he ducked his head under to see if he could see what was holding it. Even with his flashlight on, the water was so soupy and gray; he could barely make out anything. He could feel a wide piece of metal lying across Tommy's foot.

"I think his foot's under an I-beam," Collin said to Ralph as he raised his head out of the water. "We'll never move that."

Collin glanced at Tommy as soon as the words fell out of his mouth. The fear in his small green eyes penetrated Collin's soul and made his breath catch in his chest.

"You help him hold his head out of the water and I'll see if I can move some of the stuff around it."

Collin splashed back underwater and felt for the chunk of concrete that was snugged up against the other side of Tommy's foot. He grasped it and pulled as hard as he could. He wrestled with it until his lungs felt like they were on fire and he popped his head back above water. It hadn't moved. Ralph was holding Tommy's head back as far as he could. The water lapped on his chin. An eerie sound floated up out of the death trap. Tommy wasn't crying; it was more of a moan or a wail. Collin never felt so helpless. He knew for a fact that he did not have the strength to move the concrete block or the beam. He didn't know if Tommy really had any concept of what death was, but Collin did, and it had just wrapped its icy fingers around his chest.

Earlier as Collin had crouched in terror behind the door in the corner of the stairwell, he had an epiphany. He realized that the many nights he was deep in the depths of his gambling addiction and lay comfy and secure in his bed, wishing he were dead, was the biggest lie he had ever told himself. He didn't want to die. He wanted to live. But as he stared down at Tommy, he knew he would never abandon this boy. He would stay here and try to save him, even if it meant dying.

He was about to duck back under the water for another try when a blast of wind hit them. He looked up at the clouds racing overhead and the darkening sky.

"Dolly's back!" yelled Ralph.

The rain and wind assaulted them immediately. They had to crouch down to keep from being blown over backwards. Collin started to say something just as a rumbling noise caught their ears. They both turned to see the south wall of the building begin to fall. They stood frozen in place as it crashed onto the pile of rubble not more than fifty feet from them. Collin could feel the whole pile shift slightly. He instantly splashed his head back underwater and felt for Tommy's foot. His heart leapt in his throat when he felt a space between the boy's foot and the piece of concrete. He put his hand around Tommy's ankle and gave it a tug. The foot pulled free.

Collin raised up pulling Tommy with him.

"What happened?" Ralph yelled. He had a stunned look on his face.

"When the wall fell, it must have moved some of the pile," Collin shouted.

"Whatever. Let's get the hell out of here."

Collin held Tommy to his chest as he leaned into the wind and headed inside. *Christ, are we the only three left?* Guilt and elation at being alive hit him at the same instant.

CHAPTER THIRTY-SIX

The first thing J.D. noticed as consciousness slowly crept into his brain was how badly his head hurt. Then he realized the pain went down his neck and into his shoulders. Once again his mind was a blank. He opened his eyes and he still couldn't see. *I'm blind?* Panic and nausea hit him at the same time, but it was tinged with an eerie sense of déjà vu. *Now why would that thought be familiar?* He moved his arm and his hand brushed up against cold metal that felt like a round iron bar. He explored it in the blackness. Glimmers of memory came flooding back. It was a ladder. *I'm hanging on a ladder.* It took him a full minute to remember where he was, then suddenly the image of Boone standing over Carl shooting him in the head flashed through his mind. He gasped as a sliver of fear raced down his spine. He reached up and touched his right ear. He winced; it was tender to the touch.

As he stiffened, he realized he wasn't holding on to anything, but was instead hanging limply in his safety harness at an angle. Then he noticed that something else was different. *There's no movement.*

He wrenched his left arm and pain shot through his elbow. *Damn, what's that about?* He vaguely remembered being slung around inside the tank. *Oh yeah, I think I've been on a hell of a ride.* He moved his other arm and grabbed the ladder.

He pulled himself close enough to get his feet on a rung. He stood there resting for a minute; then he remembered the flashlight. He started to reach for it when a stab of pain flashed through the little finger on his right hand. *Goddamn, I am beat all to hell.* He gently eased his hand into his pocket and gripped the flashlight. He brought it out and switched it on. He checked the gauge on his air pack. It showed two minutes left of fresh oxygen. *Well, Boone or no Boone, looks like I'm going out.*

J.D. reached up, pulled the lever on the hatch above his head and pushed it open. It fell with a clang. He rested for a moment, then unhooked the safety harness and began to climb up the ladder. He slowly raised his head through the opening, holding his breath as he waited for a bullet to tear through his skull at any second. When it didn't come, he pulled himself up through the hatch and onto the bent platform, which was hanging precariously onto the tank. J.D. looked around and tried to get a bearing on where he was. The only thing he knew for sure was that he was no longer on the grounds of International Petroleum. *Well, Toto, we're not in Kansas anymore.*

After being in the pitch dark of the tank for so long, it seemed almost bright as day. He looked up and saw stars and an almost full moon overhead. Something about that was weird but he couldn't wrap a thought around it long enough to hold on to it. He was dizzy and lightheaded, as if he had just stepped off a tilt-a-whirl.

J.D. wiped his eyes and looked all around. All he could see was water. *What the hell happened?* As he gripped the rail and looked around, waves of panic coursed through him as he realized he had no idea where he was. Nothing made sense. The image of Boone's truck popped into his head. *Maybe there was an explosion.*

He pulled the mask from the air pack off and felt something wet running down the side of his face. He wiped it off and it didn't feel like water. He focused the light on his hand and saw that it was blood. He put his hand up to the side of his face and could feel a large bump and cut just under his hairline. *No wonder my head hurts.* He rubbed his forehead and felt a large knot between his eyes.

He turned and looked behind him and saw that the tank was partially lodged under what looked to be an overpass. Where and what highway he couldn't say. Everywhere he looked was water. If it weren't for the large concrete overpass rising out of the water like part of the Loch Ness monster, he might have thought he was in the bay. This was as spooky as being in the pitch dark. The more he looked around the more disoriented he felt. He could feel his knees getting weak and his mouth was so dry he couldn't swallow. He couldn't tell from here how deep the water was but it seemed to be as far as the eye could see. *This is crazy.*

He pointed his light back up to the overpass. As he swept it down the road, he caught a glimpse of the road sign barely sticking up out of the water. It had 1764 printed on it. J.D. stared at the sign. *That's impossible.* 1764 was the Emmet Lowery Expressway. It ran all the way from Texas City to the Gulf Freeway.

J.D. stood there feeling like he had suddenly been sucked into the Twilight Zone when something else dawned on him. There was no wind and rain. "Where's Dolly?" he said softly. *Oh shit, I'm in the eye* raced through his mind at the same instant as he realized the backside of the hurricane was going to show up any minute and he didn't have the oxygen left to go back into the tank, not that he wanted to anyway, and he needed to find shelter. He carefully made his way down what was left of the spiral ladder hanging on the side of the tank and jumped over to the embankment sloping gradually upward to the overpass.

"Goddamn," he yelled as he hit the ground. He reached down and massaged his right knee. He limped onto the highway where he stopped and slowly turned in a circle. At about three quarters of the way around he stopped and stared into the darkness. He could barely make out the outline of buildings in the distance. They looked vaguely familiar but he couldn't quite place them. He turned the flashlight back to the road sign and then looked back at the buildings. As he stood staring, he could just make out something else. It looked like a group of trees that were bent in odd shapes, but all their limbs were torn off. Then it hit him. They were light poles in a parking lot. *Damn, that's the Mall of the Mainland. Or what's left of it.* The realization of how far the tank had traveled hit him and made his knees weak. He guessed he was about twenty miles from IP.

J.D. stood on his island overpass and surveyed the water all around him. It was filled with debris. There were the scattered remains of houses and buildings, plus hundreds of automobiles, upside down, half-submerged, and floating aimlessly likes toys in a giant bathtub. As he looked closer he saw something else floating among the debris. He waded out into the water until he was knee deep and pointed his light to get a better look. He stopped suddenly, almost falling down. There were bodies everywhere. A young girl floated past him on her back, her dead eyes staring up at the stars. J.D. cried out and scrambled to get back on dry land as if the water were burning him. He slumped down on the highway and stared at the carnage around him. Nausea hit in an instant. He rolled over on all fours and even though there was nothing in his stomach, dry heaves wracked his body. It felt like his intestines were turning inside out.

He collapsed on his side. He squeezed his eyes shut as tears ran down his cheeks. He had never felt so completely alone. The death around him was sucking the life out of his body with every breath he took. It was too much; Boone and his gun, the hurricane, the ride in a stupid fucking tank, and water that stretched out forever in front of him was more than he could handle. Then out of nowhere he could hear his mother's voice reminding him that he was the man of the house. She had told him that when he was so distraught over his father's death. It might have not been fair to a fourteen-year-old but it had strengthened him then and it strengthened him now. As it grew stronger in his mind, he began to push the fear and horror into a place he could control.

He needed Beverly right here, right now. He needed her strength to make him believe he would make it out of this. Where was she? Where in all that lay before him were the people he loved the most; his babies, his mother, his friends and neighbors. He had to believe they were safe and dry somewhere; the alternative was unthinkable and if he dwelled too long in that direction he might as well quit now. His jerky breathing spasms slowly subsided. He took several deep breaths and struggled to his feet.

The thought of his family ignited a spark deep inside of him. *I have to find my family.* He stood on shaky legs and looked toward the few remaining buildings that were once the Mall of the Mainland and knew he had to find a way to get to shelter. He shined his light back down the road where it disappeared into the water. There were a couple of cars on top of one another and what looked like part of the roof to a house. *Maybe I can find something to float over there on,* he thought as he moved toward the water's edge. Then he saw something on the other side of the cars that he couldn't see before. It looked like the bow of a small boat. His spirits picked up and he waded excitedly into the water, but as he got closer he could tell it was almost submerged. *Shit.* He noticed another, larger, boat upside down and a couple of others that had sunk and had only the bow sticking out. Wrecked boats were all around him. It didn't make sense. *Must have been a boat dealership close by.*

The water was about chest-deep and he was about to turn back to dry pavement when what looked like a section of a picket fence floated by. He grabbed hold and dragged it onto the side of the highway. After pulling it out of the water, he could tell it was a big wooden gate. *This could work with a little help.* He looked around in the water and spotted a small piece of wood floating nearby. It was a broken piece of one-by-six, about four feet long. He grabbed it and tossed it on the gate. He then waded out to one of the submerged boats and pulled the seat cushions out.

After much manhandling, he was able to lay the gate on top of the four seat cushions. He then crawled onto the gate and sat down. With the broken one-by-six he began paddling toward the mall.

He was slowly making his way through the carnage that Dolly had dumped in the parking lot when he heard a soft moan. He froze as the hair stood up on the back of his neck. He let the small raft drift.

"Hello?" He swept his light around, looking in the cars and debris floating around him, flinching as each shadow slipped in and out of his vision. *I must have imagined it.* He started to row when he heard it again. *Man this is getting too weird.*

"Is anybody there?" he said a little louder.

"Help me," came a weak voice off to his left. He aimed his light in the direction of the sound. There was a large oak tree, or what remained of one, stuck between a pick-up truck and a pile of debris. He aimed the beam of light in the branches trying to peel away the darkness so that he could see into the deepest part of the foliage.

"Are you in the tree?"

"Yes."

J.D. maneuvered the raft closer, keeping the light concentrated on the tree. He gently bumped up against it, and leaned over and pulled some of the branches out of the way to get a better look. He saw a young woman holding something in her arms looking back at him.

"Are you an angel?"

"Well my momma thinks so," J.D. said. "But you could probably find a number of people who feel just the opposite. Can you move?"

"I'm not sure."

J.D. pulled the branches back farther and held out his hand to her. Slowly she reached up and grabbed his arm still clutching something to her chest. The raft wobbled as his weight shifted.

"Easy," he cautioned. As J.D. pulled her closer he saw she was holding a baby.

"Be careful, I have my Katy with me."

"Let me have her." He reached to take the baby from her arms. She pulled back, her eyes wide.

"Please. I want to help you."

She stared at him a moment then carefully held the baby out to him.

"Be careful."

He slipped a hand around it and gently pulled it to him. The instant he felt the baby's cold flesh against his hand and felt how stiff it was, he knew she was dead. His blood ran cold. His breath caught in his throat. Tyler's face flashed before his eyes. This baby wasn't as old as his youngest son, but Tyler was just a little thing, dependent and every bit as vulnerable. This little baby didn't have a chance out here. For God's sake, what were they doing in this tree? He could barely keep his voice even.

"Yes, ma'am." J.D. clutched the dead infant to his chest. The sadness in his heart was swift and overwhelming, but he knew he had to get his mind back in focus. There was nothing he could do for this precious life that had been taken way too soon, but he could do everything in his power to keep her mother safe.

"Are you hurt?"

"I don't know."

J.D. stared into her emotionless eyes and realized she was in shock.

"Come on, let's get you out of there." J.D. stuck out his left arm while holding the baby with his right. He slowly inched backwards to keep the raft balanced as he gently pulled her to him.

"Where's my baby? Where's my Katy?" the woman cried as soon as she was safely on the raft.

"She's right here." J.D. handed the dead child to her. "We have to get to shelter, there's more storm coming."

CHAPTER THIRTY-SEVEN

The Balinese Room, one of Galveston's most famous landmarks, had sat at the end of a long wooden pier half a block down the seawall from the Hotel Galvez for about as long as anyone could remember. In the 1940's through most of 1950 it was one of the country's premier nightclubs and illegal gambling casinos. When the local sheriff was asked why he didn't raid the club and close it down he replied that it was a private club and he wasn't a member.

Everybody from Frank Sinatra and Duke Ellington to the Marx Brothers had played the Balinese Room. In 1957 a new sheriff decided he didn't need to be a member to enter the club and closed it down. It survived Hurricane Carla in 1961 and spent the rest of the '60's and most of the '70's as a teen club featuring national and local rock and roll acts. It spent most of the '90's empty and decomposing, but it had recently been bought and was being renovated.

Most of the famous people who played the Balinese Room through the years stayed at the Hotel Galvez, so their histories were always entwined. Now they were physically meshed. One of Dolly's tornardic offspring had picked up the famous Balinese Room and most of the wooden pier it perched on, and dumped it in the two-story lobby and front hallways of the Hotel Galvez, sealing the only entrance to the conference room. The twenty-odd survivors holed up inside now found themselves entombed.

J.D. slowly pushed the makeshift raft through the floating cars and debris toward the two-story building at one end of the Mall of the Mainland. He had slipped into the water and instructed the woman to sit in the middle of the raft. She held her dead baby in her arms and stared straight ahead. J.D. swam and pushed the raft, but occasionally his feet would touch solid footing and he could wade. In the blink of an eye it was dark. J.D. looked up to see clouds covering the moon. Dolly was back with a vengeance. *Oh shit.*

"Hold on." He pushed harder. If the woman heard him she didn't acknowledge it. Within a few minutes the wind had returned to hurricane strength. The water went from calm to whitecaps. J.D. kicked as hard as he could but immediately began losing ground.

"I need your help," J.D. yelled. The woman didn't respond. A blast of wind knocked her over on her back. She looked around at J.D. with wild eyes.

"What's happening?" She tried to get up while still holding her baby.

"It's the hurricane," J.D. shouted. "I need you to get in the water and help me push the raft."

"What? No, I have to save my baby." She rolled over on her stomach and looked at J.D. He reached up and pulled the woman close to him.

"Ma'am, your baby is dead. You can't save it. You have to help me or we're going to both be dead," J.D. screamed at the woman.

 Anger spread over her face. "No. Katy is not dead." Her voice cracked as the words rolled out.

"Look at her. Look at her eyes . . . I'm sorry, but Katy is gone." J.D. tried to soften the words as much as possible. Telling her the truth twisted his stomach in knots. The woman stared at J.D. with hate. He held her gaze without blinking. Gently she moved the baby away from her chest and looked down into her open lifeless eyes.

After a moment she looked back at J.D. The truth crept into her features, her lips quivered and her eyes filled with tears.

"My baby's . . . "

"I know. I'm so sorry, but we have to get to shelter."

As if to remind J.D. that she was still the mightiest force on earth, Dolly sent a jagged bolt of lightning directly into a light pole in the parking lot. The sound of metal ripping apart jarred them both.

J.D. pointed in the direction of the Dillard's Department Store that anchored the east end of the mall. A gust of wind pushed the raft up against a half-sunken Volkswagen.

"I can't just leave her here," the woman shouted over the roar of the wind. She was crying. J.D. knew he couldn't leave Katy any more than she could. The Volkswagen was keeping them stable. He felt solid footing underneath him and began taking his raincoat off.

"Give her to me." The woman hesitated, then handed the dead infant to him. J.D. took the tiny, lifeless body and wrapped it in the coat. He then wrapped the coat around his body, pulling the arms around like a straightjacket, and tied them together. He took his belt off and secured it around the bottom of the coat and his waist, tying the coat to his back in a makeshift backpack.

"Come on," he yelled. She slipped off the raft and stood unsteadily beside him. The waves were getting stronger and holding the raft steady wasn't easy. It had become so dark that J.D. could no longer see the outline of the mall in the distance.

"I think we need to go this way." They began pushing in the direction he pointed. Not only were the high winds creating rougher water, it also was sending more debris their way. Lots of broken trees and pieces of houses sailed by or bumped into them, knocking them backwards for a bit or turning the raft away from the direction they needed to go. The lightning had returned to its high intensity light show and the noise was deafening. They pushed and kicked as hard as they could but weren't making much progress. The rain came at them like someone had turned on a fire hydrant.

The woman screamed and clung to J.D. A man's body was pushed up against her. His rigid arm, sticking out in front of him, was caught in her jacket. J.D. reached over and pulled the body loose. It floated away like a log heading for the lumber mill.

"We've got to work together." The woman nodded and they began to kick in unison. Finally they began to make some progress. After about ten minutes of hard kicking, they were both getting tired. J.D. could see a light pole that was bent almost to the water but hadn't snapped in two. It was about ten yards in front of them.

"Let's get to that pole and we can rest."

She didn't respond but kept kicking. They maneuvered around so they were in front and could rest with their backs to it. The two-story building was close enough now that it broke the force of the wind somewhat.

"We've got just a little bit farther to go." J.D. leaned close to her. She nodded and laid her head on the edge of the raft. He closed his eyes and thought of Beverly and the kids. *When was the last time I told them that I loved them?* His eyes popped open. He couldn't remember. He hadn't seen them when he left for work yesterday morning. *Good God, that seems like a week ago.*

"Come on," J.D. shouted. The woman raised her head and looked at him. "Let's get inside and then you can sleep." That seemed to sink into her consciousness and she started pushing the raft into the wind. J.D. immediately started kicking. Their progress was slow but steady. Then something rammed into the raft knocking them almost completely around. The woman screamed as J.D. caught a glimpse of what looked like a giant eye. The woman screamed again and he saw that her arm was in a huge claw. He grabbed the woman and pulled her to him. She was screaming hysterically now.

J.D. shouted as held the woman tightly to his chest. "Hold on." He tried to sound calm but his mind was racing. *What the hell is that?*

The raft was breaking up and beginning to sink from the force of whatever had hit them. J.D. got his arm around her so he could pull her with him. As he began swimming toward the building he looked back and saw the giant crab floating away with what was left of the raft. He realized it was part of a sign from a local seafood restaurant. He almost laughed out loud as he fought against the white capping waves hitting him in the face. A few seconds ago, he was sure a giant crab was about to devour both of them. The relief of not being killed by a monster rushed through his veins and energized his body. He kicked harder. He could see a doorway just a few yards away. His feet touched solid footing and he stood up, holding the woman to him.

"Just a little bit farther," he said into the woman's ear. They struggled through the waist-deep water and were soon standing inside an entrance to the mall. It wasn't quite as pitch black as it had been inside of the tank but visibility was only a foot or two. J.D. untied his coat from his back and handed it to the woman. He then found the pocket containing his flashlight and took it out. He turned it on and shined the light into the darkness. He jumped slightly and the woman gasped as the light illuminated a pile of bodies all jumbled up at the bottom of an escalator.

On closer examination, the bodies turned out to be mannequins. They looked at each other with relief on their faces. A tiny smile in one corner of her mouth was the first J.D. had seen since finding the woman.

"I'm J.D." He held out his hand.

She stared at it and then shook it. "Susan. Thank you for . . . everything."

"Sure. Let's get upstairs out of this water." They waded over to the escalator and began pulling the plastic mannequins out of the way. They cleared a path and climbed to the second floor. It was like being in the center of a cave. J.D.'s light cut through the darkness like a knife. He spotted a display of living room furniture off to his left. They made their way over and collapsed on a huge couch. J.D. leaned his head back and listened to the diminished roar of the wind and low rumbling of the thunder outside. In less than a minute he was asleep.

CHAPTER THIRTY-EIGHT

Awareness seeped into J.D. He opened one eye and started to roll over on his side when a sharp pain shot through his right knee. He grabbed it and cried out as his left leg started cramping. He felt worse than when he woke up hanging from the ladder in the tank. He felt like someone had worked him over with a tire iron. Every muscle in his body ached and he was cold because his clothes were still wet. As he massaged the cramp in his calf, he saw that the woman was lying on the opposite end of the couch with her dead baby clutched to her chest. It occurred to him that it was light enough for him to see. He looked toward the escalator and could see the light coming from that direction.

He moved over and peered down to the first floor. The water looked as deep as before and he could see the sunlight coming in through the ragged hole where the entrance doors used to be. He limped down the escalator and into the water. Surprisingly it didn't feel too cold. He waded over to look outside and blinked at the patches of blue sky. Water - as far as the eye could see. He felt like he was on some deserted island in the middle of the ocean. In the distance he could see the tank that had carried him there, still clinging to the overpass. It was the only structure in sight. He still had trouble wrapping his head around that.

The parking lot was filled with floating cars, debris from houses, trees, and bodies. Lots of bodies. And not just people, but cows, horses, dogs, cats and a number of animals he couldn't recognize. He turned away. He thought he was going to be sick again. J.D. reached down and splashed some water in his face. He wasn't sure which was worse, being out in the middle of the storm, or standing here in the clear bright day, looking at the aftermath. It was easier to go back up the escalator and avoid the whole thing. When he got to the second floor he saw the woman sitting up on the couch holding her baby. *What was her name? . . . Oh yeah, Susan.*

"I thought you had left me."

"No, I just went downstairs. I think the storm is over." He sat down beside her.

"What do we do now?"

"I'm hoping there will be people out soon. Red Cross, National Guard, somebody. We need to move so we can see them, or they can see us."

J.D. got up and held out his hand for her. She took it and he pulled her up.

"Let's find something to put Katy in," he said. He took his flashlight out and they moved farther into the store. They found the bath and bed department. J.D. got a bath towel and wrapped her baby in it. In the kitchen department he found a large basket with a handle they could lay the baby in. After taking care of Katy, Susan followed J.D. down to the first floor.

"I want to thank you again," she said as they stood in the entrance of the building. J.D. nodded.

"Do you have family?"

"Wife and four kids. Hopefully safe at my mom's house."

"Where's that?"

244

"Alvin," J.D. said, searching the parking lot for signs of life. They were silent for a while.

"You have other family?" he asked, turning back to her.

"No, just . . . " her voice trailed off as she looked down at the basket. The moment was awkward, made even more difficult by the carnage floating past them.

"Look, you don't need to be standing in this water. Why don't you go back upstairs where you'll be comfortable? I'll come get you as soon as I see somebody."

"No, I don't want to be by myself." Her voice shook slightly.

"I understand, but at least get out of the water. Go sit on the escalator. I'll be right here."

"Okay." She waded over to the escalator and climbed out of the water.

J.D. stared out at the human wreckage floating in the parking lot.

A little over an hour later, he had retreated back to the escalator from his sentry post at the eastern entrance of the Mall of the Mainland and was sitting a couple of steps below Susan. His legs were cramping and it felt good to get out of the water for a while. He was staring toward the other end of the mall and could tell most of the roof in the middle part had given way.

"People will come, won't they?" Susan asked softly.

"Oh yeah, it'll just take a little time." Just as he got the words out of his mouth he saw a flash of light coming from behind the debris in the long walkway.

"Did you see that?"

"What?"

"I thought I saw a light down the hallway."

"A light?"

"Yeah, like maybe a flashlight. You wait here, I'm gonna check it out." J.D. got up, sloshed into the water and began wading down the hallway.

"Don't go too far, okay?"

"I won't." J.D. took out his flashlight and turned it on. Light was filtering through from the caved in roof but it was still dark in the long hallway. He had gone about ten yards when he saw the light flicker again.

"Anybody there?" He stopped and listened. He could hear movement on the other side of the pile of rubble blocking the hallway.

"Yeah, who's there?" came a voice through the mound of remains of the mall roof.

"J.D. Younger. Who am I talking to?"

"Matt Sneed and John Lisle. Are you by yourself?"

"No, there are two of us."

"There's more of us back at the other end. About twenty, I think. Are y'all injured or hurt?"

"We're beat up a little, but we're okay," J.D. shouted. "How 'bout you?"

"Same thing, a few with some broken bones but nothing real serious. Let's see if we can dig a pathway through this stuff."

"Good idea. We'll need to work on the same area."

"Okay, our left, your right."

J.D. realized that Susan had waded up beside him.

"How many did they say?" she asked.

"Around twenty."

They managed to move enough wreckage to be able to see through to the other side. A black man was peering through the two-foot hole at J.D.

"I'm Matt," he said, reaching through the hole to shake J.D.'s hand.

246

"Nice to meet you. This is Susan." J.D. moved a little to the side so the man could see her.

"Ma'am," the man said, nodding. "Do y'all have a way outside?"

"Yeah, the entrance we came in is okay."

"Most of the building has caved where we are. John and I thought we would see if we could find a way out down here."

"Why don't one of y'all go back for the others and we'll work on getting a way through here."

"Sounds like a plan," Matt said.

Shortly after they left, J.D. heard a noise outside.

"That sounds like a helicopter." He splashed his way to the entrance and waded outside into the sunshine. He could hardly move through the debris in the water. The sound got louder and he looked up to see a helicopter flying low to the west. It turned and came toward J.D. He waved his aching arms back and forth. The chopper swooped in low and circled above him, splashing the water into small waves. The pilot waved and headed back north. J.D. waded back to where Matt and Susan were waiting.

"He saw me." J.D. was excited and relieved. "Someone will be coming soon."

CHAPTER THIRTY-NINE

Other than the large tree limb that had smashed through the window and seven feet of water downstairs, Uncle Harry's house and its current occupants were in good shape. Molly was the only one to sustain any injuries and they didn't seem to be critical. The bandages Jack had retrieved from his truck had worked as promised. He had checked her over as best he could and thought she probably had some bruised ribs but no concussion. He had been in contact with the Emergency Command Center and was told that the city had suffered major damage and it would probably be awhile before anyone got to them. Jack had moved Molly into a bedroom where she could lie down.

"How are you feeling?"

"Like a tree didn't like me."

"You were lucky; I think it could have been a lot worse."

"I am lucky. I have you holding my hand."

"And this time I'm not going to let go of it." Jack sat down on the bed beside her and kissed her. He told her about the strange woman he had met on his birthday and what she had said to him.

"You know that's all that I've thought about for the last few weeks and I couldn't come up with a thing that really had meaning in my life . . . until now."

"And now?"

"Us . . . has meaning to me." Jack squeezed her hand. "I was stupid once and I'm not going to do that again . . . that is, if you'll have me."

"Jack, you weren't stupid." Molly stared deep into Jack's eyes. "We were just young, and yes, I will have you." She reached up and pulled Jack close to her. "You are all I've ever wanted as long as I can remember."

It was late afternoon when J.D. saw the small fishing boat with one person steering. It slowly putt-putted through the debris-filled parking lot as J.D. waded out, waving his arms and yelling at the top of his lungs. The boater immediately turned and came toward J.D.

"I'm sure glad to see you!"

The man killed the engine and let the boat drift up to J.D. "You by yourself?"

"Nope, there's about twenty or so of us."

"Well I can only carry about five. Got any women and children?"

"No kids . . . uh, one baby, but her momma is carrying her. I think there are six or seven women." J.D. looked back at the entrance to the mall.

"Okay, I'll take what I can."

"There's more of you, aren't there?"

"Oh yeah, hundreds. We've got some bigger boats north of here. We're just working our way south little by little."

J.D. caught the look of sadness in the man's eyes. "It's bad, isn't it?"

"Son, I'm sixty six years old, lived here all my life, and I've never seen anything like this. Carla was a cakewalk compared to this thing. Just about all of Houston is flooded and it just gets worse the further south you go."

"Where you from?" J.D. squinted into the sun.

"Up on the north side near Spring. Me and my buddies are all fishermen and we usually volunteer our boats."

"I don't guess you know anything about the folks in the Alvin area?"

"I'm afraid not, other than they got hit as hard as everybody else. I don't know any particulars. You from there?"

"My wife and kids are there at my mom's house."

"Well they'll be taken to shelters like everyone else."

J.D. waded back to the front door. Once inside he told them the boat could only carry five. Everyone wanted Susan and her baby to go first, then they decided on four other women. J.D. and Matt waded out and helped them into the small boat. Susan grabbed J.D.'s hand as she sat down in the front of the boat.

"Thank you again . . . you are my angel."

"I'm glad I came along." J.D. smiled.

"Where are we going?" one of the women asked the boat driver.

"To a bigger boat that'll take you to a Red Cross shelter, but we got a ways to go."

As they watched the little boat with its crew of grateful survivors motor off, three more boats came into view.

A few minutes later, J.D. and the rest of the mall refugees were on board one of the three boats headed north. As they came around the western end of the mall and turned toward Houston, J.D. could see the remains of the racetrack that had stood on the other side of I-45. Only one corner of the four-story structure was left standing.

"Wasn't that the dog track?" J.D. asked the man steering the boat.

"Yeah, ain't much left. I heard there were a lot of folks holed up in there. Don't think many made it."

"Damn." J.D. watched the devastated building slide into the horizon.

CHAPTER FORTY

She was dying. Her outer layers had separated and dissolved into thin air. She no longer had electricity coursing through her and she made no sound. She had no shape or discernable form and she no longer had a name. Forty-eight hours ago she was the most powerful force on the planet. Today she was simply a gentle breeze blowing across a Kansas wheat field.

It had been two days since the boat had picked him up and J.D. was almost crazy. He had been taken to a Red Cross shelter that had been set up in a high school gym on the north side of Houston where he had a hot meal for the first time in two days. Then he had talked one of the volunteers into letting him help so that he could work his way back down to Alvin. In the early morning hours of the next day he had found his mother's house. It was flooded and part of the roof was missing. The double unattached garage that long ago had been transformed into Maxine's Hair Palace was nowhere to be found. There was nobody around and he noticed the absence of his mom's Suburban and Beverly's station wagon.

Disheartened, he returned to the shelter and joined the thousands of other survivors trying to find lost loved ones. He slowly walked through the hundreds of people lying on cots, sitting on the floor or standing in small clusters talking among themselves. Twice he had heard the word Daddy shouted, only to whip around and see a small child he didn't know go running to a stranger. It took every ounce of energy he could muster to keep from screaming through the crowd like a wild man shouting his wife and children's names. This was much harder than clinging to a ladder inside a fuel tank in the pitch dark and that was the scariest thing he'd ever done in his life.

J.D. spotted a small wooden chair leaning up against a wall in the corner of the gym. He shuffled over to it and flopped down. Exhaustion was setting in. His body still ached all over, but inside he felt numb. His mind flashed to the sights his eyes had taken in during the boat ride yesterday and again today. The devastation was unbelievable. Water was simply everywhere. It was like the Texas shoreline was now inside the Houston city limits and the amount of destruction and debris was mind-boggling. He was told that small towns like Kemah and Seabrook didn't exist anymore and he saw firsthand there was very little left of Alvin and Pearland. Word was that Texas City, La Marque and Dickinson were also destroyed and the two large bedroom communities, Friendswood and Clear Lake, had major damage. The latter, the home of NASA, meant the space program would be on hold for a while. Dolly had killed thousands and displaced hundreds of thousands more who were now filling the many shelters to the brim searching desperately for family and friends.

J.D. leaned his head back against the wall and closed his eyes. He thought about Beverly and his children and tears began welling up behind his eyelids. He had to find them. Nothing else mattered.

"J.D. is that you?" Hearing his name, his watery eyes snapped open. He looked around and spotted a man about his age waving at him from twenty feet away. "It is you," the man said, coming toward him.

"Jerry!" J.D. jumped to his feet as he recognized an old high school friend. Jerry rushed up to him and they grabbed each other in a bear hug.

Jerry had played quarterback on the football team and had thrown J.D. quite a few touchdown passes. They were close friends in high school and like many high school friendships, had hardly seen one another since graduation.

"Man, it's good to see you," Jerry said, taking a step back.

"You too. You homeless like the rest of us?" J.D. said with a grin.

"Naw, I'm lucky. Live up in Tomball. We're all okay; I'm just down here helping out. I've been picking up folks in my bass boat."

"Good for you. How 'bout your parents, they still down in Alvin?"

"No, thank God. Dad retired and bought a place up in the Hill Country. You aren't still in Alvin, are you?"

"No, Beverly and I have been in Galveston for almost five years."

They stood looking at one another for a moment.

"Where is Beverly?" Jerry looked around.

"I don't know," J.D. could hardly say the words.

"Aw man, I'm sorry, I . . . uh . . . fuck."

"Hey, I think she's alright. I just don't know where they are. We were separated before the storm. I was at work and Bev and the kids were going to my mom's . . . I just have to find them." J.D.'s voice trembled and he could feel his eyes begin to water again. Jerry slapped his back.

"Well hell, let's go. Where do we need to look?"

"Other shelters, I guess. They're not here."

By that evening they had been to ten more shelters with no luck. J.D. had seen a few people he knew from Alvin, but no one had seen his mom or his family.

"Man, you look whipped. I'm going to take you home with me for a good home-cooked meal and we'll start all over tomorrow."

If J.D. had been able to go on by himself, he would have looked all night, but he needed Jerry's help, so he didn't protest.

"Okay, but I want to get at it first thing in the morning."

"Sun up, I promise."

As they headed for Jerry's house, J.D. slumped down in the seat and looked out the window.

"That's where I work," Jerry said as they passed by a large white building. "I can't get use to calling it HP, it's still Compaq to me."

"How long have you been there?" J.D. asked looking over at him.

"Almost nine years. How 'bout you, what are you doing?"

"Been down at International Petroleum for the last couple of years but I don't think there's much left of it."

"Bummer."

"Naw, good riddance as far as I'm concerned. It was an accident waiting to happen. I hated it there." Boone's angry face flashed in his mind. Involuntarily, he reached up and touched the tender spot on his ear.

They rode in silence for a while.

"You got any kids?" J.D. asked.

"Leslie. She's six and a handful. I can't imagine having four."

"Yeah, it gets a little nutty around the house sometimes but I sure . . . " J.D.'s voice trailed off as he looked out the window. Jerry shifted uncomfortably behind the steering wheel and stared down the road as J.D. wiped the tears from his eyes.

"We're gonna find them, J.D. I know we are. Right now they're just little bitty needles in a big old haystack and there are lots more haystacks to check out."

CHAPTER FORTY-ONE

The next two days produced the same results as the first two days: Nothing. Lots of sad lost faces, but no familiar ones. J.D. tried to keep his hopes up but he was afraid his face was beginning to look as dejected as the ones that were staring back at him. He had spent the morning calling all the hospitals in the area but to no avail, and then they had worked their way up to cities farther north where a number of shelters had been set up.

J.D. opened the door to the Conroe High gym and stared at the mass of people lying on cots or sitting on the floor. He felt like he was in a documentary about war-ravaged refugees of some third-world country. As he scanned the hundreds of faces, suddenly one clicked in his mind. This had happened a number of times in the last few days. He would see a face that he thought he knew or looked familiar, but on closer inspection it would turn out to be a stranger. He stared intently at the woman as he edged closer. She looked up at him.

"J.D."

"Mrs. Wells," he said excitedly as he rushed over to her. It was his mother's next-door neighbor. J.D. gave her a hug.

"This is my friend Jerry." J.D. stepped back. Mrs. Wells shook his hand and nodded.

"Mrs. Wells, have you seen my mom or Bev and the kids?"

"Why, no, J.D. They're not with you?" A look of concern filled her face. J.D. shook his head.

"I haven't seen your mom since Friday morning. She was going down to Galveston."

"Galveston?" A lump formed in his throat.

"Yes, she told me that Beverly had called and said her car wouldn't start and she was going down there to get them." They stared at each other. "They never came back to the house."

An involuntary shudder raced through J.D., like someone had reached into his chest and placed a large piece of ice on his heart. He was as close to losing it as he had ever been. His breathing was shallow and the color ran out of his face. He felt his shoulders slump and he let out a long sigh. He urgently needed to get away.

Mrs. Wells saw the look on J.D.'s face and quickly said, "I'm sure they're all right, J.D. You know your mom; she's tougher than all of us put together. They're here somewhere." Mrs. Wells looked around the room like she expected they were there and everybody was just missing each other.

J.D. took a deep breath and said, "You're right Mrs. Wells, I just have to keep looking. I'm glad you're okay. And Herman?" It took all the energy he could muster to keep his voice from shaking.

"Oh yeah, he's off bending somebody's ear about the storm."

J.D. gave her another hug.

"Nice to meet ya ma'am," Jerry said. They threaded their way through the crowd toward the door.

When they got to Jerry's truck, J.D. laid his head back and closed his eyes. The surge of hope that had shot through him when he had spotted Mrs. Wells had left an empty hole in him that was now being replaced with fear and dread. *God, maybe they never got off the island.* There had been rumors that few people left on the island had survived. Thinking about Beverly not being able to get the car started made him sick to his stomach. *I should have checked it before I left for work. What the hell was I thinking?* He didn't have the energy to open his eyes when he heard Jerry shut his door.

"We got a lot more places to go, buddy." Jerry turned the key in the ignition and the truck roared to life. J.D. looked over at Jerry and gave him a weak smile as tears flowed down his face. "And after we see them all, we'll start over. They're still bringing folks in."

By now the floodwaters should have been receding but because there was so much debris from the thousands of damaged buildings and houses, the water had gone down very little. This meant that rescue operations were taking much longer than usual. As they watched the non-stop television coverage the night before, the announcers had talked on and on about still finding survivors every day, all over the thirteen-county area. People were being found alive in abandoned buildings, houses, treetops and even floating cars.

"I know." J.D. nodded his head. What he really wanted to do was to lie down, curl up in a ball and cry himself to sleep.

They spent the rest of the day walking through shelters, scanning a sea of emotionless faces. At each shelter J.D. lost a little bit more hope of finding them and by the end of the day he was totally despondent. He had beaten himself into a pile of worthless pulp thinking about their old piece-of-shit station wagon not starting. *I should have taken better care of my family* was on a one-track loop running through his mind.

That night as he lay down to sleep, all he could think about was that he wished Boone had shot him or that Dolly had blown him to Kingdom come. Anything would be better than this.

After spending half the night tossing and turning, he had finally fallen asleep in the early morning hours. Now that it was time to get up, he couldn't move. He was exhausted and mentally drained. J.D. had always been an early riser. He loved being up to see the sunrise. Now all he wanted to do was pull the covers over his head and escape into dreamland. Jerry had already knocked on his bedroom door a couple of times and told him they needed to get on the road. J.D. sat up and flopped both feet on the floor. He sat there slumped over; feeling like all of the life had been sucked out of his body. After a moment he managed to drag himself into the bathroom and get dressed.

Later they were on their way down to Houston. Jerry said he needed to pick up his boat. He had left it at the shelter where he and J.D. had first found each other. When they reached the gym, Jerry told J.D. he ought to go in and take a look while he hooked up the boat. J.D. shuffled into the gym like an obedient five-year old taking orders from his dad.

He had toured the building and the only familiar faces he had seen were people like himself, looking for missing family. Some had pictures of their loved ones on signs that they had scribbled, *have you seen my daughter?* Or *have you seen this person?* He would nod or speak to his fellow searchers as they met. Their eyes connected with a sadness that was heartbreaking. J.D. seldom asked questions anymore of the people he met. He had heard way too many horror stories. There was something about a disaster or traumatic event that just barred repeating. He didn't understand why people felt compelled to relate some gruesome thing they had seen or heard about. Maybe he'd have been as guilty if he weren't afraid that he might hear about his loved ones that way. He'd also heard joyous, heart warming stories of reunions and perilous escapes and he was glad for that person, but he couldn't listen to them anymore either.

His shoulders slumped and he walked like a prisoner making his way to the electric chair. Just as he was about to open the door to go outside, he heard a small voice behind him.

"Daddy?"

He willed himself to keep walking since he had been disappointed a number of times in the last few days and he didn't think he could take another gut-wrenching disappointment.

"Daddy-O, where are you going?" The small voice cried out a little louder.

J.D. stopped and slowly turned around. Looking up at him was Austin. J.D. fell to his knees as Austin ran into his arms. J.D. hugged him until he was afraid he would squeeze the breath out of him.

"Daddy, where have you been?" Austin said into his chest. J.D. laughed as he pulled him away to look into his face.

"Well that's a long story. I'll have to tell ya later. Where's your momma?"

"She got hurt."

The air caught in J.D.'s lungs.

"But she's alright, she's over here." Austin took J.D. by the hand and led him through the rows of cots and people. He took him to a hallway leading off of the main gym floor. J.D. heard a shriek that filled the air. Paris came running with Tyler in her arms and Dallas right behind her. They were both shouting *Daddy* as loud as they could. J.D. held out his arms and they almost knocked him down as they ran into him. Everybody was crying by this time, including J.D. and quite a few strangers around him. After a moment J.D. finally said, "Where's your momma?"

"This way." Dallas pulled J.D. down the hall. The people who had collected to witness the reunion parted to let J.D. through. He spotted a cot up against the wall. Beverly was sitting up on one elbow, the other arm was in a sling and she had a large bandage around her head and over one ear.

"Look, Mommy." Dallas held J.D.'s hand, proud to be the bearer of such a gift to his mother. Beverly's cheeks were wet with tears as she beamed up at J.D.

They stared at each other for a moment; then J.D. sat down on the cot beside her and gently took her face in his hand. He opened his mouth but nothing came out. Tears rolled down his face in torrents. He kissed her passionately and then hugged her as hard as he dared without hurting her arm. Slowly he could feel the lump in his throat loosening.

"I knew you were alive, I just knew it," Beverly said softly in his ear. J.D. pulled back and looked deep into her eyes.

"I've never been more alive in my life."

EPILOGUE

It had been a little over a month since Dolly had blown into town. Her place in the history books was secured as the worse natural disaster in the United States. The death toll was over eight thousand and counting. It would be years before the final financial total would be known, but it would be in the billions. The amount of damage was so massive; it was surreal to observe. The brain couldn't seem to comprehend what had happened. People were trying to regroup and get on with their lives but it would be many, many years before the area had any normalcy to it.

Ralph, Tommy and Collin were the only survivors at City Hall, but Mayor Collin Ramsey didn't fare as well. His political career died overnight upon the discovery of the embezzled emergency evacuation funds. Dolly took his house and his businesses and Joan took his daughter and moved in with her sister. To add to his troubles, Collin had let most of his insurance lapse because of lack of funds and was facing criminal charges over the missing money.

Though Cora and Bonnie survived without so much as a broken fingernail, both of their lives had been changed forever. Cora had become a wealthy widow. Harold had sold insurance all of his life and believed in it. And since Harold was clever enough to be killed in hurricane Dolly instead of dying a slow death from cancer, the double indemnity clauses were applicable. Bonnie had decided to take a break from radio and search for some answers as to what she really wanted to do with her life. Cora had already gotten the first of a number of large checks and convinced Bonnie to go on an around-the-world-trip, with her picking up the tab. Ironically, airplane travel didn't bother Cora's motion sickness. Bonnie had given notice at the radio station and they had spent the last week in Dallas on a shopping spree.

For all intents and purposes, Sarah was as dead as Lex, with one exception. Her heart continued to pump blood into an inactive brain as long as her trust fund pumped cash into the private sanitarium, oddly enough designed by her famous father. She had been the number-one suspect in her husband's murder, until a Detective Heath had called the Galveston police department and informed them that two of Lex's former business partners had also been murdered at about the same time. An analysis of the bullet that killed Lex soon proved that the same gun had killed all three, and Detective Heath was positive that the person responsible was a disgruntled investor from years ago by the name of Richard Hanson of Des Moines, Iowa.

The group down at the Hotel Galvez wasn't found until three days after Dolly had skipped town. They were all okay except for being quite hungry. Jeff Hankins, the night manager, had at least thought to stock the wet bar in the conference room with water and a few bottles of whiskey, but the worst of it was, their last flashlight had faded out on the second day and they spent the last eighteen hours in pitch black darkness listening to Sean whimper and complain. Jim Wells went on to win several awards for his video of the miraculous rescue of the three children, while Sean's only claim to fame would be his unscripted dive off the seawall, which made it onto Dick Clark's blooper reel.

Jack and all of his crew were picked up late the first day after Dolly moved on. Molly and her mom spent a few days in the hospital. Molly had a slight concussion, two cracked ribs and had received twenty-three stitches in her leg. Uncle Harry and Aunt Nita came through the ordeal like it was just another day in paradise and immediately went to work getting the carpet replaced and the roof repaired. Jack had to work some long days at the job but found time to help Molly get her mom into an assisted-living home. Her mom's house was completely ruined so Molly moved in with Jack until they could build a new house for themselves. They needed something that had a large back yard for their black Lab that Jack had named Flipper.

J.D.'s reunion with his family had been tempered with the news of his mother's death. J.D. grieved for his mom, but was so elated at finding Beverly and his children that he was able to get through it in good shape. Beverly told him how Maxine had saved their lives with her smart thinking and calm resolve. Jerry gladly loaned J.D. some money to buy clothes for everyone and let them use his second car until J.D's final paycheck came through. As soon as the floodwaters had receded, they headed down to Alvin.

Surprisingly, his mom's house had endured better than he first thought. The part of the roof that was missing was over a back bedroom and was easily closed off. IP Industries set up an eight-hundred number for employees to call and J.D. received his final paycheck, including a bonus for lock-down duty, the first of the week. He had gotten in touch with the American Can Company and was going up the following week for an interview.

That night as J.D. and Beverly lay in bed, he told her about Boone.

She stared at him in disbelief. "My God, I always knew something was wrong with him but I never thought he would do anything like that."

"Me neither." J.D. rolled over on his side and looked at Beverly. "I don't think there's any sense in telling anyone about this. Hell, nobody's left and what would it solve?"

"Nothing. Those families think their loved ones were killed by the storm. Why change that?"

J.D. was tired of thinking about it.

"You really think he had a bomb?"

"That box and those wires went to something and he wasn't shooting people for target practice."

265

Beverly winced as she rolled over on her injured arm.

"My hero." She gave him a kiss on the cheek.

"Ha, I was just a scared kid looking for cover. That man who saved those kids down at the Hotel Galvez, he's a real hero. Did you see that videotape they've been showing?"

"Oh yeah, its incredible."

"The cameraman that shot it was on the Today show this morning. He said he'd covered the Gulf war and plenty of natural disasters and had never seen anything like it."

"Did they ever figure out who he was?"

"One of the women at the hotel said she had talked to him earlier in the evening and he was very nice. She said his name was Richard something and he was from Des Moines, Iowa."

And somewhere deep in the Caribbean Sea . . .

She is an accident, but then so many creations are. The conditions can be exactly the same and nothing happens but today is different. The right cell merging with another right cell and suddenly energy is everywhere. Molecules acting and reacting at a frantic pace. Ions and protons smashing into one another at a random chaotic rate. The combination of water and the perfect temperature inside the natural womb she is growing in, is giving her energy and life. Soon she will be in search for more, like a hungry werewolf on a full moon night. She has no shape or form but she is growing stronger by the minute and already moving. She even has a name.

About The Author

Rod Tanner enjoyed a successful career in radio, as a DJ and in programming, including stints in Denver, Houston and San Antonio. He then spent eight years working with Atlantic Records in promotion and ten years as an independent record producer before turning to writing full time. Surge is his second novel. The first was *Double Fault,* and he has co-authored with his wife, Diana Meade, two screenplays, *Second Verse* and *Criss-Cross*. They live in Houston, Texas

Printed in the United States
34734LVS00003B/55